BUFFALOed

by
FAIRLEE WINFIELD

ISBN: 1-4392-0099-8
ISBN-13: 9781439200995

Library of Congress Control Number: 2008905716
Visit www.Amazon.com to order additional copies.

Disclaimer

BUFFALOed is a work of fiction. The characterizations and incidents presented are totally the product of the author's imagination. Names, characters, entities, products, places, and incidents are used fictitiously. Any resemblance to actual persons, living or dead, events, or locales is entirely coincidental. Characterization has required the use of some profanity.

DEDICATION

∾

For my irreverent
Grandmother Belcher and her
Great Grandson Bill

ACKNOWLEDGEMENTS

I would like to thank Elizabeth Dear who was curator of the C. M. Russell Museum way back in 1995. She graciously allowed me to visit the Russell home and studio off-season. It was during this visit, when I saw firsthand so much of what my immigrant grandmother had described to me, that I became determined to write this story. I know Granny would have enjoyed having some satirical fun with the immigrant's romanticized search for the legendary West and the idealization necessary for the creation of the all-time American hero, the cowboy.

In researching the life and times of Charles M. Russell, I turned primarily to John Taliaferro's, *Charles M. Russell: The Life and Legend of America's Cowboy Artist.* His work in turn led me to F. G. Renner's "Bad Pennies: A Study of Forgeries of Charles M. Russell Art," in *Montana: The Magazine of Western History.* Additionally, Joan Stauffer's *Behind Every Man: The Story of Nancy Cooper Russell*, provided insights into Nancy Russell's determined promotion of the Cowboy Artist's work.

For the language of the cowboy trade, their culture, their tales, and their times, I am indebted to *We Pointed Them North: Recollections of a Cowpuncher,* by E. C. Abbott and Helena Huntington Smith, and to *Recollections of Charley Russell,* by Frank Bird Linderman. Edgar R. "Frosty" Potter's, *Cowboy Slang* enhanced the chin music when I sometimes got feelin' 'zactly tongue-tied.

My sincere thanks go to Venita Blackburn, Louis Grossman, Winifred Doan, Santos Vega, and Maureen Milligan who read chapter after chapter of this novel and provided me with help and encouragement.

CONTENTS

1

Foreword by the Housemaid's Grandson
October 2001   11

2

Northern Pacific Railway to Montana
March 1904   25

3

The Electric City   43

4

Another New Language   57

5

The Elocution Lesson   71

6

The Peep Show   79

ONE

Foreword by the Housemaid's Grandson
October 2001

I think I can now, in this new millennium, reveal the secret that my grandmother, Ovidia Odegard, confided in me before her death at the age of ninety-four. Over the years the principals involved in the deception have passed gracefully into oblivion or into mythical celebrity, as the case may be, but skeptics will in any case turn a deaf ear on Ovidia's account of the events.

At stake is America's fervid reverence for the western cowboy that has popularized hundreds of movies and rests even today as a heavy buffalo robe over the entire national culture. More importantly, the reputation of the great State of Montana is, to some extent, at risk.

The dear old lady swore that the renowned cowboy artist, Charlie Russell, did not paint the famous mural hanging today in the Montana State House of Representatives. The mural is a forgery. Yes, Granny Ovidia vowed that Charles Marion Russell did not paint that magnificent depiction of *Lewis and Clark Meeting the Indians at Ross' Hole*. She claimed the State of Montana was deceived and swindled.

Although the grandeur of the work may be irrefutable, the Cowboy Artist is not the person to be credited. Albeit he was honored for the work at a special joint session of the Montana legislature, the honor did not belong to Charlie. Ovidia insisted that if you knew anything at all about Charlie Russell you would recognize that the subtle irony implicit in the painting could not have come from him.

At present, I have no wish to have the statue of Charles Marion Russell removed from the National Statuary Hall in Washington, D.C. He is, after all, the only artist represented there. I don't believe my dear Granny Ovidia would have wanted that. Certainly the seven-foot bronze statue of the Cowboy Artist should remain where it is, next to George Washington, Thomas Jefferson, Brigham Young, and Robert E. Lee in the Capitol building. Bear in mind that Charles Russell is the patron saint of the Big Sky, and his buffalo skull logo even today appears in the corner of every Montana State license plate.

Nevertheless, Ovidia revealed the chicanery involved in this fraud quite by accident. She and I had never been close, but at the time (it was in the late seventies) I was rooming with her in Las Vegas while doing doctoral research on a grant concerning the life of the Nevada Paiute Indian Prophet, Wovoka, founder of the Ghost Dance religion, "Avataric Occurrence and the Phenomenon of the Ghost Dance." The pecuniary situation surrounding the funding of my research precluded lavish spending. I needed to be in Nevada. Ovidia lived there. So, Granny and I were packed, quite literally tripping over each other, in her 1936 Clipper Airstream trailer. She had it parked beneath one of the spindly trees in the mobile home lot next to the old Showboat Casino on the Boulder Highway.

To put the deliberate trickery involved into historical perspective, I must remind you of the social and political climate of the early 1900's when the events Ovidia describe took place. The open range was rapidly disappearing. Theodore Roosevelt, in a speech to a Chicago men's club, waxed eloquent about the cowboys speaking of "their bronzed, set faces and keen eyes that look the entire world straight in the face without flinching as they flash out from under their broad-brimmed hats."

This description fit the Charlie Russell persona perfectly—the Anglo-Saxon cowboy. America needed a hero and the nation settled on Charlie Russell to be both the embodiment and publicist of that cowboy hero. A new invasion of European immigrants, the alien breeds, the Slavs and the Swedes, were being blamed for a corruption and dilution of American stock. My grandmother Ovidia was part of this alien invasion.

My previous contact with grandmother had been brief and sporadic. I remember only that during her few visits with us she had always given us astonishingly heavy, brown paper sacks full of clinking silver dollars. Her visits were also memorable for ambrosial buttermilk waffles. The problem was—she greatly disapproved of my English father. She insisted that he was nothing but a lousy drunk and a poor provider to boot. Inevitably the visits ended with angry shouts, wet handkerchiefs, and unplanned trips to the Greyhound Bus station. In truth, when I arrived on her trailer-step, Granny and I were little more than strangers.

Her habit of calling me "Billy" was somewhat mortifying. I hadn't been "Billy" since age ten. But, asking frequently for the use of my true appellation, "William," produced only a shrug and no change in her behavior. Fortunately, however, the breakfast waffles still appeared on schedule, every morning, on the tiny two-seat foldout table where we'd sit and check the horoscope magazines' predictions before venturing into the day's unknown. Yes, Granny was a fervid disciple of astrology.

My allotted space in the tarnished metal Clipper was the small "living room" with the pull out sofa bed. This was not an inconvenience really, since most of my time was spent in the archives of the university library, searching the very limited holdings of the Nevada State Museum and Historical Society, or traveling north to the old Steward Indian School near Yerington.

An excessive amount of keepsake bric-a-brac adorned all the shelves, window ledges and walls, but as is perhaps not said often enough—beggars can't be choosers. I settled quickly down among the grotesque gnomes and trolls standing guard over their chests of buried treasure and the stacks of horoscope magazines balancing precariously on the tables.

Granny always described herself a "desert rat," meaning that she needed to keep the interior of the Airstream in the high nineties during the entire winter. I'd often step outside to catch at least a brief chill before bedtime.

Progress on my Wovoka research was slow. I was far behind schedule, advisors were pushing, and my funds, limited as they were by a beggarly State of Nevada DOCA grant, started to run out. Ovidia's routine, at the time, involved daily trips to the casinos, and to ease my frustration, I sometimes began to accompany her.

I was to discover that her skill at the craps tables was legendary. Ovidia was a compulsive gambler, but a talented one. The dealers at the Showboat all knew her, and out on the strip the doormen and bellhops would hurry to help her inside, taking her arm and leading her to her favorite table.

Her mind was sharp, but her stamina was beginning to fade, so when the dice weren't behaving as she liked, we'd stop for a casino buffet meal—she loved them—or we'd move into one of the cavernous bingo parlors. She always played at least a dozen bingo cards simultaneously while she continued talking, and yet, she never missed a call.

One afternoon at the old Showboat bingo parlor, I was sounding off about the difficulties of my Wovoka research. "I can't believe it." I remember complaining. "The homeland of the Ghost Dance Prophet and this state all but ignores him. The archives have absolutely nothing of importance. I can get more information about Liberace."

"Oh, but Billy," Granny said, "You must remember, Liberace is a very important entertainer. I saw him on my eighty-eighth birthday, just this last September."

"Please, Grandma, call me William, or at least Bill."

I shook my head in disbelief. Why couldn't she remember? But someone down the table had hollered, "Bingo," and we paused to check our cards. When the win was confirmed, we discarded what wasn't producing and started to lay out a new array.

"His home state." I slapped down my new arrangement of bingo cards one at a time. The snapping sound gave a nice staccato edge to my irritation. I couldn't forget the frustrations of my research, and I slammed my fist on the table. "I just can't believe it. Historically Wokova's more important than Crazy Horse, and hell, he's all but forgotten." I needed to talk. I knew she couldn't understand this kind of research, but I needed to talk to someone. "Granny, did you know he started the half-witted notion of magic Ghost Dance shirts as bullet proof protection? He invented the Ghost Dance."

"Oh, I've seen Ghost Dance shirts," Ovidia said quietly.

"What delusions . . . what plain crap." Locked into my own problems, I barely heard Granny's response.

"A Ghost Dance shirt hung for years in the entry way of the house where I worked in Montana. Then later, we moved it to Charlie's cabin studio. Charlie Russell's studio in Great Falls—the one I helped build. The Russells, especially Charlie, held onto all kinds of old Indian stuff."

I was lost, buried actually, and it was helping me to rant on about my troubles. I blundered on. "Why in the hell did Wovoka tell the Indians that if they got into trouble with the whites, they shouldn't be afraid . . . that he'd protect them?" I watched Ovidia's bony, liver-spotted hand run down the columns of her bingo card, her thumb and forefinger clenched together as a pointer. I was trying to explain just the most broad and elementary points of my research to her. "They even believed he was their messiah, dammit."

"You know Billy, a Ghost Dance shirt was the first thing that caught my attention there at the Russell's the night I arrived in Montana because it was a little like the Norwegian dress I wore when I landed in this country," she said.

"Hell, his screwball ideas sent the Indian nations into oblivion."

Granny paid no attention to my frustration. She seemed in another world, staring off across the room.

"Antelope skin. *Ja*, I think it was antelope skin. Like an ordinary shirt or tunic, but painted a dark blue. The sleeves were loose and wide flowing. And, I remember, like in Norway, the cuffs, neck, and the hemline were bright red with a narrow band of white." Ovidia had closed her eyes behind her gold-rimmed bifocal glasses and seemed to be recapturing an image. She rubbed the center of her forehead above the bridge of her nose.

"But, my *Got*!" her eyes popped open wide. "That Indian shirt! It was covered with teeth. Big white teeth, hundreds and hundreds of them. In rows and rows sewed onto the sleeves and down in loops hanging below the waist across the front. I tell you Billy, those teeth gave me the chills. That shirt must have been full of terrifying local spirits." She looked back at her bingo cards and shook her head. "Strange and spooky that dress. All those shiny white teeth."

I looked up from my bingo cards. Her description of the teeth won my attention.

"Hundreds of teeth? What kind of teeth were they?"

"*Ja,* I don't know. Maybe antelope or elk. They were eerie. Hundreds and hundreds of animal teeth."

I was listening to her now. I'd seen pictures like that. "I guess I'd forgotten you worked for Charlie Russell, Granny. Wasn't he that well-known cowboy artist?"

"Oh *ja*, in Great Falls. Nancy Russell taught me everything. I didn't even know about women's things, and when I started bleeding one day, I thought I was dying. I had to tell someone, and Nancy explained it all to me, all about the girl stuff. But, on the other hand, Nancy was a real skint. Used to lock-up the cakes and sweet things in a big china cabinet. Locked it up with a key. She was afraid I'd steal some, so she always carried the key with her. She never found out the truth—that I didn't even like cake. What I wanted were those salty crackers she kept. She liked to be fancy and always called them 'saltines.' It seemed like a silly word. I got away with a lot of those. Nancy kept track of everything, so to fool her, I sometimes only crumbled the corners off. She always suspected there were mice in the house."

As Ovidia spoke, I was beginning to recall seeing some reproductions of the cowboy artist's work, lots of hairy buffalo and dusty looking cowboys riding unruly horses. I confess, Western art has never been a strong interest of mine, but I wanted her to continue talking. "Did you come to America to work for the Russells, Granny?"

"Oh *nei*, I didn't want to leave Norway. I knew nothing about the West and nothing of Charlie Russell. But, well, don't forget, Billy, we're ocean people you know, Vikings remember?" she paused, looked amused, and I thought she was teasing. "We do have a certain energy. We want to go out and look for things. You can't live on the sea and not long to have adventure."

"Then why did you come here? No adventure in Norway?" Listening to her chatter was putting the Wovoka research problems out of my mind.

"Well, first mother died. Looking back, it was my Aunt Anna who said my father had screwed her to death."

I choked. I pulled out my clean white handkerchief and looked down at my bingo cards pretending to check for the last number while she plunged right ahead with the story.

"Anyway, Billy, there were twelve children already, and right away he remarried my closest friend, Kristina. She was my age, sixteen. There were sure to be more children. Our farm was so remote, mostly bare rocks and cliffs on a tiny island. We were always hungry.

"Then Uncle Nils, I don't think you never met him, Billy. *Ja,* Nils Indegard, he was already in America, he sent money for my passage. He said he would find me work, and I was obligated to repay him with extra for helping me. He was my sponsor, and without a sponsor Aunt Anna said I wouldn't be allowed into America."

"You were an indentured servant?" I asked somewhat amazed.

"Oh, I don't know. Is that what you call it? But, two weeks later, Aunty Anna doused me and my trunk with some foul smelling white powder, protection against the lice, fleas, and other vermin, she said. Then just before I got on the ship, they scratched around with a sharp needle on my arm until it bled. A vaccination they called it. Anna gave me a Saint Olav amulet, and I got on a ship bound for Boston."

Granny shrugged her shoulders as if it were the most natural thing in the world to send a sixteen-year-old off on a ship alone. Well, maybe it was back in 1903, I thought.

"Hey, you must have come through Ellis Island. People talk and write about it all the time."

"*Nei,* Billy, where do people get that idea? Hell, many more of us came through Boston or even Canada. And Boston was a damned dirty city," she said. "Two things I still remember better than yesterday. A poster on the mud splattered wall of a building near the docks advertising Buffalo Bill's Wild West and Congress of Rough Riders of the World. Buffalo Bill was wearing a white buckskin coat with long fringes and he had long golden curls like a pretty girl from Gudbrandsdal. My *Got*, how I wanted to have a buckskin coat.

"And then, there was the Nickelodeon Theater. Uncle Nils and his family took me there. I'll never forget the film. *The Great Train Robbery*. I'd never seen a film before—and that last scene . . . ." Granny breathed a quiet sigh and looked up toward the ceiling where the cigarette smoke gathered heavily. "So stirring," she said. "Barnes, he was the leader of the outlaw gang, stood pointing his big revolver directly at us in the audience, and at that very moment the piano player did an ear splitting gunshot sound effect as smoke poured out of the gun there on the screen. The audience shrieked. Some of them even ran out of the theater. But my *Got*, I was bewitched. It was at that moment I knew I wanted to go to the West. I knew that was what I had to do. I'd go West, and get a buckskin jacket just like Buffalo Bill's."

"So you got there, to Montana."

"Only by chance. It wasn't that easy because it wasn't for me to decide. Uncle Nils had other plans for me. His cousin, Erik Trygstad, a widower in Minnesota with thirty-two fine milk cows and a couple of kids, needed a young girl. I started out pleading and begging Nils not to send me there. He still insisted that I go. So, I told him cows and milk made me sick. It was a lie, of course, but the next few times I was to carry the big milk pitcher to the table, I played a trick on them. I'd turn away so no one could see me and I'd stick my finger down my throat until—well, it wasn't very pretty, but that convinced him, *Gotdammit.*

"Right after that he sent me to learn English. I knew a little, but Nils made me stay in Boston for three long months studying. He sent me to a school with a bunch of Swedes, Danes and Germans. Even two students from Finland I suspected were witches. Then I found out he added the cost of the school, the English dictionary and extra board to the amount I needed to repay him.

"The next job offer was tempting. A handsome woman, Lady Catherine Amesbury, came to see Uncle Nils. Her other lady's maid from Drammen, Norway, got tired of keeping irregular hours and quit to go to work in a sweat shop.

"I met that Lady Catherine, Billy. She was glorious. She wore a large hat with long curling feathers that hid her blonde curls. So elegant—the jeweled handbag, the elaborately arranged hair, the red painted lips, my *Got*. She even had two yapping poodle dogs, one black and one white. I don't like dogs, Billy, and even though I knew I'd be cleaning up dog shit if I worked for her, I was ready to go. If I couldn't go West, I was determined to work for her. But Uncle Nils shouted, '*Nei*. Never.' He thought it was an outrageous offer.

"At the time, I didn't realize that Lady Catherine was probably a whore."

"A what?" I was shocked by Granny's profanity.

"Well I guess she'd have been called a courtesan back then, not a whore. The difference seemed to be in how much money they charged the customers. That's what Nancy Russell taught me in Great Falls when she was telling me about the differences between a harlot, a fallen woman, a sporting lady, a tart or a trollop. We didn't have all those categories in Norway, and . . . ."

"Ah, aah . . ." I mumbled trying to interrupt. There were few, if any, proscribed subjects for Ovidia, and quite frankly, I found it disconcerting to hear a wrinkled, endearing, little old lady talk like that. Before I could change the subject however, she continued.

"So anyway, Billy, it was either Cousin Trygstad's cows or the factory, and then Nils had a letter from Montana."

"From the Russells," I prompted, wanting her to talk more about the Indian Ghost Dance shirt and the Russells.

"*Ja*, Billy, from Nancy Russell. I saw it. Scribbly, poor grammar, even I could see that, but she wrote that her Charlie could charm a monkey out of a tree and that his daddy, who had plenty of money, paid all the bills. And . . . . Bingo." Ovidia suddenly called.

She had won again, and our talk ended abruptly. It wasn't until sometime later at the old Last Frontier casino, when she continued her story, that she revealed the forgery of the Montana State House mural.

The controversial nature of what I will now tell you leads me to relate our further intimate conversations as dispassionately as possible. Ovidia would sit talking in the cozy atmosphere of the casino buffet booths. She always nestled into a corner looking like a small stuffed bird in one of the red dresses that she favored. Her face was a wrinkled crepe-de-Chin, her mousey hair, light and fine. We'd finish our meal, she'd sip the coffee that she loved, but which her doctor had forbidden, and she'd talk and talk. Our conversations became something of an oral history activity.

Ovidia's English was fluent though she always retained a kind of foreignness, more in her intonation pattern than in her vocabulary, which was utterly replete with profanity learned in her early employment as a maid in the Russell household. It seemed that only Norwegian profanity held taboos for her.

Perhaps it was her foreign speech that had made both women and men tell her things they would ordinarily hesitate to tell relatives or close friends. Or perhaps her powerless status as a housemaid gave them the courage to confide.

Though I failed to pursue Ovidia's story at the time, I know it is at least partially responsible for my decision to continue as a historian of the Western United States. In the interim, I finished my work on Wovoka, suffered an emotional collapse after the death of both my mother and grandmother, and endured the many rigors of seeking tenure in an academic position, always a difficult undertaking. Considering the many hagiographies idolizing The Cowboy Artist, the truth now becomes imperative.

I'll endeavor to reproduce Ovidia's story of the events central to the forgery incident in her voice as I well remember it. I succeeded in taping only limited conversations. Indeed, she had great confidence that, at the appropriate time, I would reveal the truth. She once even told me that without knowing our true stories, we're fearful and feel ashamed.

Should you be shocked by some of the events Ovidia will depict in these pages, keep in mind as you read how unthinkable it once was to imagine any dalliance going on in the oval office, Jesus riding in the passenger seat of a Lexus, or cowboys in love with each other. Looking back,

I am sure Ovidia would have approved of taking the lid off of the State house mural hoax at last.

William Carl Andersen, Ph.D.
Albuquerque, New Mexico
October 17, 2001

TWO

Northern Pacific Railway to Montana
March 1904

I'm a Norwegian, Billy, and I'll never forget it. But there in the Northern Pacific railway station, all I wanted to do was get on the train and start being an American. An American, but more important, a Westerner. Uncle Nils and his family kept talking Norwegian and Cousin Inge-borg kept watching me. I think she knew how I felt since she could almost have been my sister. She was seventeen, so we were almost the same age and we looked just alike—the same fine blond hair and blue eyes. I think I was a little shorter and rounder though.

While we waited, she went into a crowded shop and bought me a book of pictures for the train trip. No reading, just pictures—<u>Studies of Western Life</u>, by Charles Russell. "Look, Ovidia," she whispered. "It's him." She leaned close to me, poked me with her elbow, and pointed to the book. "It's him, Charles Russell, your new employer, right there on the front cover. He is famous. And good looking, too." She giggled while I stared closely at the photograph. A steely eyed cowboy, wearing a fringed buckskin shirt, some sort of wooly covers on top of his trousers, and a huge gun strapped low on his hip. His hands were crossed over his chest in a defiant gesture like he might be ready to shoot the gun any second.

"Oh my *Got*, Inge, he looks just like Barnes in the Nickelodeon movie or maybe Buffalo Bill." We giggled nervously. "Look at the buckskin shirt. I can't wait to see him," I said, and we both broke into loud laughter which was hushed when Uncle Nils gave us one of his disapproving looks.

Inge said the book was to prepare me for what I would see in the West: wonderful scenes of flat prairies with buffalo grazing tall grass, Indians studying the broad horizon, and cowboys riding balky horses.

I thought Charles Marion Russell had to be the finest artist in the world. Of course, I didn't know anything then about him passing off the big Montana State House mural as his own painting. All that was to come much later. But if you're going to understand how it all happened, Billy, I have to tell you the story about working for the Russells from the very beginning. That's the way my memory seems to work these days.

Anyway, the Indegard family had put up a bundle of food for me to carry on the train, lots of dried white fish, flat bread, a little cheese, and some dried apples. "No *fiske* in Montana," said Aunt Borghild. "But, you may have to eat buffalo humps." Auntie Borghild was always trying to make jokes. To please her, everyone snorted, but we were all too nervous by then to find anything funny. Uncle Nils kept looking at his lavish gold watch every few seconds. He was all business.

"Now listen carefully, Ovidia, you'll change trains in Chicago, and again in St. Paul. Your English speaking is getting better, but I've written out the instructions in Norwegian. Nancy Russell is going to meet you at the train station in Great Falls. They'll be watching for your wooden trunk with the red and gold 'Odegard' town crest and the white painted flowers," he said. "And I did send them a description of you." Knowing Uncle Nils, I wondered what the description was like, maybe, "A short, plump girl, with straggling hair that won't stay in place."

I tried to listen, but my *Got* Billy, I was sure fidgety to get going to the West. When they announced the train, Nils took my arm and led me through the pushing, shoving crowd. I'd been working on my English reading too, and the station walls were covered with posters printed by the Northern Pacific Railway offering special rates to anyone who would settle in the great new Northern Pacific country. The posters claimed the best grazing lands in the world, and even said that thousands of people had made fortunes. It looked so perfect. They even had pictures of special immigrant cars to carry whole families and all their belongings. My *Got*, I was excited. I dreamed it would be a Valhalla. I was confident that I could make my fortune too, just like the thousands of people the posters described.

In an unusual show of affection, Uncle Nils gave me a penny bouquet of violets. I pinned them on the heavy wool shawl I had wrapped over the blue tunic and my long striped skirt.

"These won't last until Montana, but . . . we <u>will</u> be thinking of you, Ovidia. You'll be receiving a dollar a week from the Russell's, plus your room and board, and they will send me a dollar each week toward repaying your passage."

He helped me up the high step and into the second class coach which smelled of burning cinders and moldy, stale cheese. I found an empty seat toward the rear, facing a skinny Lutheran pastor and his wife who were reading the bible aloud. I knew immediately they were Lutherans because pinned to their black clothing they wore heavy embroidery versions of Martin Luther's Seal, the black cross, the red heart, and the white rose, stitched on the sky colored background encircled with the gold ring of heavenly bliss. It seemed a good omen.

Montana could be heavenly bliss. Yes, it would be, but, all that black clothing they were wearing. That looked awfully gloomy. Then I thought, well, maybe a good choice. I could already see that my good white blouse would soon be a sooty gray. The second class coach seats had once been some kind of heavy green cloth, but now they were dingy with coal dust blowing from the engine tender.

Cousin Ingeborg was outside the open train window, and I leaned out and threw her my small beaded Norwegian hairpin purse which she had admired. In exchange she tossed me her perfumed handkerchief.

"Be careful to hold that handkerchief over your nose when you get close to your first smelly cowboy," she shouted. We giggled nervously again, and I thought of that defiant looking Charles Russell in his buckskin shirt.

"We'll miss you, Ovidia," she called, and then the train began moving from the station platform in a series of slow, squeaking lurches. I felt an empty, hollow feeling start to grow just below my ribs. I held Inge's handkerchief to my nose and inhaled deeply so the Lutherans wouldn't notice my watery eyes. Then I watched the Indegard family until the coach rounded a long curve and they were no longer visible.

In the extreme front of the car a group of men were playing cards and passing around a brown bottle. All the train windows were now closed again to keep out the smoke and cinders, and the stink of moldy cheese and rotten fruit intensified. Babies cried, and immigrant families tried to comfort them. One family had eight children and took up almost half of the coach. I spent the day watching the rich looking farm lands as we crossed Pennsylvania. And I began reading the Norwegian translation of Owen Wister's romantic book, *The Virginian*. I must have read for hours. The story was sad, but heroic. The Wister book was teaching me what cowboys were all about. My *Got*, how I wished I could be a school teacher like pretty Molly in the book, having adventures and . . . .

Well, that night I was startled by what looked like a blazing fire in the sky, but the Lutherans assured me it was a sign of progress and prosperity because it came from the steel mills. The three screaming babies finally quieted, and the continuously praying Lutherans seemed to keep the gamblers at a distance, but I kept a close eye on them anyway. They pulled out bottles, passed them around, and took long drinks. I knew it was *rangle* because they were getting drunk, whispering and laughing, looking back at the passengers—especially at me. One left the game and came walking toward me. When he got close, I stamped my foot and glared back at him as he passed. It never pays to be sympathetic to a drunk, Billy.

I think it was sometime late the next day that we arrived in Chicago. Anyway, I still had a little cheese left, and the white fish, but that was about all. We had time in the station, so I got off the train and walked around the platform. The Chicago station bustled with activity. Venders selling fat, stinky sausages. Small boys in short pants hustling newspapers and magazines. Everyone looked prosperous compared to home. The women wore sweeping flared skirts and blouses with funny, puffy sleeves, and the men had on stiff collars and rigid shirt fronts under fancy vests with massive gold watch chains, even bigger than the gold watch Uncle Nils wore and was so proud of.

On the next set of tracks were cattle cars with cows packed so tightly they couldn't move. A tough looking guy in heavy boots walked along the top of the cars and prodded the cattle with a long punching pole. The cattle were all bawling loudly, a terrible, pathetic sound. As I watched, a cow suddenly dropped her calf, and it was trampled to death in an instant.

I was stunned. I covered my mouth and nose with Inge's handkerchief and ran inside the station's second class waiting room to the toilet services. I thought I was going to be sick. The toilet room was dirty and smelled terribly of piss, but there was running water in a basin, and I splashed it quickly again and again into my face and wet Inge's handkerchief to bathe my arms. A grimy mirror hung above the basin. I looked up and hardly recognized myself. I was pale, and the violets pinned to my tunic were wilted and dead.

I took my book, *The Virginian*, with its cover drawing of a western cowboy that had so delighted me, opened it, and spread the dying flowers inside. I closed it hard and pressed the covers heavily together crushing the violets. They gave off a fresh smell, sweet and earthy. Taking a deep breath, I stood there for a moment, and then I turned and went quickly back out on the platform.

The train for St. Paul was being called. I had started to board when I noticed a raggedy child sitting in the corner selling violet bouquets for a penny. I bought one, buried my face in it and inhaled deeply before pinning the fresh flowers to the front of my tunic as I boarded the train quickly, right behind the Lutheran couple.

Now there were fewer women in the second class car. Two hairy old men with long rifles sat up toward the front of the coach wearing greasy leather pants. Their jackets were made entirely of some kind of heavy fur. One had on a strange hat with a wide brim and flat crown. As I passed them, I thought I smelled rancid grease, or was it fermentation—an awful odor.

By now I knew the Lutherans well; I still remember their names as clear as anything, Billy—Olga and Swen Nelson. When I asked them about the stinking old men, Swen assured me the men were just trappers heading west. I remember dozing and dreaming the rest of that day that the trappers' presence and even the way they smelled confirmed my vision that the West was waiting for me.

More immigrant families were on board out of Chicago. They're like me, I thought, going west to start a new life like the Boston posters talked about. One very young couple sat across from us, Sakri and Orril Venohr. East Prussia had been their home. I still remember them because of their strange names that were so hard for me to pronounce. Sakri, the husband, confided that they had only been married a month. Orril spoke no English yet, but she smiled and nodded her head yes. Then she held up one finger patted her hand over Orril heart and then hers.

My *Got*, Billy, their story was so romantic. I've got to tell you. Sakri told me he had arrived on Ellis Island over a year ago without anyone as a sponsor, and without a sponsor, he had to take whatever work was available. So, the immigration authorities sent him to a lumber camp in Louisiana where he almost died of the heat and from all the poisonous sweet potatoes he had to eat every day. It was in the Louisiana lumber camp that he'd learned to speak English. When he finally got away, he sent what little money he had earned to Prussia so Orril could come to America. They were going to Neihart, Montana, where an uncle lived on a dry homestead. Orril said they'd soon get their own farm and live happily ever more. But you know Billy; I didn't want a farm or a husband then. All I wanted was one of those fringed buckskin coats.

As we moved west, the train swayed from side to side more violently, and I kept to my seat. I took out the book of Russell drawings Ingeborg had given me and compared the drawings to the landscape outside the smudgy train window. The pictures didn't match at all. That's how I knew we weren't really in the West yet.

Sometime during the night a group of Italian immigrants began singing to the music of an accordion. What *Gotforsaken* sounding songs, but they appeared happy. One of them moved into the aisle to dance. He circled around and around in front of me and waved his arms like a madman wildly clicking his heels in the air and mumbling some singsong words. The other Italians poked fun at him. I heard one of the old Italian women laugh and say in

English, "Ees love. Ees love." She was clapping her hands and grinning at me. I found it embarrassing. He seemed to have no shame or honor. Low class and pitiable, that's what Olga and Swen said, and I sure agreed.

In St. Paul the Lutherans left the train for good. Their mission was to establish churches in rural Minnesota. Olga hugged me and gave me some of their leftover cheese, more dried fish, and Swedish meat balls.

I was not a very dutiful Lutheran, Billy, but we stood together on the platform holding hands while we somberly repeated together the Apostle's Creed.

> I believe in God, the Father Almighty,
> Maker of heaven and earth . . .
> I believe in the Holy Spirit,
> the Holy Christian Church,
> the communion of saints,
> the Forgiveness of sins,
> the Resurrection of the Body,
> and the Life everlasting. Amen.

Olga and I exchanged our St. Olav metals, held hands, and wiped the tears from our cheeks as their heavy painted trunks were loaded onto a wagon that was to haul them away.

The St. Paul train platform was filled with mud-covered farmers moving slowly. Not the hustle of Chicago now. But, I saw my first live Indians. They were shabbily outfitted. No colorful feathers, no buckskin shirts. Not even faintly like the Russell drawings. Three of them pounded on a big drum, and others hunkered down, wrapped in some dull gray blankets. A couple of them staggered to their feet finally and began to hop and jump around. I was watching them intently when I heard a voice from behind my shoulder.

"They're paid by the railroad to do that, you know."

I turned quickly and saw a winsome young woman pointing over toward the beautifully decorated green and gold first class cars.

"A show for the tourists in first class," she said.

"I thought they were real Indians."

"Oh, they are, but . . . they've gotta make a living just like the rest of us. You're gonna see 'em at every stop. The tourists love it."

"You mean the Indians are paid?"

"Sure. Ever since Roosevelt dedicated that big old Yellowstone Park last year, the tourists have been packing into first class on the Great Northern trains. Yeah, these 'Wild' Indians are part of the show."

We stood silently together watching the Indians dance until the train for Fargo, Bismarck, Fort Benton and points West was called. I was surprised that the young woman boarded the second class coach. She was dressed so elegantly with needle-toed, high-button shoes and a tremendous puffed sleeve blouse. Cousin Ingeborg had told me it was the Gibson Girl look. I wondered why she wasn't with the well-dressed tourists in first class.

"The name's Antoinette Mathilda Walcamp, but they call me Mattie," she said as we found seats together.

"I'm Ovidia, Ovidia Odegard, on my way to work for Nancy and Charles Russell in Great Falls. He's a great, well-known cowboy artist, you know." I pressed the last of the dead violets into my *Virginian* book and took a deep breath before packing the book into my bag.

"Well, we're headed for the same place then. I got me a job dealing faro at the Mint Saloon. I hear they just sit there in Great Falls waiting to put their money into circulation." She took my bare hand in her gloved one. "I'm from Dennison, Ohio. Awful small town. Don't ever go to Ohio if you can avoid it. Don't do nothing there except thump their bibles, eat their Shaker lemon pie, and drink that damned tomato juice. It's just plain enough to curdle your stomach and curl your hair."

We watched the few cowboys and ranchers who had gotten on in St. Paul stash away their rifles. They wore tight pants and close fitting jackets with their high boots. Some had guns in their belts, but I saw no buckskin jackets. One young cowboy had leggings made of animal skins with long fringes hanging off the outside of his legs. The fringes swayed gracefully when he walked. He was the most handsome man I'd seen since coming to America. I couldn't stop watching him. Mattie poked me with her elbow, shook her head and frowned, reminding me not to stare, so I turned to watch the two old trappers in their furs who were still on board. A group of miners with heavy boxes of equipment got on board, and a new bunch of gamblers had arrived. A couple of them in shiny satin vests. Mattie called them "tinhorns." She seemed to know everything and made hushed comments about all the men in the car.

"Look at that cowboy, so bowlegged he can't even change his socks. An' that rancher, he's gettin' long in the tooth. Remember, Ovidia, most men are like a bob-wire fence, they have their good points," she laughed loudly, but I had no idea what she was talking about.

After we'd been swaying and jolting for hours, I asked Mattie, "Where are the buffalo? And the horse riders?"

I pulled out my Russell drawings of the West and showed them to her. "Look." I held the drawing up to the dust streaked window to compare. "The land looks the same, but where are the buffalo?"

"Gone," she said. "It's gonna be copper mines and wheat fields now. A bunch of sheep still around though." I guess I frowned. "Oh, stop looking so disappointed. This trip should teach you something. Ever played cards?"

"I learned on the ship. Everyday single day during the six weeks from Norway we played cards," I replied. "Once a day we could go on deck for only a few minutes, so we were packed together most of the time. Another passenger on the ship, a short little old man, saw how my arm and hand were so swollen from the smallpox scratchings, and he gave me some wet weed-like stuff to put over it."

"Was it tobacco?"

"I don't know. He told me it would draw out the poison. Said he learned it from the Indians, but I didn't believe him. We played cards to forget how long the trip was taking. *Ja*, he was a strange old man. Taught me a game he called 'Black Jack.' Said the game was named after him, Jack Tarr. But he wasn't a tar-burner like in Norway. Didn't even have black hair. Kind of white mostly, with some faded red. I thought he was Norwegian at first though."

"Hope he didn't con you outta all your life savings."

"Did he steal from me or trick me? *Nei*, he told me all kinds of stories of American history, about the great Indian battle at Little Big Horn. Said he was there when General Custer was killed. Said he lived with the Indians and told me how he was almost scalped. Scary custom, I thought, cutting off the skin of the head, my *Got*."

"Sounds to me like he gave you a cock-an-bull story. Probably not true."

"No, it's true, Mattie. He said he was with the Buffalo Bill's Wild West show in England. Told me he played an Indian, and he got separated from the show when they went to France. Had to find his way back to America working at anything he could find. He said he even went up to Lofoten with the fishing fleet. When the weather is bad, they play cards. Learned his Norwegian up there. He was real clever with all kinds of languages. "

"Sounds down-to-earth anyway."

"He sure could play cards. Taught me how to count cards and told me all about dealer busts. I prized every minute of it."

"So then, it's time for a little more practice. What're we waitin' for," Mattie said as she stood and pulled my arm. "I'll stake you fifty cents."

It was an enormous sum. "Old Mr. Tarr told me I was a canny gambler. He said I had both watching skill and intuitive analysis. I'm not sure what he was talking about, but I'll be careful of your stake, Mattie."

"Jus' come on." She pulled me up and toward the fancy looking gamblers. There were shouts of excitement from the group when we joined them. Mattie did all the talking. She sure knew how to handle gamblers.

After a few hands of poker, she suggested Black Jack. I sat with my back against the wall and waited watching the players carefully. I could see that Mattie was what my shipmate, Jack Tarr, had called a "locator." What she did, Billy, was watch the position of one card and she only bet when she knew the play favored her. I played cautiously, betting little, but concentrating. I was worried about losing Mattie's stake.

Mattie caught my eye and whispered, "I believe you musta had a good teacher."

A conductor passed through the coach lighting the kerosene lamps, and Mattie proposed a break. In the grubby toilet, shared by all the second class passengers, she taught me a lesson about gambling I never forgot.

"Rule number one—know who you're playing against," she said. "This is the way it stacks up with these tinhorns. I've been watching their nervous tells. Only one player out there, Morgan, the one with the tobacco-stained handlebar mustache, is a professional gambler. The young fellow in the yellow satin vest, Virgil, he's a real tenderfoot. Seated hisself so that his cards are reflected in the train window. You always know what he has. The old gent, Hoss, well, he's not so bad, but probably never was too smart. Notice how he uses an overhand shuffle. And, Mr. Satin Brocade Vest there, I think they call him Edgar, the one with the fancy gold chain, he thinks he's good, but check the careless cuts he makes. Not one of those four can give you any trouble. Now, let's pick up the pace. You're doing fine."

I must admit I thought Mattie knew everything. When we returned to the game, I was pretty agitated. So far, I was doing all right. By late that night, my winnings amounted to only thirty-five cents, but I felt I was just getting started. We took another break and when the play began again, the professional gambler, Morgan, was dealing. The tenderfoot, Virgil, hollered, "Hit me again." Morgan flipped down the card and Virgil yelled, "Oh damn it. I'm over." Then it was my call.

I had a soft fourteen, an ace and a three-spot. "Hit me." And I drew a nine for a count of thirteen. With a glance I confirmed that the dealer's up card was a six. And I didn't even hesitate saying, "I stand." Morgan, of course, had to hit his sixteen count, got a seven and went bust. He was clearly irritated. The tenderfoot, Virgil, left the group to retire, and I began gaining ground. I can't forget this because it was my first big night of real gambling, though certainly not my last.

You <u>do</u> gamble, don't you, Billy? I wondered 'cause you looked kind of puzzled when I said I stood on a low thirteen count. You see I knew old Morgan had to hit a sixteen. I was betting he'd go bust, and he sure did. I'm going to have to start teaching you something about real gambling, Billy. Sure this bingo is slow, but you know, sometimes it suits me just fine these days. So where were we? Oh yeah, on the train coming into Great Falls, I remember.

By sunrise, there were only three of us left in the game, Morgan, Hoss, and me. Mattie had taken her winnings and was stretched out asleep across two of the seats wrapped in her woolen cape. The deal had passed to me after a natural, a beautiful king and an Ace of spades. That gave me the advantage I'd been looking for. The old man, Hoss, had scrupulously cut the cards. My *Got*, I'll never forget that hand.

I squared the deck, and the players placed their bets. The stakes had gone up, almost a week's salary for me. My up card was a paint, a ten count. The professional, Morgan, looked hard at me. I just held his gaze. He slid his cards face-up under his bet and doubled it. He'd held a seven and a four for an eleven count. "Do you want to double down?" I asked quietly.

"What's it look like, dammit. Deal." Morgan said.

"One more then," I replied calmly.

Jack had taught me to never get emotional over a card game. I flipped the card out face-down, while Morgan was whining, "I beseech you sweet JEE-sus."

Old Hoss, his voice quivering, was whispering, "Gimme that nine, gimme that nine. I'm beggin' ya. I'm beggin' ya. Hit me. Hit me with the big nine spot."

I peeled off the top card from the deck. It was an eight.

"Sommabitch." moaned Hoss.

I turned over my hole card. It was another paint for a twenty count.

"Push. Be damned," said the old guy. He'd been holding twelve in the hole. We both held a twenty count and as dealer, I took the push. "Now, if you'll excuse me, I'm through for the night," Hoss said, and he shoved his bets toward me.

Morgan said nothing as he pushed his stack of silver dollars toward me. His single face-down card had been an ace. Either way, count it high for twenty-two, or low for twelve, Morgan lost. To be honest, I was pleased. I knew then I'd make my fortune in the West.

No, Billy, I'm not off on a tangent talking about gambling. Don't get impatient with me. I'm telling you all this about the gambling because it is important to the story of the State House painting fraud. You'll see that as soon as we move along with the how the deception came about, but anyway we were almost to Great Falls by that time, and . . . .

About that time, the conductor moved through the coach calling, "One hour to Great Falls. An hour to Great

Falls." Everyone began stirring. Mattie sat up from where she'd been sleeping across the seats. She stood, shook out her woolen cape, and pointed toward the train windows. Surprising, but outside I finally saw the Russell drawing complete with a few buffalo.

Up in front from the first class coaches, we could hear the crack of rifle fire. And then came the smell of gun powder. I opened the closest window to see what was going on. Looking forward I saw rifle barrels protruding from the first class train windows and black smoke drifting back toward us. The shots came fast and loud. The two old trappers in our carriage now watched from the car steps. They were shaking their bearded heads in disapproval. Through the rifle fire I could hear their gravely voices.

"Well shit."

"What the hell? Them poor buff's probably some of the last of the sixty million."

Two buffalo staggered and fell. The small herd was running parallel beside the train trying to outrun it without success. Two more went down. Only a half dozen remained, and when the lead bull fell, the rest finally turned away. The shooting continued more rapidly now and only stopped when three more dropped, and then it was silent except for the grinding of the iron train wheels.

Mattie was awake and standing in the aisle by my side shaking her head. "Now you know what happened to the buffalo," she said.

THREE

The Electric City

When I stepped off the train in Great Falls, the first thing I noticed was the cold. It was late March, and a biting sort of dry cold entered my lungs and seemed to burn every time I inhaled. Mattie said it was the change from spending days in the overheated train.

The railway station seemed overly large and barn-like. When I looked out the smudged windows, I could see a tall smoke stack belching a steady stream of thick black smoke, not exactly the West I had anticipated.

"They call it 'The Big Stack.' The pride and joy of the Boston and Montana Copper Smelter," said Mattie.

The scene spoke of progress and expectation, and once outside the station, the town looked modern. Not aged like Boston, but up-to-date. The streets were wide and slushy from a recent snow that still lingered gray and dingy with soot in the shaded corners and below the wooden boards of the three-foot high sidewalk.

Mattie and I stood on the platform waiting for our belongings from the baggage car. The usual group of shabby Indians hung out at the station trying to decide whether or not to put on their show. Watching them didn't cheer me. Seeing the buffalo killed had left me with a gloomy feeling I couldn't shake. "My *Got* Mattie, but this isn't what I expected." I shook my head as I addressed her.

"Paris Gibson calls it the Electric City. He's the man got the place started," Mattie answered. "Everything's modern here. Gibson says it's going to be the Pittsburgh of the Great Northwest. That's why I'm here. My job down to The Mint Saloon's going to be a good one. Nothing but drinking tea from a shot glass an' dealing Faro an' Monte for a while." Mattie grinned and the dimples on each side of her cheeks appeared. "Anyway Ovidia, I expect that before long that cute little Cupid feller with his bow and arrow is gonna cinch up one of those mining engineers for me, or maybe a wealthy rancher."

"You mean you're looking for a husband?"

"Sure thing, Honey, I bet you ain't gonna like being somebody's housemaid—even in the great cowboy artist's house. Hell, with your blonde hair and big blue eyes, you could come along down to the Mint. Bet they'd be happy to let you deal. Hell, those bar regulars, why they'd hover around you grinning like weasels peekin' in the henhouse door."

"I'd like to Mattie, but I owe the money. Uncle Nils has given his word, and I'm obliged to pay him back. Besides, I sure won't put up with things I don't like. I told Uncle Nils, '*Ja*, I have to hire out, but I'm nobody's servant. I'm not going to empty any slops.'"

"Well, stick to it," she said nodding and giving me a hug around the shoulders.

I was shivering. I still don't know whether it was from the cold or the shock of seeing Great Falls for the first time. Everything seemed so, so . . . industrial. Where were the trees, I wondered, and the cowboys?

The Montana wind went right through my wool shawl. Colder than a witch's tit we'd say in Norway. The spring time mud had discouraged the arriving first class tourists from crossing to the ritzy three-story brick hotel down the street. While they huddled together waiting, the group of squalid Indians finally began hopping around dancing to the beat of their huge drum. Finally a handsome horse drawn Northern Pacific carriage arrived, and the contingent of mining engineers, along with the stylish tourists in their boots and high crowned hats, started boarding.

"You'd better save some of your winnings to buy some real warm clothes as soon as you can," said Mattie.

"I'll try. I don't look American, do I? People stare. I'll need to send money to Uncle Nils to speed up repayment, but . . . maybe a warm coat." I stamped my feet to try and warm them.

Mattie turned and set out boldly edging her way between the tourists toward the board sidewalk in front of first class. She didn't hesitate a minute. She simply pushed ahead and waved to me as she boarded the fancy first class carriage. When the carriage pulled out, the Indians abruptly stopped their howling and their war-dance and hunkered back down covered in their dingy blankets. Now that I knew the railroad and Paris Gibson paid them, I wasn't surprised by their actions. They were part of the Western atmosphere.

Only a few smelter employees remained outside the station talking with a tall man in a worsted sack coat. He looked rangy and American to me. But he did have glorious white-blond hair like the men from Norjfiord. . . . He was old though. I guessed he was probably at least thirty. I watched him hand out some cards and then leave the smelter people and walk toward me, so I turned and moved away to the other end of the station. He caught up with me though and even started walking right beside me. In my opinion, he was being very arrogant.

"Evening, Miss. Name's Carl. I'm here rounding up strays, an . . . ."

"I'm no stray." I interrupted him stamping my foot. I turned, faced him directly and spoke precisely and clearly. "Mrs. Charles Marion Russell is meeting me . . . the wife of the famous cowboy artist." I tried to speak with dignity, but I knew my Norwegian showed. I couldn't stop the Norwegian sounds from slipping in.

"Well, in that case, Miss Brunhilde, I've known Mr. Charlie M. Russell for a long time, and believe me, he's as slow acting as wet gunpowder."

He knew I was an immigrant. I stamped my foot again. I'd freeze him out.

As I turned away to look up the muddy street, I saw a large, noisy beer wagon pulled by six matching Clydesdales rumbling toward the station. Painted on the side of the wagon in big red and gold letters was a sign that read, "BRUNSWICK SALOON," and below in smaller letters, "Private Lounge for the Ladies." The driver was dressed in handsome British tweeds, but he looked short and portly, with large drooping mustaches. I tried to take no notice of the beer wagon, but the odor absolutely commanded my attention.

When the wagon had pulled up right in front of the station, the driver called down from his high seat. "Sorry Miss. Late again, I'm afraid."

He couldn't be talking to me. I ignored him.

"Miss Odegard? Are you expecting Mrs. Russell?"

What could he possibly want with me? And, where was Nancy Russell? I began to feel anxious.

"You are Miss Odegard, aren't you?" He yelled down again. "I had to deliver old Charlie Russell home from the Brunswick, and Nancy asked me to come find you."

Before I could answer, the rangy blond man stepped forward and interrupted. "So, it is Miss Odegard, is it? I knew all the time you had to be 'Brynhilde.' You can't disguise that foot tapping and the painted trunk." He pointed rudely at my luggage. He was teasing me now, just hoping I'd respond, but I was determined to pay no heed to him.

"It's here, Miss Brynhilde," he said grinning. "Your carriage awaits. Sent by the 'famous cowboy artist.'" He swept his arm in a kind of salute and made an exaggerated low bow. I knew I wasn't going to like that man, but he just kept at it. "Your royal carriage, along with your gracious driver, Albert Trigg, from the Brunswick Saloon, come to fetch you directly to the Russell palace."

The wagon driver hefted his pot belly over the side of the beer wagon, climbed down, and the two men exchanged slaps on the back.

"Ah, Miss Odegard, don't let this scalawag politician tease you. He's running for reelection to the State Assembly and he'd do anything for a vote. Charming the constituents

is his middle name, but Carl Holmes is what they call
him."

So he was a 'Holmes,' just as I suspected. Just as Norwegian as I was, not American at all, but, my *Got,* he
looked so American. I remembered Uncle Nils telling me
that Norwegians, who didn't even have a town name to
give themselves, took the name Holmes.

Did you know that, Billy? Back then, at home in Norway, we didn't use second names, not in those days. Just a
first name and the name of the town or farm we were from.
Seems kind of strange now, I guess, looking back on it. But
then I had to laugh because 'Mr. Holmes' wasn't a rancher,
or a cowboy, or even a smelter worker. He was just another
Norwegian, like me.

The two men finally loaded my trunk on top of the
beer kegs. It looked like it could clearly slide off and my
uneasiness increased as I battled to reach the high step of
the wagon. The problem was, I couldn't, but I didn't want
any help from them. Before I knew what was going on,
the two men grabbed my elbows. Then while I kicked and
struggled, they flipped me up onto the high wagon seat.

"I could have done it myself," I protested.

"Easier than throwing a calf. You be careful around
Miss Odegard here, Albert. She's a gal with sand in her
craw."

I wanted to respond. To put Carl Holmes in his place,
but the smell of the beer wagon and my worry over the
safety of my trunk left me without English words. I pulled
Ingeborg's handkerchief from my handbag and covered my
nose.

Carl gave Albert Trigg a salute and shouted, "I'll slide off and cool my saddle down at the Brunswick later tonight."

Trigg nodded and snapped the reins over the horses' backs, and they jolted forward. To avoid looking at Carl, I buried my face in the handkerchief and looked away as the wagon lumbered slowly down the wide street through the mud. My *Got*, I didn't want to see Carl Holmes standing there giving me another bow.

I told myself to concentrate on the street crowd, mostly a motley group of Indians, a few cowboys, miners, and tourists. The tourists were dressed like Easterners with stiff shirt fronts, but they had their pants shortened and tucked up into those high lace-up boots they seemed to fancy.

"You're watching those spiffy tourists, are you?" asked Trigg.

"I sense that they're watching us," I said. "Are we part of the show?"

"Well, ever since John Muir wrote all that stuff about the glories of nature making you truly immortal, they've been flocking here. And then too, the Great Northern has to tout their new Glacier Hotel up at the park. Lucky for us, most of them stay over here in Great Falls for a few days. Good for business it is."

"Well then, Mr. Trigg, if they're looking for the glories of nature and fancy it so, why were the tourists shooting buffalo from the train?" I asked.

"Part of the sport. Part of what they come for—not much left to shoot at though."

I turned away. I couldn't talk about the buffalo. Instead I watched the mining people on Central Avenue dressed in heavy woolen three piece suits with coats to the knees. Most of them had round flat hats with small brims, or they wore those stiff black things the people in Boston had called Derbies. I was afraid to embarrass myself by asking Mr. Trigg if that's what they were. Near some shops, a group of stylish women walked carefully on the wooden board sidewalk. Their heads were covered with great flower gardens in full bloom and it was still winter here too. I smothered my snickering in Ingeborg's handkerchief, but Trigg saw me watching them.

"Oh, they're wives of the Boston and Montana smelter managers. Out shopping, all dolled up in their hats and gloves. It's spring time you understand." I didn't because it still looked like winter to me.

Trigg's business interests prompted him to point out all the saloons. "Now across there, Miss, is The Mint. Old Sid Willis owns it. Always sits by the door chewing a cigar. Cheap food in there. Tourists seem to like it. Then over there across the street, that's The Maverick that the mining workers patronize. The Silver Dollar is that fancy decorated one back there with all the electric lights, right across from The Mint. The quality always goes there, mining engineers and such. I think Bill Rance, the owner, has them all fooled with his fancy gold headed cane and *boulevardier* manners."

"Well where do the cowboys go?"

"Not many cowboys left, Miss Odegard. Over yonder's my place, The Brunswick Saloon. Most classy establishment in town. Charlie Russell used to paint in the little back room there. Thought he liked it, but then he got married. . . . All of us told him. 'Charlie,' we said, 'you're making a mistake getting married. You're taking on an awful responsibility.' Mame, that's what he calls his wife Nancy, she's got a bad heart. Often faints just dead away. Probably had rheumatic fever."

"Is Mrs. Russell sickly?" I asked.

"That's not exactly it," Trigg hesitated and then continued slowly in his charming English accent. "But, she stays in bed considerable."

"She's not suited for physical work?" I asked.

"Maudlin, just simply maudlin that's what it is. She often talks about the rosewood coffin she bought when her mother died in Helena . . . ."

"Her mother died?" I interrupted. "My mother died too. That's why I'm here." I began to feel a sympathetic kinship with Nancy Russell.

"Yep, I believe it gives her a feeling of dignity—that rosewood coffin. Talks about it all the time. Nancy likes dignity . . . ." We were leaving the downtown and entering an area of smaller shops and brick apartment buildings.

". . . Then after Charlie's mother died, his old Dad, Charles Silas, came out here. Saw how they were living. Didn't make him too happy. Charles Silas is a real English style gentleman. He has a big estate in St. Louis you know. Russ and Nancy were living in a rundown shack over in Boston Heights."

I had a moment of panic. Boston Heights? Boston? I had just come from Boston. Why were the Russells living in Boston? The sound of the beer sloshing around in the casks whenever we hit another rut in the street was making me feel seasick.

"But . . . I thought this was Great Falls, Montana. What is Boston Heights?" I managed to mumble.

"Where all the low-class smelter workers live."

Trigg was talkative. He lit a big cigar. The acrid odor of the cigar mixed with the sour smell of the beer. I was getting dizzy, but he kept on talking.

"The daddy, that's old Charles Silas Russell, built them a real nice house. Trouble is—Nancy really wanted something better. She's determined to live up on Smelter Hill. It's the finest neighborhood. But only for Boston and Montana Company engineers."

"What difference does it make?" I asked.

"Well, Nancy will never get voted into the Shakespeare Club or the Maids and Matrons unless she lives in the right neighborhood. Where they live isn't bad, but Little Chicago, that neighborhood would keep you out forever. A real calamity that place."

I was trying to remember all those names: Smelter Hill, Little Chicago, Boston Heights. Was all this important? How could I understand it? And, who were the Maids and Matrons? Maybe there was some kind of American royalty I'd never heard about.

Trigg cracked the reins over the horses again, and they picked up the pace as we entered a residential neighborhood. The land was almost totally flat, and once we left the two-story buildings, the big smoke stack of the smelter in the northeast was always in view. Frail little sapling trees grew in the yards and some sparse grass, but the only things that seemed to be actually growing were the telephone poles that lined the side of every street.

The beer wagon turned onto a street with a sign that said, Fourth Avenue North. Trigg pulled up on the reins and stopped in front of a modest, two-story, clapboard house with a large front porch. He pointed to the house. "That's it. That's the Russell's palace," he said.

"Oh, Mr. Trigg, this <u>does</u> look like a nice house. It <u>is</u> a palace." I was pleased. It looked comfortable, and as Trigg helped me from the wagon, my anticipation increased. At least there wouldn't be cows living on the ground floor, and I couldn't wait to see if Charles Russell looked like the picture on the front of my book.

Albert Trigg helped me down from the wagon's high seat, and we followed a short gravel walkway toward the house. Our footsteps were making crunching noises on the gravel, but as we approached the building, I could hear muffled snoring sounds. Asleep in the far corner of the porch near the door was an old Indian wrapped in a striped blanket.

"Hey, up-and-at-em, Young Boy," Trigg said giving the Indian a shove with the pointed tip of his western boot. The Indian managed to sit up on his haunches, but stumbled as he tried to stand. "Make yourself useful now. I'd be pleased if you'd get that trunk from over there in the wagon and fetch it on around to the maid's room." The Indian gave a hand signal and shuffled off toward the wagon.

Groans and grunts seemed to come from inside the house as we got nearer the door. I hesitated, and the sounds increased in volume. I stopped before I got to the door, but Mr. Trigg moved on ahead. He reached for the door handle, turned it, gave a shove and pushed the door wide open without even knocking.

That scene, Billy, what I saw when the door opened is drawn in my memory with indelible pencil. I'll never forget it. Charlie Russell stood in the little parlor right off the entry, shirt off, half-naked, his bare torso twisted at a contorted angle, one arm raised as if to throw a spear. Instead of a spear though, he held a long handled paint brush. He was looking backward over his shoulder into a large mirror as he twisted and turned. Meanwhile an Indian woman in full buckskin costume squatted on a dirty red and yellow blanket in front of him. She held a long pipe and wore a great many beaded necklaces. Heavy turquoise stones hung down from her earlobes.

Charlie grinned at us and moved to pick up a glass. He raised his drink in a salute to Trigg mumbling something that sounded like an Indian language. And then he opened his mouth and laughed madly.

I was stunned. A stuffed parrot and a great horned owl stared down at me from a high shelf. Several saddles were heaped in the left corner along with a buffalo horn head-dress. There were stage drivers' gauntlets made of short black fur that looked to have come from a dog. Horse bits, headstalls, reins, stirrups, spurs and other stuff I couldn't even name covered the entry way and streamed into the dining room and the parlor.

Indian blankets, spears, animal skins, guns, and buffalo skulls decorated the walls. Ropes and feathers hung from the antlers of a deer head hanging over the mirror. Paints, paint boxes, brushes, easels, and art gear were mixed in with the cowboy and Indian items on the dining table. One easel had an unfinished picture of an Indian buffalo hunt. And, the Ghost Dance shirt with all the teeth, the one I told you about, it was pinned to the wall facing the entry doorway. The house was chaos.

"Hou how hourk," Charlie kept grunting, as he waved his hands and used Indian sign language to signal something to Trigg. Trigg frowned, but returned the hand signal. Russell then turned from Trigg and addressed me.

"You look as scairt as a rabbit in a wolf's mouth."

At this moment, before I could answer, I got my first glimpse at Nancy Russell. She was slowly descending the narrow stairs in a flashy red and black, lace-covered dress. She looked like a harlot.

"Oh my, dee-ah," she said, as she held out her hand to me. "I'm just so sonnabitchin, damned glad you're here."

And with this, Charlie spotted his Mame, gave her a sly look, grabbed her buttocks, and as she squealed, he hooted and chased her up the stairway. They both disappeared amid screams and laughter.

I guess I <u>was</u> "as scairt as a rabbit," Billy. I suspected they were both lunatics. Uncle Nils had sent me to keep house for the mentally deranged, and there was nowhere else to go. Run from the house? To where? To the Mint Saloon hoping I'd find Mattie? The Indian, Young Boy, appeared at this moment with my painted trunk. The sight of it brought some solace.

"Ah, ah well, you may need a bita' help getting used to things around here," said Trigg. "My wife, Margaret, and I live right next door, down there to the left. Whatever you need . . . just ask."

I followed Trigg and the old Indian as they carried the trunk through the kitchen and into the small maid's room. The kitchen smelled as strong as sheepherder's socks, and the roaches ran races on every flat surface. The two men carried the trunk into the room off the kitchen and left quickly.

I entered what was to be my room and slammed the door to keep the stink from the kitchen at bay. The room was tiny, but the last of the evening sun entered through two narrow windows facing the small barn. I raised the windows and looked around. Everything was dusty. The iron cot had a dirty white cotton coverlet. I circled the room stamping my foot in disgust.

On the wall were glitzy Victorian-style pictures of wood nymphs. Ugly things, tiny fairylike ladies with wings perched on branches trying to catch butterflies. This can't be the West, I thought. The pictures looked like Norwegian river sprites, and they could very well have been evil ones. I ripped them down and tossed them out the window.

I grabbed my bag and took out the Russell picture book Ingeborg had given me in Boston, the *Studies of Western Life*. The western illustrations were more like what I wanted and had expected to find in the West. I carefully tore out several pages and poked them onto the nails where the wood nymphs had hung. Afterward, I stepped back and looked at my decorating work with approval. Yes, it would work. "I'm here. It will be fine. I'm here in the West," I said out loud.

It was then that I noticed them, the bead covered Indian woman and old Young Boy. They were watching me through one of the open windows. "How picturesque." I grumbled as I crossed to the window, slammed it shut, and pulled down the roller shade. I thought I was going to cry for a minute. I really felt like crying, but then strangely, I don't know why, Billy, but I started to laugh instead.

FOUR

Another New Language

Like you say, Billy, throwing those pictures out the window when I had just arrived at the Russell's was a bold thing to do, I suppose. Sure, they could have been important or valuable. But, nobody ever said a word about the disappearance of those wood sprites. I think maybe the Indians took them. Hell, maybe they sold them to one of the saloons.

Anyway, I never saw those pictures again. It turned out that Charlie was a salty old romanticist and did a bunch of racy stuff for the saloons. That's one of the reasons he was so popular and one of the reasons Nancy was so often damned annoyed. She believed all the world loved Charlie, and she didn't want to share him. But I didn't know all of that at first. That night I was worn-out from the train and dismayed by so many newfangled ideas and whatchamacallits. All I wanted to do was fall onto that iron cot with the spotted old coverlet even though it didn't look too snug.

Trouble was, the ashes had blown in the train windows and I sure felt grubby. *Got,* I even thought I could hear Aunty Anna's voice coming clear over from Norway grumbling in my ear like the train wheels, 'cleanliness is next to *Gotliness,* cleanliness is next to *Gotliness,*' over and over. I finally pulled myself together to search for the bath or at least some water to clean up a bit, and I didn't know where the *vassen closet* might be. Maybe out by the barn.

I left my room and started wandering around the house. Where were the Russells? The house was totally silent. It was getting dark, but the house was full of Paris Gibson's electric lights. Strings hanging down from the ceiling in every room. I found I could pull on one and it became day light. No dangerous candles, no messy oil lamps with chimneys to clean. Amazing.

Right off the kitchen I discovered a real bathroom. A wonder, better than the one at Uncle Nils' house in Boston. The biggest bathtub I'd ever seen, all shining white, with animal claws for feet and handles that turned to fill it, one for hot water and one for cold. No buckets to carry. Not even a pump. The place was indeed a palace.

I turned on the water, and while the tub was filling, I tried out the toilet. No *vasser closet* out by the barn here, thank *Got,* but I thought there should be some lime powder to throw in. I searched around, but there was none, so I guessed it wasn't necessary with all the water sitting there and all. Hanging down from a large box suspended over the white bowl was a thin gold chain. I yanked on it, and water gushed down with a loud whoosh, scaring me to death, and—well, everything went away, everything. If I had any doubts, or choice, about staying on at the Russell's, they disappeared right then. I could put up with

Mr. Russell's "Hou how hourking" easily since there sure wouldn't be any slops to empty.

I took off my dirty clothes, folded them neatly on a wooden chair, and got into the hot tub. What comfort. I could feel the warmth finally reaching my bones. I leaned back. This would be different from our old farmhouse in Nordfjord. *Nei*, that farm—it had been so crowded—I tried to picture the place in my mind. I remembered only a desolate, remote place, on the small island of Odegard. The house had been stout and square, and it looked like a two-story barn with grasses and wild flowers growing on the roof. Actually, it was a barn since the animals were brought into the lower floor at night and stayed inside with us all winter. Without them, we'd freeze and starve which we almost did anyway.

But the smell—that's why I don't like cows. You have to constantly clean up after them. I'd rather eat nothing but boiled potatoes and skip the milk. When I was little, I thought the cows were crazy. When we'd let them out in the spring, they'd stagger around stupidly, totally blind. With my twin brothers, Emil and Hans, I'd tease them by shaking blankets until they ran around in circles. Of course, we didn't do this when father was around.

Luckily, father was gone a lot. In the winter he went fishing at Lofoten, and then later he began coming to America for the winter to work as a stone mason in Wisconsin or Minnesota. He'd stay for six months or so, earn a high salary, and then return home to Odegard using his new American words like *gootamorn, gootafanoon, hiee, koofa-ka-fee-plees*. I'd repeat the words. It was our game, when he was in a good humor, but most of the time he wasn't. It helped me with my English though when Uncle Nils sent me to those classes in Boston.

Well, I knew I didn't have to worry about that anymore, but sprawling there in the tub thinking about those
poor cows made me sad. I remembered how wasted and
gaunt they were by spring. Their eyes so cavernous. I could
remember how they stood during the long winter, endur-
ing in the dark stalls, and suddenly I knew I missed my
home in Odegard because hot tears were running down my
cheeks. I closed my eyes and could picture that house with
the grass growing on the roof and the family all standing
there surrounded by the cows.

But the bath water was getting cold. I shook myself,
pulled the rubber plug and listened to the swirling water
gurgle away. With it, my memories of Norway spun down
the drain too and were put aside. Life would start new for
me here in the West with the cowboys, the Russells, and
what was left of the buffalo.

The next day I was up well before dawn. The nasty stink
of the kitchen seeping in under my door needed attention.
I had to do something about it. I dressed quickly in an old

gray skirt and woolen tunic. Just outside the kitchen door a bucket and some rags were piled inside a kind of shed.

Before taking them in and getting to work, I walked out onto the thin grass and stood outside looking at the morning star low on the eastern horizon and at the white smoke clouds coming from the smelter to the north. I heard the horses snuffling quietly in the barn and pictured them watching me. Maybe they were quietly talking about the new housemaid. The West appeared so silent in the morning and the air smelled nice. A new kind of scent of something I couldn't identify. I took in several deep breaths. "This is it." I said aloud. "The West." And I turned back toward the unpleasant smell in the kitchen.

As I scraped the grease from the stove, I day-dreamed. This place could be Valhalla yet, if only these people who seemed so irresponsible could learn how to organize and do things right. I'd need to teach them.

The wooden ice box reeked of mold, and the water pan under it was overflowing. Trying to empty it, I accidentally sloshed water all over the boards of the kitchen floor, but that just made it easier to scrub. I was making progress on the kitchen. As I worked, I repeated English words aloud, carefully practicing my pronunciation like Uncle Nils had suggested. I wanted to get rid of my Norwegian accent.

Just after dawn I heard heavy clumping on the stairway and Charlie Russell thumped into the kitchen in his high heeled riding boots with the floppy mule ears, fully dressed this time. No buckskin shirt and wooly pants like in the picture on the cover of my book though. He looked more up to date, but splashy, even though the boots had plain tops and plain black stitching. He wasn't turned out like the engineers or tourists I had seen yesterday on Central

Avenue, but he did have the same hard looking eyes as on the book cover.

Instead of a six-gun strapped around his hips, he wore a long, red, hand-woven sash that I later found out was a Métis sash used the by Indian half-breeds. He sure didn't look like a half-breed though because his hair was light and sandy colored. The sash wrapped twice around his waist and tucked up on the left side with the long tassels hanging down almost to the floor. Indian-style, I guess. Gold and silver rings with colorful gem stones adorned all of his fingers, and a sack of Bull Durham bulged from the pocket of his white shirt. Instead of a tie, a faded scarf was tied loosely around his neck. It took me awhile to realize that this was going to be his customary attire. No jeans in those days, at least not in Great Falls, just dark trousers of some heavy material.

"Wahl, if it ain't the scairt rabbit." He stopped just inside the kitchen doorway, and we stared at each other. "So . . . if ya ain't gonna run on off, I better know who you are."

"Ovidia Odegard," I said. He unsettled me, and I knew I would have to get over it.

"Owidi what?" He spoke from the side of his mouth. . . . Now that's no name for a good lookin' little package like you, rosy cheeks, blonde hair an' all. Sounds more like the moniker you'd put on your best sow."

I was momentarily embarrassed and then annoyed. I stamped my foot. "Well, Mr. Russell, your wife sent for me, so you'd better get used to saying 'Ovidia' because I'm going to be around here for some time. The name is a common one in Norway." He hadn't noticed the kitchen cleaning I'd done. He hadn't smelled the coffee, and he didn't seem to care that I had taken out and polished the fancy electric chrome waffle iron.

"Don't get your steam up. Hell, you'll soon see I'm mostly all gurgle and no gut. Right now I'm so damned hungry I could eat a sow an' nine pigs an' chase the ol' boar a half-a-mile," he said.

"I'm not sure what you're talking about, Mr. Russell. Sows and nine pigs? . . . A boar?"

"Wahl, dammit. I heared you talked English. Don't ya? I'm trying to tell you my stomach's so shrunk up it wouldn't even chamber a liver pill."

"Why do you talk like that, Mr. Russell? You're from the city, aren't you? . . . St. Louis, Mr. Trigg said. Right here in America. Mr. Trigg told me yesterday your father is quality."

"Wahl, old Albert, he's as full of verbal lather as a shaving mug."

"He said you went to expensive private schools."

"Wahl Owidi, I try to hide it. Try to hide it. Sides, it never took. My thinker is plumb puny. They all tol' me that."

He started to sit down at the kitchen table but stood back up abruptly coming toward where I was standing by the cook stove. "Come on," he said, "I gotta show you sumpin'. Teach you 'bout how things are round here. Show you what I do exactly, 'fore you get any big ideas from the Triggs or even from my darlin' Mame." Charlie grabbed my arm and hauled me into the cluttered dining room.

In the morning light, I could see that the walls of the downstairs rooms were covered in dark paneling and even darker woodwork, but it was hard to tell since there were so many strange objects hanging all over. He rummaged through a pile of Indian necklaces made of bones, shells, and Chinese coins that were on the dining room table. "They's here someplace, dammit."

Pushing aside some bottles of turpentine, varnish, and shellac, and some half-finished canvases, he finally found a couple of pen and ink drawings on some heavy paper. He snapped on the dining room lights and shoved the drawings on top of some animal skins. "Now I want ya to lookie this. You might's well understand, it's what they all want from me. An' that's what my sweet Mame'd even like fer me too. I call it *My Studio as Mother Thought*," he said.

The drawing showed an artist's salon. A prissy look-ing artist in a cravat and quilted jacket stood before an enormous easel working on a painting of a foreign looking woman with a big jar balanced on her head. The artist's black hair was slicked-down and he had a large handle-bar mustache that twisted to sharp points on either side of his nose. To his side, a fancy lady in high collar, bil-lowy sleeves, and feathered hat was watching him coyly. The studio had a real uppity look: a Victorian lamp, Japanese parasol, heavy draperies, and some of the wood nymph drawings like those I had torn off my wall the night before. On the floor was a large, bear rug. To me, the whole thing looked pretty silly, but then I'd never seen an artist's studio. I covered my mouth with my fist to stifle a giggle.

"An' now, lookie this one, Owidi. Here I be. Few years back now. Best time of my life. In the shack. Up in the Cascades, Jake Hoover's old' cabin, pleased as a heifer with a new fence post."

I had to suppress a titter at this one too. It was clearly Charlie Russell himself in his riding boots and Métis sash, blond hair all tussled up, sitting on a wooden crate in a log cabin before a tiny little easel painting a picture of a man on horseback. Watching the artist in wonderment this time was not a lady with billowy sleeves, but a scruffy looking Indian brave wrapped in a blanket and holding a long pipe. The artist's paint box and saddle were strewn on the plank floor of the shack. Looking at it, I realized the cluttered scene looked much like the muddled dining room of the Russell house, although the current house was certainly no shack.

"Ya see it. That's what I wanted. All you gotta do is understand that's all I want now. My own shack. Nothin' fancy."

"But Mr. Russell, this house is so comfortable. Running water, electricity . . ."

"All I ever wanted was to be a cowboy. An' I almost didn't make it. Give 'em all plenty of grief. Them city bastards, shit . . . sent me out to herd sheep, and there's nothing dumber than a sheep 'cept a man as herds 'em. . . . Dirty little buggers, always gettin' their selfs lost and going—baa, baa, baa. And Old' Pike, he's the St. Louis relative what got me the sheep job, brought me out here an' then told everybody, 'Kid Russell's nothin' but lazy and irresponsible.'"

"But you had a buckskin shirt? That's what I'd want."

"Yeah, but no wrangler job."

"Why did you need one?"

"Hungry. That's why. After I was tossed outta the sheep job, I was damned hungry, an' this old trapper, he snuck up on me. 'Whar ya keep your grub?' he asked me. 'Ain't got none,' I said. So, ol' Jake Hoover took me in, and I stayed up in that Cascades shack of hissen off and on fer three years. That cabin of hissen—better than any king's domain, Owidi. The smella' them logs, big ol' stone fireplace. Never been so happy. Like to be there today, goddammit. Now how about some coffee that'll kick up in the middle an' pack double?"

When we got back in the kitchen, Young Boy, the old Cree Indian, and a kid who looked about thirteen were stomping in through the back door.

"Hou how, Chief," the kid said. And then, he looked at me and started his hands and fingers waving around like swallows after mosquitoes. I thought maybe the young kid was . . . well, not all right in the head.

Charlie put his hand on the boy's shoulder. "Joe here's trying to tell you he's hungry. See, he's kinda hard-a-hearing. We use a lotta Indian sign talk around him, but he reads lips pretty good." Charlie turned to look directly at the boy. "You kin talk some too, can't ya Joe?"

"Sure kin, jus' caint hear ya none too good. Not since I had that meningitises couple years back."

"He's from over in Dewey, Oklahoma, name's Joe DeYoung. Lives with us and helps around the place feedin' the horses, the chickens, an' the furnace in exchange for drawin' lessons. Says he want to be a painter."

"Shore do. Chief here is teaching me." Joe sat and tilted his head into the palm of his hand mumbling, "God, Chief, I gotta headache so damn big it won't fit into a hoss corral. I done drunk too mucha that joy juice out there on the Pablo. Shore was some buffalo hunt." His hands fluttered again as he talked.

"We all took it kinda heavy, Joe. The high drammer of the hunt puts a thirst into ya. Last buffalo hunt we're ever likely to see, I'm thinkin'." Charlie sat down in front of the coffee I'd poured.

"God, I got lit-up like a honky-tonk on a Saturday night," said Joe. He shook his head back and forth and moved his hands in circles.

"Wahl, they're moving the whole damned kit an' caboodle Pablo herd outta here and up into Canada. Gettin' rid of the last of the buffalo so what used to be the Flathead Indian reservation lands'll be open to a danged bunch of sod-busters and their dirty little sheep," Charlie grumbled.

"An' then, Chief, I made a mistake. I started givin' your old buddy Frank Linderman hell with the hide off. Shoulda knowed better. Frank don't take to no teasin'."

"He's weasel smart, but coldern'a Montana well driller."

"After the photographer took our pictures, I was still playin' Indian and swung my hatchet 'round takin' off Frank's Indian wig. Made him so mad he coulda' swallowed a horny toad backwards. Tol' him I didn't mean no harm. 'The liquor jus' musta' done eat its way plumb down to my boot heels,' I said. Wouldn't take my apology. Tol' me, 'Joe, you smelt out the wrong hound's butt this time.'" Little Joe put his head in his hands and groaned pitifully.

"Guess he's up for reelection this year too," said Charlie. "An' he's havin' to squeeze the dollars 'til the eagle's squawkin an' . . ."

I slammed down a pitcher of molasses interrupting Charlie and pointed to Joe. "What was this young child doing? Off drinking alcohol and killing buffalo? Why he's just no more than a kid."

"He onny looks that way," Charlie replied and he laughed.

I looked closely across the table at Joe. He wasn't even as tall as I was. Maybe only about five feet, a cleft chin as smooth as a baby's, and a narrow brimmed cowboy hat shoved back on his head. He dressed a lot like Charlie, white shirt, boots, heavy dark trousers, but he had a childish looking bow tie at his neck.

"You jus' don't know him yet, Owidi," Charlie said. "May not look it, but he's twenty-one, rides broncos better'n most, and worked the rodeo circuit with Tom Mix. Drunk or sober he can run circles round them buffalo."

"Shit Chief, the bunch is really gonna miss those hunts," moaned Joe while his hands flew in all directions. He looked at me. "Whar's the grub?"

The waffle iron had been plugged in while I was listening to the conversation. I suddenly smelled something burning. The first waffle was almost black, but it seemed to make no difference. As I started to throw it away, Joe grabbed it, tossed it onto a plate, poured the molasses all over it, and wolfed it down. I'd used the sour milk, eggs, and wheat flour recipe like we did in Norway. As fast as I could turn them out, the three were flooding the waffles with molasses and butter and they disappeared. Made me wonder what they'd been having before I arrived. They sure could eat. Young Boy had brought in a side of bacon from the storage shed and sliced it into thick slabs with his hatchet, and they went through that too. All washed down with strong coffee. I couldn't understand most of their conversation. It didn't seem like the English I'd practiced in Boston.

Joe waved his right hand back and forth, pointed his index finger at me. He kept flicking the hand open and closed. I thought he was still hungry.

"He's askin' your name," said Charlie. "He wants you to start learnin' Indian sign talk. We all do Indian sign around here, even Mame."

Struggling with English was going to be hard enough, and now it seemed that to be a part of the West I'd have to learn to wave my arms around, flick my fingers and learn some pesky sign language. It seemed foolish, but I faced him and tried to speak clearly. "Oh—vee—de—ah, Ovidia," I said. Then I looked right at him and repeated his gesture, wave hand, point at him, flick hand open and closed. They seemed amused.

"Joe DeYoung," he said quite clearly and grinned at me, pleased, I guess, that I was learning. He turned and waved at Charlie signing a question and said, "Where Wise Woman?"

Charlie motioned toward the stairway pointing with his nose. He pushed back from the table, got up, and rummaged around until he found a glass. He picked a dried-up looking lemon from a basket near the sink and carefully prepared a concoction of lemon juice and hot water from the teakettle. Then he put the glass on a tray, searched for a napkin, found one not too badly stained, and carried the tray out and up the stairway. This was to be his routine every morning. Even on her good days, Nancy would prove to be a notoriously slow riser.

FIVE

The Elocution Lesson

I cleared the kitchen of the old Indian, but the deaf buffalo hunter wanted to hang around. Joe stirred more sugar into his black coffee. "I'm gonna miss those hunts. Peaceful as a church out there on the Pablo in the morning."

"Until you start shooting."

"Jus' a game. Charlie and the bunch like to play Injun. I think Charlie wishes he were one. He says he lived with the Bloods for a while, but nobody knows for sure. Shore wish I coulda done that. The Chief's got a strong urge to understand 'em though. It's old Frank Linderman who rightly knows 'em. Knows sign talk perfect too. Lived eight years with the Flatheads. Got mad as hell at me on the hunt this time. His luck's running kinda muddy. I tol' him, he was acting like he was raised on sour milk."

I finished clearing off the table and started wiping it down with some strong smelling soap I'd found in the shed. That seemed to chase Mr. Buffalo Hunter off. I'd heard enough for one day, and hardly understood what they were talking about anyway. Sows, and eagles, and hound's butts, and horn toads? And all the time hands and fingers flying all over the place. Was this the West? I needed to clean and cook, but I'd barely started doing some organizing in the dining room when two women burst in through the front door. People in the West always forgot to knock.

"So you're Ovidia," the older woman said. She couldn't wait to start talking. "Call me Margaret. Margaret Trigg. Nancy will be so glad you're here. Albert said we should come over and see if you needed any help. This is my daughter, Josephine. You must be overwhelmed by all this." She waved her arm around at the chaos.

She was talking very fast with British accented English, just like Albert. Both women didn't stop at the door; they pushed right in, headed toward the kitchen, and sniffed around. I could see that any organizing would have to wait.

"Wonderful my dear, you've managed to make some order out of this already. Marvelous. Isn't that right, Josephine? Now, you must leave Charlie's painting supplies just as they are. He'll be down shortly to begin work. He only works in the morning, you know—right there in the dining room. Nancy wanted to use the dining room for entertaining buyers, but . . . ." Margaret moved around the house as she talked. Josephine and I followed.

"After dinner at noon, they both rest. Then Charlie visits with his cronies at the saloons, 'the bunch' he calls them. He says the light isn't right for painting in the afternoon. Well, I'm not so sure about that but . . . .

"Oh dear, just look at that. I told Nancy not to put that red flocked wall paper in the living room and dining room. Especially the dining room. It makes the place look like a bordello. And now, you see, look, it's getting spotted from all that paint."

"Now, Mother, please don't talk like that." Josephine finally spoke. "You know Nancy is trying. Nancy's like a sister to me, and she thinks of you as her lost mother."

Josephine's voice was tiny, like that of a small child, but she looked like she was old, way over twenty anyway. In Norway she would have been called *enkel*, or plain. Her hair, done up on top of her head in a tight knot, emphasized her receding chin. I thought at first she must be almost blind since I'd never seen such thick eyeglasses. They were set into heavy, dark metal frames that seemed to pinch her nose painfully.

Josephine turned to me and smiled. "We come here every day, Ovidia. Mother's giving Nancy elocution lessons. I help too. I'm a children's librarian. Nancy's trying to improve her reading and her grammar."

"*Ja*, but Mrs. Russell hasn't come down yet," I finally said.

"Of course he needs a studio . . . I told Nancy that. And, now she wants a baby. Oh my dear, that would clinch it. Thank the good Lord God they can't have any. God-be-blessed. Poor dear."

Margaret hardly ever stopped talking. She was a heavy, large woman with gray, curly hair piled up under a dark blue bonnet with a red ribbon. I thought maybe she was wearing a uniform. Long skirt and jacket, also dark blue, with a high stiff collar emblazoned with a large gold letter "S" and gold shields. Her jacket was decorated with gold buttons and ribbon braid.

They both headed back to the kitchen, Josephine trailing her mother closely. I took the kettle and poured hot water into a china teapot. They were having a cup of tea when Nancy finally appeared. Her light colored hair was loosely arranged and caught in a soft knot. She was tall and plump but had a tiny waist and wore a skirt that draped gracefully at the hips. In the morning light she appeared quite winsome, but her expression looked tormented and she addressed the visitors in a whiny voice.

"Oh, Mother Trigg, Mother Trigg, yesterday was hell on earth. Those Eastern tourists. They always want to see Charlie's work, and then they come here to snigger." I poured her some tea, and she looked pleased. "Ovidia, dear, you're going to be a life-saver. I'm so glad you're here." She clasped my hand in both of hers and eased into one of the wooden chairs at the kitchen table.

"What went wrong this time, darling? Will it help if you tell us?" asked Margaret.

Nancy sighed. "Well, I had taken out the painting, *Where Tracks Spell Meat*, you remember, the one with all the snow and the dead elk. I was relating that wonderful story about Cha'lie being taken in by the old trapper, Jake, and how he was able to study the wild animals alive. The husband was so interested, but the wife said, 'Why who would want a dead animal on the wall?'

"The husband was rather obliging. He told her, 'But look at the action. The cold, the hunter, the look of triumph.'" Nancy mimicked the husband's deep voice. "And the wife turned to me and said, 'What about some colorful Indians?' I said that everyone calls Cha'lie the White Indian and that he shared a tepee with the Blood Indians back in eighty-eight. She didn't seem interested. And then, I said proudly, 'Cha'lie's, the *sinee kuater nona*.'"

"Oh dear, you meant *sine qua non*, didn't you," Josephine whispered.

I had no idea what she was talking about, but Margaret and Josephine both caught their breath with open mouths and then tried to hide it. Josephine struggled to suppress a giggle.

"Oh shit. Hell, Josephine, I guess I said those swanky words wrong again because they raised their eyebrows and exchanged comical glances." Nancy's voice became more strained and shrill. "On the way out the tourist's wife said, 'The artists that I admire are all in France.' Oh, bullshit. Cha'lie's an artist. Not a damned illustrator. What in the hell can I do, Mother Trigg? Why don't Cha'lie care about these things."

"Now my dear, you must understand. People from the East . . ." Margaret began.

"Have certain standards," Josephine interrupted.

"Yes, very socially . . . well, stratified. Class consciousness, dear," said Margaret.

"Snooty," added Josephine.

"The 'quality' speak and act in particular ways."

"Elocution, etiquette, table setting. It's all so important. Mother Trigg can teach you, can't you Mother?" said Josephine.

"Then the 'quality' from Black Hawk will get to know you too," Margaret added.

"You'd be invited to join The Maids and Matrons." Josephine smiled and clapped her hands together.

Nancy's expression was changing. The idea appealed to her. I remembered that Albert had mentioned The Maids and Matrons the day before during the ride to the Russell house.

"Oh, bullshit. I don't . . . . Yes, yes. I <u>do</u> care," said Nancy.

"Dear, please remember . . . I've mentioned it before; the profanity must go. Lips that utter such words never, ever, enter the best salons, my dear," said Margaret. "Now let's get on with our lesson. Where's the society page, Josephine? The first step." She pulled a copy of the local newspaper, *The Great Falls Tribune*, from her satchel and opened it to the "Spray of the Falls" gossip column.

I wasn't sure what they were doing, but it looked like they had practiced this before. First Margaret would read, in her precise English accent, and then Nancy would try to mimic exactly what had been said.

"The Maids and Matrons met in the garden of Mrs. Paris Gibson," said Margaret.

"The Maids and Matrons met in the garden of Mrs. Paris Gibson," repeated Nancy.

"That's wonderful," said Josephine. "You sound just like Mother."

Margaret continued reading. "Miss Evette Gibson entertained the group with a selection from *La Vivandiere.*"

"Miss Evette Gibson entertained the group with a selection from . . . aaah."

"*La Vivandiere,*" prompted Josephine.

"*La Vivandiere.*" Nancy groaned.

"*Ja,* you can do it," I said.

"Next month The Maids and Matrons will meet at the home of Mr. and Mrs. William Buchanan on Smelter Hill." Margaret pronounced the words distinctly.

"Next month the Maids and Matrons will meet at the home of . . . . Oh my God. How I wish I could join them."

"You're doing fine," said Margaret. "Just listen carefully and repeat what I say.

"The Mint Saloon is drawing many new patrons," Margaret read, then stopped.

"The Mint Saloon is drawing . . ." Nancy started to repeat, but hesitated.

Margaret continued reading slowly, "with, with . . . Charlie Russell's . . . peep show . . . *Joy of Life*." She became silent and looked up from the paper at Nancy. Josephine gasped and covered her mouth with her gloved hand.

"Oh no." cried Nancy. "Oh no . . . no, no, no. I told him . . . I've begged him."

Margaret continued reading. "*The Joy of Life* . . . probity prevents a comprehensive description . . . ."

"Ooh dear," groaned Josephine as tears started down her cheeks.

Margaret paused again and then continued reading in a befuddled voice. "Whether or not Charlie Russell's art will come up to the standard of the St. Louis exhibition and be hung in the great art gallery is problematical."

Nancy howled, and Margaret got up and wrapped her arms around her. Josephine wiped her teary eyes, and I stood and tapped my foot. I wasn't sure what it was all about, and I didn't know what a peep show might be, but it was clear that something was not going as well as expected.

"Oh dear God, why didn't I marry someone like John Alexander, a real artist?" Nancy sobbed. "I'll never be invited to The Maids and Matrons. Cha'lie only paints those fucking cowboys and Indians."

While Margaret, Nancy, and Josephine were dabbing at their tears, there was a rattling at the kitchen door and Carl Holmes, the tall Norwegian from the station platform, came bounding in smiling. He spotted the "Spray of the Falls" newspaper column open on the kitchen table, looked at the red eyes and wet handkerchiefs, and immediately suspected what had happened. His expression changed.

"Well now," he said slowly putting his hand gently on Nancy's shoulder, "You know, Nancy, when it comes right down to it, you can join the Maids and Matrons if you like. But you'll have to bear in mind; no amount of plotting will ever get Charlie to join the Mutts and Muttons."

Nancy looked up at him, hesitated, and then grinned. She perked right up, her eyes sparkled, and she even giggled a little while Margaret muttered "Bless the Lord, Amen."

"You ladies are going to have to understand. There's no use conspiring to get the cowboy artist to do anything he's gonna take issue with. He'll just hunker down and be about as interested as a hibernating' bear."

SIX

The Peep Show

Charlie appeared each day right after his noon dinner and a short snooze just as Margaret Trigg had predicted. He'd come from behind the barn riding Neenah, his ill-natured bay gelding. They'd be clipping along in good spirits and pass around the back of the house up toward the big front porch where Nancy would be waiting. She'd stand there frowning with her right arm raised and two fingers extended in a "V." When I saw this, I thought it had to be some more of the Indian sign talk that they used all the time, but I found out later it was a common American gesture meaning "two."

She'd say, "Two Cha'lie." She always pronounced his name leaving out the "r" sound. Then she'd go on, "That's all now, remember Cha'lie, remember. Soon as you get back. . . I'm gonna ask you, two?

"Gotcha, Mame, darling. Two's all." And he'd ride off without ever looking back, but she'd yell after him anyway.

"Remember, Cha'lie. Eastern tourists. They're buyers . . . and all those mining engineers . . . and the National Park people." Nancy never forgot sales.

The Russells gave me half-day off on Thursday, and I'd take the Number Ten Line electric streetcar downtown to Central to meet Mattie. My friend from the train, you remember, I told you about her—Mattie. You do remember her, don't you, Billy? I told you about her before, the girl on the train . . . the one who went to work at the Mint Saloon. Well, she knew how Charlie spent his afternoons.

But my *Got*, that yellow streetcar itself was an adventure. Here I was in the West, and there were streetcars. I thought there would only be horses. If the streetcar was crowded, I had to stand, and when the car went around a curve, it would swerve sharply. The first time this happened I fell into the lap of a grumpy fat lady who seemed annoyed even though I repeated several times, *om forlatelse, om forlatelse*. The conductor in his stiff blue serge uniform with the shiny brass buttons came over and showed me how I needed to grab one of the leather straps hanging from the brass bars that ran the length of the car. Even when it was crowded, everyone was very polite trying to avoid tumbling into each other, and the men always gave their seats up to the ladies. If they didn't, the conductor would tip his billed cap graciously at the lady and glare threateningly at the man.

Mattie and I usually went shopping, but before that we'd meet at Lulu Disher's soda fountain, and sit in the tiny wire chairs at the marble topped tables gazing at the pink cupids painted on the walls. Mattie sure admired cupids. She was always looking for a husband, a "Mr. Right," she called him, but so far she'd only found deadbeats and drunks since starting her new job at the Mint Saloon. She told me she was fattening her bank roll though.

We'd exchange the latest gossip while we stirred cherry-flavored soda-water with straws and watched the bubbles swirl. The soda turned our lips a bright pink, and I'd look at my reflection in one of the big oval mirrors and admire the color. Mattie knew just about everything that happened there in Great Falls, and I even though I knew Uncle Nils and Aunty Ann wouldn't approve of my nattering about my employers I had to ask Mattie about what Charlie did down at the saloons every afternoon.

"Oh hell, I'll tell you what your 'Cowboy Artist' does when he comes to town every day. When he gets down to Central Avenue he ties his horse to the rail outside the Mint or, sometimes the Brunswick. Everybody in town recognizes the horse and knows him, Ovidia, and passers -by call out greetings and slap him on the back and act like they was close enough to use the same tooth pick," she said. "He spends the afternoons with his cronies. Lotta old has-been cowboys and ranchers. Call themselves 'the bunch,' and don't mix much with the mining people or regular farmers.

"Old Sid, who owns the place, he's got a passel of Russell's paintings hung toward the front of the saloon. Sid's always begging Charlie for more stuff. Says it gives his place a real Western appeal, especially his more racy pieces. Right now, the tenderfoot tourists are just eating up the peep show."

"Tell me, Mattie. What's a peep show anyway? Mrs. Russell got real disturbed about it." I didn't like to admit it, but I was curious. I wanted to know what the peep show was all about. So far, I only knew that Nancy was sure distraught when she heard about it.

Mattie laughed and stirred her soda bubbles. "Yeah, I'll bet Nancy weren't too pleased. Not something that endears you to the Maids and Matrons. You really want to hear about it?"

"Sure. Don't just laugh, Mattie. Tell me. There was an article in the *Great Falls Tribune* newspaper, and when Margaret Trigg read it to Nancy, she was nettled—she howled and cried and carried on—having a fitful time."

"You really gotta see it, Ovidia, but course I can't take you in there. It's up front in the saloon. The tourists all huddle around it sniggering and poking each other in the ribs with their elbows."

"Must have to do with sex then," I said. "American people are peculiar about that."

"Try to picture this. It looks like a plain tall box at first. In big gold letters on the side of the box, and there's a sign that says, *Joy of Life*." Mattie eyes flashed. She put her handkerchief to her mouth to keep from laughing and looked around to see if anyone was listening.

"Oh, just go ahead and tell me."

"Well, inside the box is a Russell painting. It looks like any old typical Russell painting, an innocent looking Indian Brave guarding the door of his teepee. Then, to the side of the teepee, there's a cow pony and a dog standing there waiting obediently. When you first see it, it looks just like any of his other paintings." She lowered her voice and began to whisper.

"But—you put ten cents into a slot, and watch out. The teepee door slowly swings open and there's this cowboy *en flagrante*, typical old missionary position, with the brave's daughter, or hell, who knows, maybe it's the brave's wife. It's a pretty explicit coupling, Ovidia. Those pea-green tourists just howl."

I wasn't sure I was getting it. Why would Charlie paint that? I thought he admired the Indians. *Got* in heaven, wouldn't it be offensive to the Indians. And, Charlie always went around saying he wanted to be an Indian. He loved it when a tourist looking at one of his paintings called him "The White Indian," and he was always dressing-up in Indian clothes. I'd even seen him dressed up as a squaw, and there was this picture postcard photo he seemed to treasure so much I had to be careful not to lose it. He and this other cowboy, both dressed like Indians, and Russell squatting there dressed like a squaw. All that Indian sign language and costumes and . . . .

"*Gut Got*, Mattie, that peep show doesn't seem like . . . well, like . . . the West," I grumbled.

"Ovidia, that's exactly the West, but that's not the whole peep show." She leaned in closer to my ear grinning. "There's a shocker still to come. Sometimes the tourists don't even see it at first, and when they do, they just holler. If you look closely and check out the dog, you see that even that shitkicker's got a hard on," Mattie whispered. "Biggest joke of the peep show." She covered her mouth again with her handkerchief and giggled. I just groaned.

"Oh, all those Eastern pilgrims just howl and head back to the bar to order another round of drinks. It's a money maker for Sid, that's for sure. He's beggin' Charlie to do more stuff like that. Offered him his back room for a studio. Charlie tol' him Trigg had offered <u>his</u> backroom at the Brunswick, and that he'd given his word that Trigg was next. Sid's pissed as hell, but comps Charlie's drinks anyway."

"Charlie does need a place to paint, a real studio," I said. "He has only the entry way and dining room now and worse yet, Nancy has nowhere to show the paintings, and entertain, and sell to those tourists. Does he take just two drinks?"

"Hell no."

"Nancy swears Charlie only has two drinks every afternoon."

"That's a bunch a horse pucky. When those old sidekicks of his get together, they keep that damned Finlander guy who tends bar busy as a beaver building a new dam. . ."

"A man from Finland tends the bar?" I interrupted.

"Sure—does a good job too."

"Oh Mattie, be careful. He could be a witch you know."

"Nah, not old Tony, his real name's Isaac Talvi, but he's dark like an Italian so that's why we all call him Tony. Gotta say, your Charlie Russell usually holds his liquor well though. What with the peep show and right now the Annual Montana Stock Convention's in town I've got a roll big enough to choke a cow. The Convention's brought all of Charlie's cronies are here. Those ex-cowboys are all drinkin' and bemoaning the bygone days when there was cattle and no sheep. Back-trailin' talk they call it. They get real sentimental and forget how much they're spending for my company. The Russell bunch hang out at a big table in the rear of the saloon. Won't wear the Stock Convention badges 'cause some of the badges are hangin' on sheep men."

"What difference does it make? Americans have crazy ideas about things—where you live, where you work, and even about animals. Sheep and cattle are all live stock aren't they?"

"Not to those guys. Hell, they get real upset about sheep men. I overheard that the Jew, Lewi Kauffman, even ripped a couple of convention tags offen a couple of the bunch, Ballie Buck and old Tommy Tucker. Both of 'em old-timers. 'Course Ballie, who's a half-breed, was already drunk, and Tommy, he's gotten so squat and fat he can hardly squeeze into his old fringed buckskins. Kauffman used to be one of the biggest cattlemen in Montana until ten or fifteen years ago. Now he's an overweight butcher."

"He's not your Mr. Right then, I guess," I teased.

"Hell no. Those cowpunchers are serious about their strong distaste for sheep. They joke, but—I overheard Charlie askin' Kauffman if he knew sheepherders become queer. A bunch a fairies, he said. Then he says, 'some go as crazy as a parrot eatin' stick candy,' and the whole table of 'em just roared."

"Doesn't sound like what I expected. My idea of a cow-boy is someone polite talking . . . and, and, humble, and courageous, and modest, and noble. Strong and manly, not silly peep shows."

"Well, you'll learn. Keep your eyes open. It's not the way you dreamed it, sweet gal. Everybody thinks Charlie's a pretty good guy and funny to boot."

I thought about that for a while, but it still didn't make much sense. "Maybe Sid Willis could be your 'Mr. Right,' Mattie. He's a business man after all, not a cowboy."

"God no, not with that stinkin' cigar, but I've got my eye on one of the bunch. He owns the Lazy KY ranch up near the Canadian border. Con Price's his name. A real cow puncher, and everyone says he modeled for Charlie's painting, *The Hold Up*. Supposed to look like the infamous Black Hills stage robber, Big Nose George."

"Does he have a big nose, Mattie?"

"Well, yeah, I guess he does."

"My grandmother always said to look for a man with a big nose."

"<u>My</u> grandmother told me it was big feet," said Mattie. We both snickered and stirred the bubbles in the last of our cherry sodas. "But you can count on it, he's big." Mattie tried to keep her mouth closed when she took a sip, but started to snicker and blew a fine spray of pink soda from her mouth.

"The pilgrims all tell Con he's immortal 'cause a that painting. They ask him to come stand beside it. He wears that same buff colored hat with the high crown like in the painting and even carries a pistol on his right hip. They're all putting on a show anyway, even if they're not paid by the railroad." Mattie smiled and gave the cupids a long fixed look.

"It's intoxicatin' just to see him, Ovidia. But do you know who'd be a catch? That Frank Linderman, he's in the state legislature. But hell, he's already taken. Sells insurance and some of the bunch say he writes books about Indians. Lived with the Indians plenty too, but doesn't go around dressing like one—only Charlie does that."

"Joe and Charlie talk about him, but I haven't seen him."

"Those Crees that hang around back of the saloon all call Linderman the 'Man Who Looks Through Glass.' Guess it's cause of those big round eye-glasses he wears. He an' Charlie have something going though. They're always huddled there at the Mint, and Frank looks like he's begging and pleading."

"Nancy doesn't consent to Charlie's cronies hanging around the house much. Especially those old cowboys. She does like Carl Holmes though. He's been dropping by at all times of day lately. He teases Nancy and makes her feel like a young girl. Maybe he's there to see Josephine Trigg? She spends a lot of time at the house."

"Maybe he's there to see you, Ovidia."

I felt my cheeks flush. "Oh *nei*, not me. I don't even like him. He's too much of a know-it-all. Besides, I'm too busy bringing some kind of order to that place to laugh at his teasing jokes. Untidiness doesn't suit me. I want everything in its place and ready to use. You can't be slack over cleaning."

"He's good lookin' though," Mattie said, and she looked at me with suspicion. I changed the subject.

"Nancy's determined to see that 'Cha'lie,' as she calls him, is a real artist. She hates it when anyone says he's an illustrator. She's all business."

"Well, she's gonna have a time. Charlie's about as hard to pin down as smoke in a bottle. But meantime, no cupid's gonna ever find you, Ovidia, unless you get some shoes that don't look like a couple of clodhoppers."

After the sodas, we'd go to Jacob Heikkila's Dry Goods store to look around and shop. I wondered about buying ready-made clothes, but Mattie said it was becoming the thing to do. I liked the smell of the place. I think the smell came from the oiled pine floor. You could look out the big front windows and watch the shoppers passing by. But when Mattie told me Jacob Heikkila was from Finland too, like the bartender, it worried me. All those witches living here in the West, right here in Great Falls.

Jacob was handsome though, with light brown hair falling down over his right eye and little lumps of muscle at the corners of his mouth on either side of a square mustache. It was his wife, Johanna, who made me fret. She even looked like a witch, dressed all in black, and it wasn't because she was a Lutheran either. Her forehead was high and her tiny black eyes always seemed to see through my clothes, and her mouth—just a tight straight line below her nose—no lips at all.

No matter how I tried to convince her, Mattie wouldn't believe that people from Finland were witches. I knew I couldn't trust them though. So I always prayed to Saint Olav before I entered the store.

I did buy some real American clothes as soon as I could. All I had at first to wear were the things I'd brought from Norway, and I knew they looked strange so I was using the good cloth from my old dresses and remaking what I could. People thought the blue tunic that came to my knees was odd. They'd stare. And then, that long skirt of green, blue and red stripes, it didn't look American. I wanted to get rid of the scarves and have a hat like Mattie's so I'd look up-to-date.

With the money I'd won gambling on the train, I settled on a long, dark blue skirt, full, with small pleats around the waist line. I bought a matching blouse with long sleeves. It had ruching and smocking down the front with three big white buttons and a high white collar. The material was silky and soft, and as an extravagance I even got a small blue straw hat with one large flower, not the whole rose garden. Mattie wanted me to buy more engaging dresses, but I hadn't the courage yet and I disappointed her by not buying some pointed toe, high button shoes, but shoes in America cost more than a cow in Norway. My "clodhoppers," as she called them, would have to do until colder weather or more cash came in. She did say I looked American in my new outfit, though. Later I even had my picture taken wearing it. I sent the picture to Aunty Anna in Norway and she wrote that I looked like a prosperous Swede.

"Never worry about wearing showy clothes," Mattie advised me. "The women you see on the streets in dark gray and black are usually the real harlots. Whores are mostly real modest and try not to draw attention to themselves when they're out in public. And those women dressed so showy, I sometimes think the upper class behaves more like strumpets."

Oh sorry Billy, I'm afraid I get carried away thinking about Mattie and shopping and the clothes we wore in the old days. I thought that Mattie knew just about everything, but I'll get on with it. . . . Dammit all, I can still remember how shocked I felt to find out that a pair of shoes cost more than a cow. . . . Now, what was it? *Ja*, it was the forgery I was telling you about, wasn't it?

For my Aunty Anna with love, Ovidia

SEVEN

Brighten the Corner

Well, Billy, I'd almost forgotten to tell you about this, but it's important. One afternoon, after shopping, Mattie and I were walking down Central approaching Trigg's Brunswick saloon when a group of uniformed musicians came marching in military order up the center of the street totally unmindful of the mud. The leader was carrying a large flag which he waved in time to the music and the singing. As they got nearer, I could hear the words they were singing. Maybe a Whitmonday holiday, but it wasn't the right time of the year. They almost shouted the song.

> Brighten the corner, where you are,
> Brighten the corner, where you are,
> Some poor sinking sinner
> You may guide across the bar,
> Brighten the corner where you are.

The marchers came to a halt on the Brunswick Saloon corner and a large crowd was gathering near where the musicians had circled.

"My *Got* in heaven, Mattie, it's . . . that's . . . Margaret Trigg." We were still a half-block away when I recognized her gray hair frizzing out from under the dark bonnet hat with the red ribbon band. It was a uniform she was wearing. No wonder I thought her clothes were so strange. Dark blue serge, heavy material with the stand-up collar and the coat trimmed in yellow braid.

"She's drawing so much attention."

"Sure as hell she is," said Mattie. "It's meant to be conspicuous. Didn't Nancy tell you? Margaret's a Brigadier in the Salvation Army. Her mother was one of the *Hallelujah Seven* sent here from England years ago to preach the gospel of redemption."

"*Gut Got*, Mattie, I didn't know that. How am I going to understand? I thought that . . . . I thought Margaret was some sort of society lady."

"Yeah, it's Margaret Trigg all right," said Mattie. "Now you'll understand the uniform. She may not be society, but she's sure an agent of God's sovereign will—sent here by the Salvationists to redeem all the drunkards. They put on quite a show. Both the drunkards and the Salvationists. Do good work around here though. Don't matter who it is. They're ready to help—service of humanity, they say."

By the time we reached them, the troop was finishing another song and had formed a semi-circle near the entry to the Brunswick Saloon. With all the noise of the trumpets and drums, quite a few drunks were drifting or staggering out the double doors. The Salvationists had laid the big bass drum flat inside the semi-circle and Margaret stood in the center of the group. She was rattling a tambourine in one hand and holding a bible over her head in the other.

"Praise GOD." she shouted in a high pitched loud voice.

"Praise God." the crowd responded.

"Praise JESUS."

"Praise Jesus."

"These are troubled times, friends. Hard, hard times."

"Amen." answered the crowd.

"We are beset, beset by the evils of SIN."

I thought I saw her glance at Mattie, but Mattie appeared unaware of any pointed attention.

"Yes, friends, and we are beset by the evils of ALCOHOL."

"Amen." I said surprising myself at why in the world I was joining in the crowd's response.

"Are any among you afflicted?" Margaret bellowed in her deepest voice. Honestly, Billy, I thought I must be among those afflicted even though I didn't know what I could have done. Maybe the gambling. I started to move forward with a couple of men who had come out of the saloon, but Mattie grabbed tight to my elbow keeping me where I was standing.

"Let him join together with us. Let him then pray to Jee-sus to be saved of his sins. Let him learn to fight the Devil who spreads hell fires across God's bountiful land. Let him be redeemed in the blood of the lamb," and as the music started again softly, two young shabbily dressed men who looked like mining company workers knelt down beside the bass drum and removed their low-crowned plug hats.

Margaret approached them slowly and placed her hands upon their heads speaking more quietly while the golden trumpets crooned and a saxophone moaned. Coins and silver dollars began thumping down onto the surface of the bass drum. Margaret moved toward us through the crowd stopping often to pray with those who appeared to have an affliction.

"Come on, Ovidia," Mattie whispered, "Let's go before she wants us to visit the soup kitchen. I'm not ready to serve soup today, or to be saved either, and neither are you."

We moved back down the street and turned at the next block to see the flag with the big red letters, *BLOOD AND FIRE,* waving on down Central toward the storefront headquarters with a mass of people following. I turned and took Mattie's arm.

"But Mattie, the Salvationists are opposed to drinking alcohol, aren't they?"

"Yeah sure, and that's why Margaret has them parade in front of the saloons. It's to save the sinners."

"But, Mattie, her own husband, Albert, he runs a saloon."

"Yeah but, he doesn't drink. He's been saved. He just sells it."

"But, wouldn't that be a sin too—misdirecting others?"

"He don't look at it that way. It's his business, and besides he keeps it clean and has a side room for the ladies and families at the Brunswick. I don't know. I guess he figures that if they're gonna have it, they need to have it in a respectable, safe place where the wives can enjoy themselves nearby." Mattie looked back down the street and shook her head. "I'll admit it does cut down on his business some, having Margaret preaching against alcohol right there on the doorstep."

"And, they're both so friendly with the Russells."

"Hoping someday Charlie and Nancy'll see the light and be saved and quit drinking. But, Charlie, he likes his nip of barleycorn too much. Meanwhile, since Charlie is from a good English family, the Triggs believe the English must stick together. And they sure love Charlie. They'd do anything for him."

We walked on silently for a while. I was wondering if maybe I was "afflicted" with the gambling. I loved the feel of the stiff cards in my hands. Sometimes I even practiced shuffling just to enjoy the sound and the touch of the cards.

"You might as well know about the Triggs, Ovidia. Local gossip has it that Albert had a fine big bar over in Michigan, but it folded—lack of customers. Having those soul savers beating the drums and tootling their horns outside the front door of a saloon ain't no way to increase business none.

"But remember, Albert fancies himself a real gentleman. I'll give him that. And he adores that homely daughter of his. The Triggs keep looking for a suitable husband for her, but they'll have trouble finding one since it's only Charlie that she adores."

Those afternoons with Mattie left me confused sometimes and full of strange new ideas I needed to absorb if I wanted to be an American. I'd return to the Russell's place mixed up, excited, and usually covered with the powdery gray soot that continually poured out of the big stack at the smelter, but I knew I was beginning to find my way around Great Falls.

American westerners behaved strangely. Beating drums in front of saloons, peep shows, and Nancy told me that Indian women were called "prairie chickens." So, what could that mean, I asked myself.

Evenings when Charlie returned from the saloons he sometimes wobbled. Once he fell off Neenah out at the barn before he could dismount. Fortunately, Young Boy was always there to help him. Then he'd head for the front steps and plunge up the first three catching himself on his hands and pulling on up using the railing. Nancy never lost her aplomb when this happened though.

The household had its routine in spite of the often comical behavior. After supper, Nancy would do book-keeping, she kept track of every penny. She would send out letters promoting Charlie's work while he looked at picture books or leafed through accounts of Lewis and Clark's exploration of the Missouri River.

When I'd cleared up the light supper things, I'd fix a big pot of coffee. Then Young Boy, Joe and I played Black Jack, or Poker at the kitchen table. I tried not to think of what Margaret Trigg might say about the gambling. Besides the stakes weren't high, so maybe it didn't count as gambling after all. I wondered what the Lutherans, Olga and Swen, would have thought. The Russells never played cards, but usually one or two of Charlie's bunch would come by and join us. Carl Holmes began dropping by regularly. He'd go in the living room first, tease Nancy some, tell Charlie about the latest cattle deals, and then he'd join the game. Because of the card games, I came to know Teddy "Blue" Abbott and the Dane, Olaf Selzer, but I'll tell you more about them later.

EIGHT

Intrigues at Fourth Avenue North

I was beginning to make some small changes at the Russell household, but the dining room where Charlie did most of his painting was still chaotic and overflowed with painting equipment, canvases, and western cowboy gear weeks after I had arrived. I'd managed to organize the upstairs rooms. The three bedrooms and a small room Nancy called the "trunk room" would now pass my old Aunty Anna's spick-and-span test, every corner done down on my hands and knees. As I told you, Billy, untidiness doesn't suit me and never has. The drawers and small closets all smelled of the mothballs that I had scattered everywhere. But, the work at the Russell's was easy compared to shoveling cow dung out of the ground floor of our house in Norway in the spring.

If only I could figure out how to steady the unpredictable dispositions of the Nancy and Charlie, the place would be a palace. All Charlie wanted to do was spend time with his bunch talking about their wrangling days. He got grumpy if he couldn't. It seemed to me that he was kind of work-shy. And Nancy, she was always edgy and easily annoyed.

For example, Billy, the upstairs bath had only a sink and toilet, but the downstairs bath—my *Got* how Nancy worshiped it. The porcelain bathtub was her *besettelse*, I guess that's like an *obsession* in English, but it doesn't translate exactly right. Anyway, each day she'd scrupulously inspect its "majestic eagle-claw feet." That's what she called them. The slightest spot on one of the mighty claws tied her in a knot, and she'd come hollering for me with hot words and indignation. Josephine Trigg told me she thought that the bathtub made Nancy forget the tobacco worms she had to pick-off the plants as a child in the fields of Kentucky. It made her feel upper-class, and I guessed that was what everyone in America wanted. Outside of the porcelain tub, Nancy didn't seem to care much about housekeeping or cleanliness.

Then Charlie, he was supposed to work every morning. Instead he usually played cowboys and Indians noisily with a group of neighborhood children. He outfitted the kids with feathers, beads, and war paint, then dressed himself up like a chief or one of Nancy's "prairie chickens." Anyway, the kids and Charlie all ran and yelled, whooping around the current painting on his easel. Then under Charlie's instructions, he always played the chief, the children hid behind the velvet Victorian sofa or Charlie's favorite living room chairs made of buffalo horns. The kids would hunker down quietly pretending they were waiting for the settler's' wagon train to approach and then burst out

screaming and howling and shooting toy arrows all over
the place.

I couldn't understand why the children weren't frightened by those grotesque buffalo horn chairs Charlie loved
so much. The horns made them look to me like big grouchy
insects ready to grab the first passerby. I imagined the six
black horns on the seat would trap the unsuspecting visitor
while the four pointy horns on the back of the chair could
suck the living blood from the victim. Fearsome things.
But, this was the West. Even the chair legs were made of
buffalo horns, and the speckled red velvet upholstery only
added to the bloody image. Every time I looked at them, I
remembered all the buffalo that were shot from the railroad
train and wondered if they had found this useless destiny.
Had they ended up as living room chairs? *Gut Got*, how
terrible—and sad.

One morning I was trying to clean in the dining room
working around Josephine who was there as usual printing menus for the Great Falls hotel restaurants. Joe was
hunched at the other end of the table struggling over his
art lessons and watching Charlie with a worshiping look
on his face. I looked at the chairs and then at Charlie. I
couldn't stop my tongue and finally dared to ask, "Where'd
those things . . . ah . . . those unusual chairs, come from,
Mr. Russell?" I pointed to the living room and even signed
a question with my hands. That always put him in a good
humor.

"Well, Little Package, glad you asked. I'll tell ya. But
it's a long, sad story. Them things is made by the Cree Indians over across the Missouri River. They gather up them
horns out on the prairies. Ya gotta understand, the Cree,
like Young Boy here, they ain't got no home. Their original

huntin' ground was up on the Canadian plains west of the Great Lakes, but they been pushed ever westward."

"Isn't land always good for farming? Don't they have government land?"

"Not exactly. They were sposed to go live on the Black-feet reservation. Problem was that the two tribes had been rivals. There was long-standing hatred 'tween 'em, but hell, the government agents, they don't understand or care anything about that. And then, the damned fool Crees sided with the wrong people. They up an' joined the rebellion of the half-breed Métis in their fight for an independent homeland. All of 'em wanted to go up to Saskatchewan, but it finally come down to nothin' . . . now nobody wants 'em. Neither the United States nor Canada'll have 'em. So they're homeless. Survive by selling off their remainin' possessions and make these here fancy chairs, hat racks too, of old buffalo horns and bones and stuff they find out on the prairie."

"Did you side with the half-breed Métis, Mr. Russell? Is that why you always wear that sash?" I asked him.

". . . Mebbe . . . it has to do with a whole lotta things. Sure, mebbe it's solidarity with them exiled Indians and half-breeds. Mebbe it's religion. They was all Catholic ya know. More likely it's 'cause of the land they was from— the Judith Basin. God how I loved that place. And they loved it. They settled up in the Judith."

"Is that where the log cabin you lived in was?"

"Yeah, but hell, mebbe I wear this Métis thing jus' cuz I always like being the court jester of the roundup. I dunno. Here in town ya see 'em all the time, the Cree people, feeding their selfs by rummaging in the garbage cans. It's son-of-a-bitching humiliatin' god-dammit." He swung around and faced the dining table, "Oops—oh, sorry Miss Josephine."

He looked at Josephine who was sitting at the far end of the dining table and cleared his throat. She glanced up through her heavy eye-glasses from her painstaking printing on the large stack of papers. Charlie seemed uncomfortable as he moved toward her. Leaning in closely, he touched Josephine's hair with his shoulder, and I heard her take in a quick gasp of breath.

"Your printin's a thing a beauty, Miss Josephine," he said looking over her shoulder.

"Oh Charlie, I can't even draw a straight line." She was blushing as she blurted out her reply.

Nancy who never missed a trick was standing unnoticed in the dining room entry watching closely. "Why Josephine. I think you have a crush on my Cha'lie," she said suspiciously and narrowed her eyes. Josephine looked flustered, but Charlie didn't move.

I sensed we might be in for an ugly scene, so I pushed well into the dining room quickly to interrupt. "You know how everyone loves Charlie, Mrs. Russell," I said cheerfully. "But come to the kitchen now, *ha det travelt* everyone, *haste.* Hurry on, smorgasbord's ready in the kitchen." I pointed in that direction and made a big show of the Indian sign for 'eat,' and as I expected, Joe broke the tension by pushing away from his art lesson and immediately getting up.

Nancy looked annoyed and brusquely shooed the children out of the house. "You kids get going now, outta here, dammit." She turned back to Charlie and took his arm. "They keep you from working, Cha'lie, and my Grandpa Blue always said to protect what I have . . . ."

"You have me, Mame," Charlie interrupted. "You got me cinched up to the last hole. An' you look jus' as pretty as a little red heifer in a flowerbed."

"Well, I know you love kids Cha'lie . . . and . . . I'm gonna make it up in other ways." Her expression was sad, but when he grabbed her around the waist, it changed to delight. She squealed as they moved into the kitchen. We always ate dinner there because the dining room was full of painting gear.

While all the others were moving into the kitchen and settling down, Josephine whispered to me, "She's upset. No sales since they got back from the 'big tepee' . . . New York." She made the Indian signs for "big tepee" and when she moved her extended palms rapidly apart to sign "big," her thick eyeglasses bobbled up and down on her long straight nose. We had to stifle our laughter.

"Park Hotel menus?" I asked pointing to the stack of papers she'd been working on. "How many?"

"One hundred and twenty-five—each one a little gem. They're all part of Nancy's bargaining. Twenty dollars total."

"Why do you bother Josie?"

"You just said it, Ovidia. Like everyone, I find Charlie irresistible."

We had become close friends in the past weeks, and I suspected that her feelings for Charlie came from a special relationship. I could tell she didn't enjoy doing all the lettering on Nancy's commercial illustration projects. But in fact, neither Nancy nor Charlie Russell could write anything without careful attention and extreme effort and even then with many errors. Josephine confided that the results were often comical. They must have been because even I could see their mistakes.

You know, Billy, it's funny but English writing never quite came to me. Reading was easy. But why had I supposed that everyone in American could read and write? Okay, okay, I'll get back to it. Next I need to tell you about the studio or "the shack" as it came to be called because without the studio, the forgery of the State House painting could never have taken place. And hell, that's why I sometimes feel responsible for the whole fraud. Because, I was the one that contrived to get the studio built.

The plot to build Charlie a real studio began some weeks later. It must have been late June, or was it July? I'm not exactly sure, but by then the weather had turned very hot. Carl came by after supper one evening. Like I said, he was making a habit of visiting the Russells and always with something urgent to tell me that turned out to be nothing at all and I suspected it wasn't just the card games he enjoyed.

"'Scuse us folks," he'd say. "Got something outside here to show this stubborn Valkyrie," and as usual, he ushered me outside to sit by the barn. Nancy didn't mind as long as I had finished the supper dishes.

I remember that particular night when I first had the idea for the studio. The summer sky that night was still a bright blue even though the sun had almost disappeared. Young Boy stood leaning against the rough barn boards wrapped in a red Whitney blanket with a wide black stripe. He cradled a long rifle wrapped in a beaded buckskin cover and wore leggings heavily beaded with a teepee design. It seemed strange because Young Boy never wore real Indian garb. Just his faded shirts and old serge pants, but that night he was acting as Joe's model. Joe squatted beside him in the alkali dust practicing his drawing lessons by sketching in the early evening sparkle. The light seemed perfect. Young Boy's skin gleamed a vivid bronze with deep shadows falling under his high cheek bones and under his dark brow line. Joe was signing and talking hurriedly to Young Boy as he worked.

"Shit, Young Boy, I thought I was doing purty good and then the Chief tol' me my drawin's all wrong. Said my buffalo looked like a damned mule in a hailstorm. Said buffalo ain't got their backs arched up like that. Said I had to start out all over agin."

Young Boy nodded his head and signed "yes" with his clasped hands.

"Watch me. I do jus' like the Chief says. You see, Young Boy. Charlie says you gotta do it like this." Joe took his pencil and moved it rapidly over the paper while Young Boy watched. "And then that stuff there in the background . . . he tol' me, no need for detail there. Understand . . . ."

We exchanged sign language greetings. By then I knew quite a few signs. The Indian signing was a theatrical ritual of the Russell's household. Maybe it made Charlie feel he was still in touch with the Indians—I don't know—but I used my thumb and forefinger to make the incomplete circle for "evening sun" and then extended and lowered my arm before signing "good." Carl signed too, but he scowled and jostled me off toward his long lumber wagon that was pulled up behind the horse stalls next to the barn.

"I can't believe you haven't had enough of this yet," he grumbled.

"Why Carl, I'm just beginning to tidy things up around here. You know I've a debt to my sponsor Uncle Nils."

"You'll never 'tidy-up' around Charlie. Unless you get him outta the house."

We'd reached the wagon, and Carl reached under the high seat and pulled out a small bouquet of violets. I was pleased by his kindness and held the flowers up to my face to hide my self-consciousness. I wasn't used to receiving flowers, and I remembered Mattie had suggested Carl was probably romancing me.

"When are you coming up to the Belt Mountains with me?" he asked. "I want to show you my place up there." I ignored the question as I buried my nose in the flowers, turned away, and walked toward the two open horse stalls where Charlie kept Neenah and old Monte. Carl followed closely and wrapped his jacket around me as the sun disappeared.

I looked at Carl. "Did you know, Charlie once told me what he liked best was Jake Hoover's place," I said. "That cabin up in the Judith I think."

"What are you talking about, Ovidia? That filthy log cabin? Don't tell me Nancy wants to send him up there to work."

"'A king's domain,' he called it."

"He's living in the past. Wishful thinking . . . he and his saloon-bunch cronies still dress up and play at chasing a few tired buffalo around for God's sake. Then they call it a buffalo hunt. And all this Indian sign language, hogwash."

We'd reached the horse stalls, and I pulled some sugar out of my apron pocket and gave Charlie's old horse, Monte, a lick. Carl reached over and stroked the horse's faded forehead.

"Charlie's gotta give everything a western spin. Even his damned horses. Has he told you the story about of Monte yet?" Carl asked. I shook my head and grinned, but teased him by making the Indian Sign for "yes."

"Well, I'll tell you anyway. Charlie lets it be known everywhere 'round town that Monte was a Crow Indian buffalo pony, which I doubt, but as he tells it, a Blackfeet warrior named Calf Rope stole the pony from the Crows one night. Trouble was, while Calf Rope was escaping with the pony, he was killed. So, as was the Indian custom, Calf Rope's fellow warriors shot the pony so his spirit wouldn't have to walk in his afterlife. But, the damned pony survived the bullet wound and became what the Indians call a 'ghost horse.' But then, since the pony was supposed to be dead, no Indian would ride him. The pony's medicine was too strong. Story ends with the Indians playing a trick on Charlie, a tenderfoot white boy newly arrived from St. Louis. They sold him the horse. And of course he's been riding Monte every since."

"Is that true?"

"I doubt it. It's a good story though. Makes Charlie appear to have strong medicine." Carl leaned over the stall.

"But Carl, I think it's a wonderful story, *vidunderlig*. A real western story. I wish there were more of them."

"Hell, Charlie's got hundreds of them. None of them true. Just look at this. Carl stroked Monte's stiff mane. "Poor ol' Monte," said Carl. "A real Indian Ghost horse? Well, maybe, but Monte's still trying to hang-in when he musta knowed all time that Charlie never was much of a cowboy. They was always only nighthawkers you know . . . no fault of Monte's though."

"What's a 'nighthawker?'"

"God, Ovidia, don't you know? . . . Guess you wouldn't. It's the lowest form of cowboy. All nighthawkers did was keep the horses together filling their bellies with grass during the night so as they'd be ready for the real wranglers in the morning. Charlie's no good at roping. Even Jake Hoover said he was sure no roughrider at all. Always afoot in the saddle when it came to real cowpunching. But don't get me wrong. I know I'm critical. He's a good enough guy, but never was a real cowboy."

"Yes, but the West, Carl, those stories, the cowboys, and the horses, and the Indians, and Charlie, the Cowboy Artist. That's America, and he can paint it," I said somewhat breathless with anticipation.

"Whoa—look over there, Ovidia." Carl took my shoulders and turned me toward his lumber wagon. "That's America, that's the West. Those new telephone poles. Progress. The Electric City."

"But . . . the Cowboy Artist. He can make the West permanent. He could . . . help me, Carl. Nancy wants him to paint and stay away from the bunch in the saloons. I've asked Joe and Young Boy to start looking for material to build a studio. We can do it."

"Nancy'd never spend the money."

"We'd have to do it cheap."

"We? Where's this we stuff coming from? An' Charlie'd prob'ly resent it. I've told you he's stubborn. I don't think he likes that palace of a house they got now. He's pigheaded."

That's it, Carl. Why not? The studio doesn't need to be a palace. Only a cabin. A log cabin studio. Just like Jake's place only right here, right here in the yard—on the extra lot. And you Carl, you thought of it. A log cabin studio."

Carl looked bewildered. In my excitement about the idea of the log cabin studio, I threw my arms around Carl and kissed him, very quickly, on the cheek. My mind was racing with plans. Carl was quiet, but it seemed the crickets were singing, "Okee, okee," in American English to tell me it would work. Charlie'd get his studio, Nancy'd sell more paintings, everyone would see the real West and the cowboys. I'd have my buffalo dream and maybe my buckskin jacket with long fringes.

I guess I'd pushed Carl some. I lied. He hadn't thought of the cabin studio, I had. But it would work. I knew it would. Was this another affliction? Gambling, now lying, deceit. What would Margaret and the Salvationists say? I believed Mattie would say it was all right. All I wanted to do was help the Russells.

We walked slowly back to the house past Carl's wagon load of telephone poles. An hour or so later, I looked out the back screen door and saw Joe, Young Boy, and Carl inspecting the wagon load of telephone poles and signing. It looked like an Indian sign language parley, so I closed the door softly hoping it wouldn't make the usual slam.

Sales in the Big Tepee

By the next day, I was having misgivings about a studio for Charlie on the empty lot next door. I wasn't sure I was doing the right thing with my plans for the log cabin studio. What was really going on in the household? As far as I could figure, Nancy was an ambitious social climber. One thing I was certain of, she goaded and pushed Charlie to create more artwork. She yearned for him to become wealthy and famous. I thought he was already, but I guess not in Nancy's eyes. Her long suit sure seemed to be pushing sales. She never gave up, but she didn't seem to be having a great deal of success.

And Charlie? It seemed he didn't care about fame or fortune at all. It looked like all he yearned for was to be with the bunch, his cowboy friends, or I guess they were now all ex-cowboys. If Nancy would just build the cabin studio, it could solve both of the problems. He would have his bunch in the log cabin, and she could have the Victorian parlor and dining room for her sales. It was just a question of how to get everyone to agree. I tried to isolate the problems involved in getting the studio: money number one, and Charlie's stubborn nature number two. It seemed simple.

While I was preparing the trout Young Boy caught and delivered to us for our evening supper, I overheard Nancy's muffled conversation with two new tourist customers in the living room. When I peeked in, she was rustling pages of a messy looking scrapbook that she pulled out from under some bottles of Higgins India ink.

"We've just come back from New York," she said. "Cha'lie got raving reviews. *The New York Press* said, 'A Westerner of the old school who stalled off the night stampede.'"

I could hear a stranger's deep voice. "Look at this my dear. Now that's energy." I knew the Eastern tourist must have been looking at *Redskin Raiders* because that was the painting currently on the living room easel.

A sweet melodious voice replied. "Oh but—so exhausting. And so, so—utterly gloomy."

"You can almost hear those galloping horses' hooves beating."

"But, I love John Alexander."

"My God. I think I can smell the alkali dust from the hoof beats," said the deep voice.

"Well Sir, my Cha'lie knows a horse's physique from firsthand experience. And he can . . ."

"But dearest, Alexander's work is so, so . . . noble. I adore the angels, and the Greek gods and goddesses," I heard the soft voice interrupt Nancy and then fade away.

There was some more murmuring and then the sound of the front door closing. I kept cleaning the trout and waited thinking Nancy would come in for her tea. When she didn't, I went to the living room to find her drooping in the arms of the fierce buffalo horn chair. She was sniffling.

"More gods and goddesses?" I asked. Nancy merely shook her head. "I'll get you some tea, Mrs. Russell."

"And my medicine, Ovidia, the large blue bottle in the bathroom medicine cabinet."

Her neurasthenia was acting up again. I hurried the tea and retrieved the bottle and a spoon. I didn't want her to faint since we were alone in the house. The medicine was laudanum. I'd asked Mattie about it and she told me it was good for just about everything: depression, anxiety, chronic fatigue and even tuberculosis. It always helped Nancy. I settled the tea tray on the table next to the ugly insect chair. Nancy opened the medicine bottle and ignoring the spoon, took a swig. Then she splashed an ample nip of the medication into the tea.

"Oh sit down, Ovidia. You're always so busy, busy. I need you to sit. I've been exhausted ever since we got back from New York. What a horrid stinking place. Sit down." I edged into the arms of the other creepy buffalo chair.

"God, that shitty hotel, The Park View, with no park and sure no damned view. Cold, damp room, looking out on a sooty black airshaft. Gas explosions, no quiet. And nothing but those 'illustrator' friends of Cha'lie's. Marchand, Crawford, and damn—I can't even remember the other guy's name. Oh sure, they was nice enough. Shared their studio with Cha'lie. Except that fat pig Remington. Thinks he owns the throne when it comes to western art. An' he never, ever, even lived here. How in hell could he sit a horse when he weighs more than three hundred pounds? You know, Ovidia, one of the New York papers said Cha'lie'd push that fat old whale offen his damn throne."

"The newspaper called him a 'fat old whale?'" I asked amazed, but Nancy didn't answer. She was ranting, her face red, and she took the medicine bottle and poured another splash of laudanum into what was left of her tea.

"Would you like another cup?" I asked.

"No, jus' sit still and listen. Mebbe you'll learn sumpin." I wanted to get back to the trout, but I didn't dare. Nancy seemed lost. She was staring blankly into space, her eyes bright, and the pupils looked very black and large.

"Well, first off, we got there and I had to rent a basement gallery near that damned No-View Hotel. Would you believe, I had to go out on the street and collar anyone I saw there on Forty-Second jus' to get 'em to look—anyone, just anyone.

"Pretty soon we ran out of money for even that. So Cha'lie, he moved in to work with those 'illustrators.' They was damned lucky to have him, Ovidia, cause they got a chance to soak up some authentic western details of art.

"Well sure, I guess Cha'lie learned a little from them too. Did you know my Cha'lie never went to art school? Well he didn't." Nancy stopped talking and gave a heavy sigh. She picked up *The Great Falls Tribune* from the marble topped side table and began fanning herself. She looked flushed. I thought she was through talking and started to get up.

"Sit still. I spent four damned months pounding the pavement looking for sales with book and magazine editors. But, hell, I got 'em. I never give up, Ovidia. So, they didn't like me much, but I got 'em. *Scribner's, Leslie's,* and *Outing,* they all promised to use Cha'lie's illustrations. But goddammit Cha'lie he ain't no illustrator. He's an artist. An' dear God, I only managed to sell one sonnabitchin painting the whole time."

Nancy sat quietly now. I worried. It was better when she was talking. She was still staring with a kind of glazed look. I wanted to say something to break the silence, but what? I didn't know how to reassure her. I only thought it might help if their lives were a bit more organized. The buffalo chair I was sitting in seemed to be squeezing me tighter, and then I saw the corners of her lips begin to turn upward in a slight smile. It soon became a real grin and her eyes started to lose their glassy look.

"Cha'lie hated New York. Said it smelled worsen a cow shed. Noise gave him headaches. One day he even got lost. Wandered around for hours. After that, all he wanted to do was come home.

"And then, thank God in heaven, I found our dear, dear friend William S. Hart again. After two years. It was a miracle. He's a famous New York actor, you know. Ovidia, you gotta believe, he's the most handsome man in the world. Well, except for Cha'lie. But oh, Bill Hart has such a long straight nose, and those eyes, they jus' poke right through you."

Nancy's cheeks seemed flushed, and her hands went up to her hair tucking in some stray ends that had fallen from the coil at the back of her neck. Suddenly she had a flirty sort of look in her eyes.

"Bill was working in a New York production, and he took me and Cha'lie to get our first look at the ocean. Far Rockaway Beach, he called it. Isn't that a romantic name? Far Rockaway Beach, on Long Island, that's where we went. It was a cold, cloudy day with great angry breakers smashing up high on the shore. I'll never forget. Cha'lie was delighted. He actually waded in the freezing surf, boots soaked, his sash jus' dragging in the water, Stetson blown off by the wind. Meanwhile Bill and I, we jus' sat together there rubbing each other's hands to keep them warm. I looked into Bill's eyes and, and, I can't describe the sensation . . . I was, I felt like, a pretty young girl again." Nancy grinned and got up from the buffalo horn chair and swirled around the room before sprawling onto the Victorian sofa. She closed her eyes and I thought she might be falling asleep. I started to get up and head back to the trout.

"Sit down dammit." she said. "Later Bill hooked us up with a reporter. Shit, that interview was damned frightening. Cha'lie wouldn't talk at all at first, but then he started one of his stories. Tol' the reporter about a how he an' Pike Miller was surrounded by a war party of Piegan Indians. The usual Cha'lie embroidery, but lucky for us, the reporter took it even farther. What he said in the newspaper was, and I'm gonna quote this, he said, 'Cha'lie was 'a new type of American painter an' hardly a man to care for pink tea.'

"Cha'lie felt better after that, and then he did his first real sculpture. We had twenty-six castings made of *Smokin' Up*. Better than any of fat Remington's crap. And—right now—that old Remington's gettin' famous for his bronzes. Gossip says he has to hire an obedient, citified Indian to model for him on his fancy New Rochelle driveway. He's nothing but a joke," she giggled.

"Frederic Sackrider Remington, huh, fat in the middle and poor on each end, that's him. Cha'lie never, hardly ever, uses models. He <u>knows</u> what he's doing."

I finally brought Nancy into the kitchen for another cup of tea and after that and poured myself some coffee.

Tea's never been my drink. I was starting to think that what was important to the West was to keep the tough cowboy image that the newspaper man in New York has talked about. While I worked on the trout, Nancy kept talking.

"You know Ovidia, those New York professionals, even though they are 'illustrators,' they sure could mix colors. Course Cha'lie, he always has to have the top hand, he told them all right. He said, 'You should see what Injins can do with colors. Nobody can do color like the Injin. I can't anyway. You hear say the Injin can't draw. But, shit, his hosses look like hosses and his buffalo look like buffalo.' Cha'lie loves to tell those Easterners 'bout his Injins.

"He 'jus needed to get out of the No-View Hotel more. He always needs to be with a bunch of men so they can swap stories. Those 'illustrators' learned a lot from Cha'lie. Never forget, it's only Cha'lie who's an authentic western artist. They all loved him. And, I'll admit it, he picked up some ideas from those guys about how to mix colors and avoid gloomy dark looking shadows."

So, she did understand he needed to be with the bunch. It seemed like my chance, so I put the trout into the hot skillet and as it crackled, I suggested hopefully. "Maybe he needs a place here where he can work and still be with the men swapping stories. If he had a studio of his own, you could entertain the Eastern customers here in the house."

"Oh no. None of that shit. I'm not gonna let him go back down to those rooms behind the bars. Not even to the Brunswick, Albert's place. I have to protect what I have like Grampa Blue always said."

"Maybe a studio right here on the lot, right next to the house. Everything could be so much more organized. And, and . . . wouldn't the light would be right in the afternoon so he could paint right here, all day long. And . . . and see his men friends too." I was hesitant, but excited. It was the first time I'd had the nerve to suggest the studio to Nancy. But her expression was forbidding; she didn't seem to be buying the idea. I hurried on with my pitch.

"You could have a real gallery right here in the living room. A place to entertain the tourists, and Paris Gibson, and his wife, and . . . maybe even William Hart when he comes through Great Falls." That brought a light into her eyes.

"Would cost way too much." She shook her head and the loose wisps came back down along with a big tortoise shell hairpin.

"Maybe not," I said as I leaned over to pick-up the hairpin. "Carl said a cowboy artist' should have a studio built out of logs, like a log cabin."

"Well, Ovidia, that might be nice, but you have no idea about how scarce and expensive logs are anymore. The damned railroads used 'em all, and then the goddamned smelters. Not hardly a tree left in all of Montana, I betcha. Scarcer than hens' teeth."

"Maybe something that looks like logs." I was thinking of Carl's telephone poles. "Maybe telephone poles. Carl had a whole wagon load of them," I said.

"Shit, I'd just have to sell a helluva lot more paintings, and there hasn't been a sale since we got back from New York."

"Carl said he didn't know what he was going to do with all those telephone poles."

"If only Cha'lie's paintings are accepted for the St. Louis World Fair. That'd bring in the sales. He'd be an important artist then. I'm hopin'. I submitted six paintings, an' the deadline was way back in March."

"Oh, Mr. Russell is sure to be accepted," I quickly reassured her since her expression had turned sour again.

"Well, I don't take no chances. I wrote Cha'lie's daddy. He's very important in St. Louis, you know. Knows all the important people. Owns the Parker-Russell Mining and Manufacturing Company. Real quality they are. He promised to write to the fair officials on his company stationery for an answer."

"Then, I bet it's certain he'll be accepted. Later, when he has his studio where he can work all day, you'll have the house so you can sell a lot more paintings." Nancy tended to become distracted easily, and I didn't want her to lose the idea of the studio.

"Think of what a charming place a log cabin studio would be. A real 'Cowboy Artist' studio. The tourists would love it."

"Do you think Cha'lie'd really like it?"

"Oh, I know he would. He always talks about Jake's old cabin and hunting and trapping. He'd feel comfortable. Then, he'd get more work done."

"An' Carl has the telephone poles?"

"Oh *ja*, he got them for Paris Gibson and the Electric City, but now Mr. Gibson says there isn't a need for them. Mr. Gibson says not much new business is coming into Great Falls. He expected a lot more. Carl's told me he's stuck, and he'll sell 'em cheap."

"Well hell, at least I'll talk to him. But, you may as well warn him—I'm gonna want a good price. And then . . . maybe Cha'lie won't like the idea—he's obstinate— wouldn't move his camp for a damned prairie fire."

"Try reminding Mr. Russell of how much he loved Jake Hoover's old cabin," I suggested.

So you see Billy, I was moving things forward toward an end that I couldn't have imagined that day while I was cooking trout for supper. Now I had both Nancy and Carl ready to negotiate on a log cabin artist's studio.

The Log Cabin Studio

The advantages a log cabin studio could provide had taken root in Nancy's hawk-eyed conscience. I think she pictured how fine it would be to have both a fancy tea room for the customers and still keep Charlie close enough to make sure he was working. That very night when Carl dropped in, he and Nancy had a secretive conversation out on the vacant lot beside the house. When I carried the garbage out I saw Nancy gesturing and pointing with her arms spread at a ninety degree angle. Late the next morning Margaret Trigg came by for the usual elocution lesson and I caught them whispering in the dining room. By that evening Nancy was huddled with Joe and Young Boy outside by the barn.

It was Carl who gave me the official news a few days later. It was settled. Nancy was moving ahead on her brilliant idea. She had decided on a wonderful gift for Charlie's birthday. She would build a log cabin studio for the Cowboy Artist, and she'd have it built with telephone poles.

Charlie, at first reluctant, had agreed on the condition that it would be built just like the cabin he had shared with Jake Hoover. He didn't want anything bigger or more elaborate or fancier. That meant the poles had to look like logs and the studio had to have a big stone fireplace. Nancy squirmed over the price Carl asked for the telephone poles until she received news that Charlie's oil painting *Pirates of the Plains* had been accepted at the St. Louis Exposition. It would hang in the Palace of Fine Arts, and three of his other painting would be hung in the Montana pavilion. Her mood was definitely on the up-swing. A place in the magnificent Palace of Fine Arts at the Louisiana Purchase Exposition would guarantee sales and Charlie would be on his was to fame and fortune.

"It's gonna be fine," she told me. "I'll sell more paintings and the trades people won't be askin' Cha'lie some damn fool questions and gettin' him started telling about cowboyin' or livin' with the Blood Indians. And the bunch—hell, they can all jus' go out to the cabin and smoke and eat their beans, bacon, and bachelor bread. 'Cept you've gotta help me, Ovidia. We've gotta watch 'em. Not too many hangin' out there, and I don't want no Scamper Juice drinking."

"Oh, I'll help, Mrs. Russell."

"An' those wannabe artists like Olaf Seltzer, and Joseph Sharp, and that damned Ed Borein, thank God I won't have 'em hangin' around the dining room anymore trying to soak up being cowboys. I'll have time for the more important things like business and dealin' art. I'll be Cha'lie's business manager—and his agent—both. I'm the damned wagon boss around here."

Early the next Sunday birds were chirping quietly in the morning sun, and smoke drifted slowly up from the big stack as usual. When I went out to empty the drip water from the ice box, I could hear church bells sounding in the distance and the snuffling of the horses out in the barn. I poured the cloudy water on one of the struggling sapling trees and stood a minute breathing the western air before I went back inside. The house was quiet, and I got out the flour from the big metal bin for the waffles that I prepared every morning. I was reaching up to get eggs from the cooler when I heard the rumbling of a wagon in the yard and three sharp piercing whistles. Startled, I dropped one of the eggs and it broke on the pine floor boards and began seeping into the cracks. "Damn it," I mumbled and reached for the cleaning rag I kept hanging by the sink, but before I could wipe up the mess I heard more whistling and a loud crashing noise, and then the sound of trotting hoof beats.

"Hey buckaroo. Careful there!"

"Better catch them doggies fer they stampede right inta the street."

The yells were coming from back behind the barn. The ground seemed to be shaking. I rushed out the back door and saw six or seven men dressed in full, dusty cowboy gear riding their horses around the yard, twirling ropes, whistling and shouting. Albert Trigg and Carl were standing in front of an overloaded logging wagon full of telephone poles trying to calm two stomping Clydesdales.

Crouching on top of the wagon, Young Boy and Joe DeYong were struggling to release the chains holding the poles in place. It looked dangerous. As the poles finally came tumbling off the wagon, they both quickly jumped aside while the load crashed down the slight slope and began rolling toward the house.

"Kee-ryst, they're moving faster'n squirrels in a cage," yelled Trigg.

"Whoa, whoa there now." squawked a trim, gray-haired little cowboy with a big dark moustache. "This's dange'rous as squattin' bare-assed in a nest a rattlers,"

"Watch it there, Teddy Blue. Ridin' through this brush ya need a suit made by a blacksmith," hollered a big, tough looking wrangler with forearms like barrels bursting out of his stained buckskin shirt. The cowboys were behaving like a bunch of school kids, whistling at the logs and shouting to each other.

"My *Got*, they're pretending like they're roping steers at a roundup," I screamed to Charlie as he slammed out the back screen door hustled toward the middle of the twirling ropes. He was in his night shirt and boots, but he didn't seem to care by the look on his face and his pleased, crooked grin.

"Hey Russ. These damn poles is thorny as Arizona cactus. They's no controlling 'em," griped a tall guy in a high crowned white hat sitting a fancy stepping black stallion. I remember him particularly because I suspected this must be the Con Price that Mattie was so sweet on. Good looking but with a gigantic nose.

Nancy had come out the back door with an Indian blanket wrapped over her nightdress and her hair straggling. "Albert. Albert Trigg. And you there Carl Holmes—up on that wagon. What in the hell's going on? What will the neighbors think?" squawked Nancy. Joe kept Indian signing and yelling, "Build it, build it, Jake's cabin, a studio," from his perch on top of the wagon.

In the middle of this pandemonium, Margaret and Josephine Trigg appeared from their house next door carrying baskets. Margaret was in her usual blue serge uniform and bonnet. I raced to the kitchen knowing we'd need to feed this crowd, and soon Margaret and Josephine came in with Nancy to help. We put together some quick biscuits and jerked beef for the cowboys who had finally corralled their horses and put away the ropes. They didn't seem much like any cabin builders or carpenters I'd seen in Norway, and they sure weren't stone masons like my uncles, but they had rolled up their sleeves like they were ready to work. Con Price had taken off his white hat and even seemed to know what he was doing.

In the kitchen, Nancy looked a little pasty-pale. She had agreed to the cabin studio, but I don't think she understood, or didn't want to know, that to keep the costs down Carl had talked Charlie's drinking bunch into doing the job and they were determined to make the event a celebration.

We were frying up bacon, frying eggs, and boiling beans when we heard the trumpet music. "Thank God, they're here. I knew they'd come to give a hand," Margaret said looking satisfied. She wiped her hands on her apron, put her bonnet back on and went out to welcome her Army. They were coming up Fourth Avenue North with banners flying and drums beating. By now, all the Fourth Avenue neighbors had lined the street to see what was going on. I could hear the Salvationists singing and drumming as they approached.

> Stand-up, stand-up for Jesus,
> Ye soldiers of the cross,
> Lift high his royal banner,
> We shall not suffer loss . . . .

Nancy retreated to the bathroom for her medicine while Josephine and I started carrying food outside for the troops. With Margaret's help, the whole Salvation Army Corps of twenty or more, in full uniform, had camped on the north side of the house. The soldiers took off their heavy blue, gold braided jackets. A very tall, thin man was leading them in testimony. "That's 'Hallelujah Pickles,' mother's adjutant," Jose whispered and we watched as they took over the construction of the south and east cabin walls. Young Boy had gathered a few of his Cree brothers, and the cowboys and Indians worked the north and west.

Well, yes, Billy. This does have to do with the forgery. Without the log cabin studio, it all couldn't have happened. So I have to tell you about it. It was a wild, wild day, Billy. Like a real circus. I remember every detail, even now.

The Salvation Army "lassies" set-up their outdoor cook stoves and began boiling coffee and frying doughnuts. They filled a couple of clean refuse pails with hog fat, rolled out the spiced dough with an empty wine bottle, cut it with a baking powder tin, and poked in the hole with a round camphorice container. Once things got going, they fried seven doughnuts at a time and not only the workers but the whole population of Fourth Avenue North came over to try them. I noticed Con Price making trip after trip to get doughnuts and wondered whether it might have been the lassies he was more interested in.

"Who's that little gray-haired cowboy?" I asked Jose.

"You mean the short fellow with the big moustache?"

"*Ja*, the one who seems to be in charge."

"Teddy Blue, they call him. Teddy Blue Abbott. Why are you asking, Ovidia? Are you interested? He's about your size." We both looked over at Teddy Blue and sniggered. I was embarrassed. I couldn't understand why American women were so interested in match making. Was that all they thought about?

"*Nei*, Josie, I was curious, that's all."

"Well, he's a Texan. Born in England, but he came to America as a child. He was with one of the first cattle drives. He may be sawed-off, but he's tougher than any of them. Better keep your eye on him."

I laughed and walked away to pass some doughnuts to Young Boy and his group of Cree. They had started working with Joe DeYong to caulk the spaces between the logs as soon as the first two rows were set in place. I watched as one of the Cree stood or knelt on each side of the wall. They used a kind of twisted loose fiber, pushing it tightly into the spaces between the logs with sharpened white bones.

But, you know, the fiber wasn't oakum like we used on boats in Norway. I moved toward Young Boy to look at it more closely. The stuff they used was twisted, not unraveled, and the pile of it didn't have the same smell. My *Got,* I realized it was hair. Thick, wooly and matted, a dusty looking brown color. I pointed at the stuff and signed, "What is it?" to Young Boy. He signed back. "Hair." That's what it was. And then he signed "buffalo." Buffalo hair. And the tools. I could see now that they were buffalo bones.

Well, Billy, I was sadly reminded again of the train trip and the useless shooting for sport that had taken place. The Cree Indians were the scavengers. They did the clean-up, collecting what the tourists discarded and then cleverly selling it back to them. Cunning as foxes really. Perhaps more devious than I had at first imagined, and the notion made me smile.

Children dressed up in Sunday best were running all over. Boys in knee pants with ruffled white blouses and long black stockings and girls with satin ribbons streaming from their long hair. The flags of the Salvationists were snapping in the light breeze giving a rhythm to the humming of the two-man crosscut saws. The air smelled of coffee, doughnuts, bacon and red cedar logs. It was all intoxicating. I hurried back and forth from the house carrying pots of beans, tin plates and cups. The scene reminded me of *Syttende Mai* in Norway—the Seventeenth of May.

Do you know what that is, Billy? Course not, but I'll tell you. It's the day we Norwegians celebrated our freedom after four hundred years of control by the damned Danish.

Josephine and I were in the kitchen when we heard the crowd cheering. We hurried outside to the cabin site and saw the hefty cowboy with the barrel arms struggling to lift one of the poles into place with no help.

"Ya' got about as much chance as a jackrabbit at a coyote convention," Hallelujah Pickles taunted from the Army side of the cabin.

"Easy as throwing a two-day-old calf," the cowboy grunted. His high-heeled boots began to slide in what was now becoming a deep mud-bog. The watching crowd groaned, but he managed to slip the long pole up and into place. With that victory for the cowboys, the crowd yelled their praise, and Hallelujah Pickles rushed over to pump his arm.

Teddy Blue hollered over to Hallelujah, "Easy. Jus' like a kitten hoppin' over a caterpillar—praise the Lord." and all the Salvationists roared.

"Like lickin' butter offen a knife," said Charlie as he clapped the tough cowboy across the shoulder and grabbed his hand.

"Who is that big guy?" I whispered to Josephine.

"Johnny Matheson. A jerkline freight wagon driver. He can manage ten or twelve horses plying the route from Fort Benton to Judith. But he's no favorite of Nancy's. She's tried to house break him, and she can't."

Later that day, Matheson relieved himself in the backyard. Nancy caught him with his fly open and threw the iron skillet she was carrying at him. She was outraged.

"We've indoor plumbing now, God damn you," she screeched as Johnny ducked back around behind the horse stalls.

I was starting to understand that Nancy ranked everyone on an "up or down" social scale. To me it seemed a strange kind of measure. It was based on how much each person lived a style of life that revolved around the idea of appearing very wealthy. Frequently her social scale included where the person came from. Most of the cowboys were "down," and most of the Salvationists too. The Triggs were different. They were "up" because they came from England, so although Albert owned a saloon, he was at a level higher-up than the other saloon keepers like Sid Willis who only came from Arkansas. The Triggs never played down, nor had they lost, their European sensibilities. Even Josephine kept her family's British accent. I guessed that Teddy Blue's English birth wouldn't help him. He had lost his accent and talked just like the rest of the cowboy bunch. Nancy sure doted on anything rich, famous, or English. I didn't really understand yet all the things that could put you up or down, but I suspected that the Indians were at the very bottom, even below immigrants."

ELEVEN

Charlie's Promise

Early that afternoon I was admiring how fast the cabin was taking shape when I heard the sputtering sound of a gasoline engine. A bulky motor car came speeding down Fourth Avenue and stopped right in front of the log cabin construction. Teddy Blue seemed to be following me around a lot, so I asked him about the noisy auto. He was real captivated by it. Said it was called a truck—a brand new 1904 Studebaker truck. Paris Gibson, who was definitely on Nancy's "up" list, had arrived. Over his handsome wool suit and vest he wore a loose, pale colored, linen duster, and instead of the usual derby hat I'd seen him wearing in newspaper photographs, he wore a tight fitted leather helmet that buckled under the chin. Glass goggles strapped around his head over the helmet and covered his eyes. Naturally everyone gathered around. Paris jumped out from under the flashy gold plated steering wheel.

"Wha'cha got in that dern skunkmobile, Paris?" said Charlie out of the side of his mouth as they exchanged claps on the back.

"It's called a lorry, Russ. Just in from Detroit. And that's a damned funny looking corral you're building." Paris had a deep raspy voice that commanded attention.

"It's my surprise for Cha'lie, Paris," Nancy said. "Every true artist needs a private studio." Nancy had hurried over to greet Paris, and was practicing her elocution lessons by speaking carefully.

"Oh hell, Mame, you know I'm just a no-count illustrator," said Charlie addressing Nancy while reaching for his sack of Bull Durham. He cleared his throat and began to roll a cigarette. "I ain't no artist."

"I heard about it, Nancy," said Paris. "Heard you plan to have a damned trapper's cabin right here on North Fourth. Frank Linderman told me and we decided we'd best come and give you some expert advice and help on that fireplace." From the far side of the Studebaker a gangly individual, about Charlie's age, seemed to be unfolding. He appeared very tall and slim in his close fitting pants and narrow jacket.

"Ho Ho, Hi-eeeeee," he called to Charlie, and taking off his broad brimmed hat, he dusted it across his knees.

"Ho Ho, Hi-eeeeeeee, 'Sign-talker,' you old son-of-a-bitch. Look who Paris drugged in, Mame. I'll bet you been keepin' the legislature in line down there in Helena, Frank. Giving them sheepherders hell, I suspect." Charlie grinned and grabbed Frank around his shoulders.

When Nancy looked at Paris Gibson she glowed and simpered, but on seeing Frank Linderman her eyebrows went up and she got a particular tight curl at the corners of her mouth with her nostrils flaring slightly as if she smelled something foul. I had noticed the look before, and I thought it had to be part of her up or down rating system. Whenever she met one of Charlie's old cronies, it was the tight mouth and raised eyebrows. I guessed from Nancy's look that Frank must be one of the bunch even though he was in the State legislature—probably an ex-cowboy.

Barely nodding to Frank, she put on her best social face and addressed Paris Gibson politely. "And how is Mrs. Gibson? I haven't seen her in such a while. That was such a lovely tea she had in you all's garden. She certainly knows how to entertain."

"She's feelin' a little punkish lately in the overly warm weather, I'm afraid."

"Well, please send her my regards . . . I hope . . ."

But Paris had already turned away from Nancy toward the back of the truck and hollered at two Chinese sitting hunched on top of a load of pavers and stones. "Dump 'em right over here boys. And then, get going on that fireplace—there over yonder on the south wall. Chop-chop." He motioned toward the cabin and clapped his hands. The Chinese quickly jumped down, their traditional long queues flying, and began unloading the lorry. They were to be the stone masons who would build the fireplace and pave the floor.

Teddy Blue moved in between Gibson and Linderman and reached up to wrap his arms over both their shoulders. He pressed them over toward the construction. "Wahl, you see there," he pointed, "we been workin' so damned hard we're drowning in our own sweat. Come on an' let's set an' jaw awhile, Paris. Teddy nodded toward Charlie. Hell, an' if we're lucky 'The Buckskin Kid' here'll tell us one of his famous stories 'bout Jake Hoover's pig." "Bet you never heared that'un, Frank," boasted Teddy Blue.

"Why hell, Teddy, only two or three hundred times. At least a couple a times every dern hunting trip," replied Frank. Everyone laughed, but Nancy didn't look amused when the bunch moved toward the cabin where they hunkered down on top of the logs.

"Brought you boys a little refreshment to start the shack off right. Just like my name, it's right out of Paris. Time to paint your tonsils." After Nancy turned toward the house, Gibson had pulled a bottle of brandy out from under his duster coat.

All right, Billy. I am staying on track, dammit. All of these events lead up to how and why the forgery took place. You have to understand the way everything set-up to make the forgery possible, and even necessary. Can you cut me some slack? Isn't that what they say now on television? Cut some slack. And, warm up this damn cold coffee from over there on the buffet line.

When I returned from the kitchen with cups and lemonade, I noticed the bunch were still talking and passing around the bottle that Paris kept hidden under a log. The Salvation Army soldiers were under Margaret's close order drill taking either a coffee break or some lemonade after circling to pray. Only the Indians and the Chinese continued work. I could hear the bunch laughing and loudly telling their tales over by the unfinished cabin.

"Yeah, an' 'member that time . . . the fourteen-horse span comin' up outta Belt. . . . Three days an' we didn't turn a wheel," boasted Matheson in his deep voice.

"You sleepin' in the cook cart an' me in the Murphy wagon . . . the roar of that storm jus' rockin' my cradle. Coldern' a witch's caress," said Charlie laughing.

"More backtrailing,'" Carl whispered to me. He'd come up from behind me, and we walked toward the house. "Well, how 'bout it, Little Valkyrie? This suit your fancy? Your idea you know. Too bad old Jake himself can't see this . . . even down to the stone fireplace. Not that Jake ever cared that damned much about his old cabin, but it'll suit the cowboy artist's public image. You happy?"

"Almost, Carl, but we're missing the Buffalo Skull—for the front door. Charlie's symbol. And . . . and . . . those big old horns. You know. Joe says he's got to have them. For the roof." I wasn't giving an inch until it was perfect.

"Damn, Miss Ovidia, I believe you kin chew up nails and spit out tacks," Carl responded.

I didn't laugh. I had to taunt Carl, but I was pleased with the building. Paris Gibson had quickly bought into the trapper's log cabin studio. Maybe he thought it would help tourism though it sure didn't look like it belonged in the "Electric City." Nancy could cheer up now that Paris had given his approval. She might even get an invitation to join the Maids and Matrons. At the least, she'd have the bunch out of the dining room.

Charlie's words came floating down from the cabin, "Did I ever tell you about Jake Hoover's pig? . . . Well, one spring a ranchman traded old Jake a little suckin' pig for some elk meat. He was a tiny, little thing, black as . . . ." His voice was drowned out by groans and hollers.

"Not again."

"Oh no ya don't, Russ." yelled Matheson. "I'd rather heft logs than hear that'un again."

"Not even if I'm as sober as a muley cow," said Con Price.

They all got up and moved to pick up their tools again, but before going back to work, Con wandered over to the lassies and begged a cup of lemonade.

The drinking hitch was over, and the besotted bunch rolled back to fitting and laying the cabin's cedar logs. Linderman and Paris drove off after cranking up the Studebaker leaving the Chinese to work on the fireplace. By late afternoon the windows had been set into place and the front door framed up. Before sundown, the Cree Indians had set the roof of split logs into place. And the Salvationist soldiers had the log supports in for the covered porch that extended across the front side facing the street. By evening the cabin was nearing completion when Frank Linderman returned. His team of four trotted up noisily pulling a wagon load of elk horns and a couple of buffalo skulls. I remember watching Frank and Charlie going into their ritualized greetings, Indian signs and all.

"Ho. Ho. Hi-eeeeeeeee, Running Antelope," called Linderman.

"Ho. Ho. Hi-eeeeeeeee, Sign-Talker," responded Charlie with the usual ceremonial greeting. Linderman jumped from the wagon, Indian signed to Charlie, and they moved off to inspect the cabin.

Why did grown men do this? Was it some sort of boyman ritual I wondered? Every time the two met. All the signing and the Indian greetings. Josephine told me it was a vision held over from the old yellow-back novels they both read as kids. The library had plenty of them, and later she even gave me a couple written by Ned Buntline and one I remember well by Harry Castlemon. For me they were breathtaking reading. Exactly the West I expected and was looking for, but not like the West I saw everyday around Great Falls.

The Cree and the Chinese who were working late began to unload Frank's wagon in front of the cabin. All those bones made a huge pile out front by the sapling trees that struggled to take root on land I suspected wanted to be a treeless prairie.

Carl was so pleased with himself. "Just like you ordered, Miss Ovidia. Buffalo skull complete with horns and spit nose, and a couple dozen elk antlers. Unless it's the Cree, no one can find this stuff like Frank, our distinguished senior State Representative. He's the resident Indian expert. Don't tell Charlie I said so, but Frank's got him one-up on living with Indians. Flatheads, Blackfeet, Cree and Chippewa. Some say, whether slanderous or not, that Charlie's yarns are spun to order like his illustrations."

"Well," I huffed. Carl always found ways to annoy me. I was trying to break the habit, but found I was stamping my foot anyway. "Nancy tells me Charlie lived with the Blood branch of the Blackfeet. And . . . and, she says he almost married a little 'prairie chicken.'"

"My goodness, Miss Ovidia, where <u>do</u> you get such language? 'Prairie chicken?' You're beginning to sound just like the Russells."

"So! That's what I've heard."

"Not a very nice thing to say though."

"It's nicer than 'squaw,' isn't it? Nancy says that squaw means 'cunt.'"

"Whoa now. Hold up a danged minute. Where are you getting such language? Do you know what that means?"

"*Ja*, Nancy told me."

"Well, what does it mean then?"

I turned away from Carl. I was self-conscious. I knew I'd said something dreadful.

"Well, tell me," Carl insisted.

Now I wasn't sure anymore. "I . . . I . . . think it's a word that means a lady's private parts. Nancy told me. She did, dammit." I started to walk away, and Carl took my arm and pulled me back.

"Whoa. Slow up there Little Miss Valkyrie. Nancy knows a lot, but sometimes things are better left unsaid. Maybe you're learning the wrong things. Too much, too fast, and your teacher—maybe she's not a real good judge of what English you should learn. Ask Margaret, or Josephine, or your friend Mattie even if you don't understand." Carl picked up the largest buffalo skull with the black horns still attached and the bones bleached chalk white.

"Oh hell, come on now, don't sulk, help me. Let's get this damned buffalo skull hung over the doorway. Foolish trademark anyway. Like trying to keep the dead alive." I followed Carl to the door of the new cabin carrying a hammer, large nails and some bailing wire.

"Charlie says it was a prog—nos—ti—ca—shun. Is it okay to say it that?"

"Ovidia . . . I can see you'll always say whatever you want to anyway, so go ahead."

"He told me that the first time he came up to Helena by stagecoach they got to the top of a rise and had to stop the stage to blow the horses. When the passengers got out to stretch their legs, like any kid he was poking around back from the trail and under a clump of buffalo grass he found his first buffalo skull. He said it was sent there to tell him to stay in Montana. That's how he tells it."

"Yarn spinning, I'd call it."

Carl bent over and put a squared section of log down in front of the door frame as a riser. He climbed up and hammered in three nails while I twisted the bailing wire around the back of the skull to provide a hanger. I noticed Carl's hands had beautiful long tapered fingers as he reached down to grab the wire as I lifted the skull. He hooked it neatly over the nails, and we stood back silently admiring our work. Charlie and Frank were talking inside the cabin.

"Yeap, I got it, Russ. Contract's right here in my pocket. Title's going to be *Indian Why Stories*."

"You got more guts than you could hang on a fence, Frank. Them there in that New York, why they're as fulla wind as a bull in corn time."

"Scribner's . . . it'll be Scribner's fall publication. Say they'll take it as is, but they're pounding me hard on the back for Charlie Russell's illustrations—and I don't know. Listen Russ, I <u>can't</u> have 'em back out on me now forgod's sake. I'm committed. Remember, I asked you way back in aught-three when I was just getting started. You promised."

"Well shit, Sign-Talker, all ya gotta do is ask. You know I'll back ya till old Sittin' Bull stands up."

When Linderman and Charlie came out of the cabin, they were clapping each other on the back and grinning.

TWELVE

Inside the Shack

After the log cabin studio was completed it took me several days to move all the Indian objects, cowboy gear, mounted animal heads and skulls, and painting equipment out of the house. Joe and Young Boy pitched in. Even Josephine helped while Charlie hung most of the studio walls with his Indian gimcracks. Compared to the front hall alcove where he had worked in the house, the cabin-studio was spacious, about twenty-four feet by thirty. I think Charlie was having some trouble adjusting to it at first, but he sure liked the low ceiling and the big stone fireplace. He said it was just like Jake's place. He never called it a studio though. He always called it his shack.

One morning Charlie finally decided he was ready to try it out, and he did an unusual thing. He asked Josephine to pose for him. Most of the time he wouldn't, or couldn't, do people's faces. Once I had heard Frank Linderman say jokingly that he couldn't, and Teddy Blue always teased about Charlie having only one face he could paint so he had to put it on every head. Nevertheless, Josephine was thrilled to pose for him. She blushed charmingly and smoothed her hair back into its tight knot. Then she sat totally motionless on a stool in front of the fireplace. I don't think I could have kept still for so long.

Before giving the sketch he'd done to Josephine, Charlie signed it—no buffalo skull in the corner this time though. He sat hunched over a low table writing a dedication instead. It took him a very long time. When he finally finished, he paused to roll a new Bull Durham, and then he sat back smoking and watching the small fire he'd set in the new fireplace. He seemed dog-tired. That evening after Charlie had gone back to the house, Josephine and I were still busy organizing things in the studio when she showed the portrait to me.

"Read the inscription, Ovidia."

The portrait was a small pencil sketch that had an intimate feel. Josie was looking down as if reading and her hair though piled high revealed soft wisps falling down the back of her long thin neck. I had no trouble reading the dedication.

"To Miss Josephine . . . Myth is the Mother of Romance and I am her oldest son."

A bit slushy, I thought, but that was Charlie's way. The writing itself was the usual Kid Russell scribble. He couldn't print at all, but the portrait had a kind of intimate charm. It showed a warmhearted Josephine. Thick glasses and all, but it held a curious appeal that made her unusually attractive.

"He's a hopeless romantic, isn't he?" she whispered.

I looked up from the portrait and saw that Josephine had started trembling while she watched me studying the drawing. I was afraid she was having palpitations like Nancy and might even faint. I grabbed her arm and helped her outside onto the wide studio porch and made her sit in the evening breeze that had turned fresh and cool. She seemed feverish. I pulled my Chinese sandalwood fan from my apron pocket, the one daddy had given me before I left for America, and started waving it rapidly in front of her flushed face.

"What's wrong, Josie? It's a beautiful portrait and a sweet, sentimental dedication," I said putting one arm around her narrow shoulders.

"I don't like to talk about it, Ovidia. I just don't want to talk about myself. You must have noticed how I always let Mother do the talking. Men frighten me—all except Charlie." She was speaking fast.

"I know it's wrong, but every time I see him strange things happen to me. When I'm printing his poems—or even those awful menus—something deep down in the region below my ribs squeezes together and then flips completely over and, and . . . I almost faint. I know I'll die a virgin." Josephine moaned and sniffled.

"Oh, now don't say that, Josie. Everything will be fine. Nancy says that Will Ridley has been courting you. Why I know your mother Margaret and Albert think he's a fine young man."

"They may think so, but I don't. I don't love him. I have an aversion to Will Ridley. He stinks of printer's ink. I'm already over eighteen. . . . Oh dear God, I know I'm not pretty. I don't even try to be."

"You look lovely in Charlie's sketch. You are lovely."

"It's my eyes. I know it is. Without these thick glasses I can barely see across the room." I passed her my handkerchief, and she dabbed at the tears pooling up under her spectacles.

"Things were so easy for me when I was younger and Charlie just worked in the back room of Daddy's saloon. I only saw him once in a while. I loved the way he called me 'Miss Josephine.' But then . . . but then . . . he got married. I was only fourteen, yet my heart was broken. I always thought he'd wait and marry me, but Nancy . . . Nancy trapped him. She wanted a wealthy husband. She wanted to live at Oak Hill his family place in St. Louis. She was determined to climb the social ladder. And, Ovidia, I didn't even care if he had a dime. I don't even care if he's foul-mouthed . . . anyway, he does try to be careful around me."

Josephine was sobbing softly, and I stayed quiet and stroked her shoulders and back. It seemed better for her to go ahead and cry it out. Margaret was at her Wednesday night prayer and revival meetings, and I hoped Albert was still over at the Brunswick Saloon. I was relieved to know that Charlie was having his usual evening drink, his sheep-dip as he called it, up at the house and that Nancy was tucked in at her new desk in the living room painstakingly composing letters to *Harper's* and *Collier's* magazines. Margaret had composed one perfect letter for her, and she copied it over and over just changing greetings and addresses. It took all her attention. I stayed quiet listening to the sobs.

"And then," Josephine snuffled, "to make things so much worse, they moved into the house two doors down from us. Oh dear . . . it's so hard now that I see him almost every day.

"Do you remember Ovidia, that day when I was writing the menus and she said I had a 'crush' on Charlie? A crush. What a crude way to put it. Just like her. An ex-servant girl with a bad reputation. I've heard the whispers . . . about why she can't have children. How could she say something like that to me? And, she's always huffy with him . . . .

"Well, I know that I have more in common with Charlie than she does. We both of us love tales of knights and ladies, gnomes and fairies, and everything that is medieval and romantic and English. He is truly a sentimental romantic, you know. That's why Charlie likes to come over and spend hours and hours looking at our pictures and reading our magazines, and my, how he enjoys the journals of Lewis and Clark. Nancy, well, she only wants him to paint, paint, paint. No poetry, no chivalry."

Her emotions were shifting from weepy to vexation and that seemed like a good thing.

"Josie, you've had a long day, and we've both worked too hard getting the cabin organized. You'll be feeling better tomorrow . . . . How about this? Tomorrow we'll go down to Jacob Heikkila's Dry Goods. We'll find a lovely frame for the drawing, Josie. You look so charming. Your Daddy, Albert, will want to have it in a central place on the mantle." I helped her up, and we headed down Fourth Street toward the Trigg's house. She was quiet now.

"Charlie is like an older brother to you, you know. He and Nancy call your parents Mother and Father. Charlie's always saying, 'Mama Trigg this,' and 'Mama Trigg that.' All of you are very close."

"I try to remember that, Ovidia. I try to call Nancy 'sister.' But it's so hard. I'm afraid my feelings are too strong. But—I'm trying to settle for that. I have to."

Oh *Got*, Billy. I guess I am deviating from the central plot again? I know I am, but I can't seem to help it. I keep remembering how things were then. How everything stacked up before the forgery. Charlie was so lethargic, and I recall he was drinking a lot. Nancy was having trouble with sales after the New York trip. It made her a nervous wreck. She was always taking that medicine. But anyway, like I told you, we got the studio built and that helped. You know, Joe DeYong and I took that scary Ghost Dance shirt with the hundreds of antelope teeth down from the wall in the entryway of the house and hung it in the studio next to the stone fireplace the Chinese had built. I wonder whatever could have happened to it.

So, every morning The Cowboy Artist would head right out there to the shack after taking his "Mame" her water with lemon juice and her medicine. "Goin' to the shack," he'd say, and that was about the last we saw of him around the house. It was always, "the shack."

When Joe finished looking after the horses and doing his other chores, he'd head on out there too. Charlie'd give him his art lessons. When Young Boy finished up, he usually hung out there too. He'd turned up with a bunch of old Cree Indian beaded shirts and even a huge painted buffalo robe that he gave to Charlie while we were fixing up the cabin studio. Charlie gave him old painting supplies and some mineral spirits that he could use for paintings on the Cree lodge skins, though Young Boy signed that there were not many real Indian lodges still in use. Most Cree just hung out in the hovels the government provided on the reservation or else they lived on the streets behind the bars.

We settled into a routine that pleased Nancy. By afternoon, there would sometimes be four or five cowboys and wanna-be-cowboy-artists out there in the shack watching Charlie work. The locals like that young kid from Belt—oh, what was his name—Erik I think, Erik Heikka, he was there two or three days a week when he probably should have been in school. Just about every artist passing through from California or New Mexico or New York came by and sat in the studio soaking up the "Western" atmosphere, eating beans, and sopping-up Charlie's stories. They came as sightseers, Joseph Sharp, Ed Borein, Charlie Beil, Oscar Berninghaus and a whole bunch I can't even remember. They always left the studio as authorities on the West.

Charlie never minded an audience. In fact, he seemed to thrive on it. He'd just go on painting or sit and listen to the "backtrailing" or whatever they called it. One day I asked Joe how Charlie could work with so much going on, and he explained it to me. "Charlie kin go back into an earlier time and lose himself completely in those past activities and people and dress. It's funny, almost like he was still there, like when he was night-wrangling over on the Judith. Like some kinda spiritualism. Sort of a self-hypnosis. Nancy calls it 'the Great Silence.'" Of course, you have to remember, Joe idolized Charlie.

And Charlie'd even cook over the fire for all his visitors: boiled beans, fried bacon, and some bannock bread. It was my job to sweep out and clean up the studio, tidy things up, and make sure the place was supplied with things Charlie might need. I was a good organizer. I even kept a supply of Bull Durham stashed in a tin box above the fireplace, but I drew the line at cleaning up spittoons. Nancy stuck Young Boy with that job. Some still liked a jaw full, not all of them rolled their own. Secretly they brought their own special hard liquor refreshments, "conversation fluid" Charlie called it.

Not long after the studio was built Olaf Seltzer, the immigrant Dane, began to hang out there. You'd have thought Charlie was running an art school. Olaf soon weaseled his way in to become Charlie's number one understudy. Because he was from Denmark, he thought he had a great deal in common with me. Well, he was sure as hell wrong about that. I didn't much like him. The Danes are almost as bad as the Finns. Never trust anyone from Denmark, Billy. In Norway, we knew that their true ambitions always amounted to having the total say-so. But, hell, I guess all of us had dreams, especially the immigrants.

Olaf sure did kiss-up to Charlie though, and it made Joe mad. Joe told me that Olaf wanted to be just like Charlie. One day after Charlie had taken off on Neenah, I went in to tidy-up and resupply the studio. Right there, big as you please, I found Olaf Seltzer sitting on Charlie's favorite working stool copying a painting Charlie had just finished. *The Bolter,* he'd named it.

"Painting a roundup scene are you?" I asked.

"I tink I gonna call it, 'Yassoing a Yong 'Orn.'"

"You ever been to a roundup, Olaf?" I asked.

"Don't matter. Charlie tell me dat I need vork all over canvas. Not finish one figger atta time. He say it vork better dat vay. I do yast like he say."

"But your horse right there looks like it's standing still, Olaf."

"Don' madder. He's anatomy perfect—precise."

"The steer, he looks . . ."

"Perfect anatomy," interrupted Seltzer.

"Awfully bright colors for the prairie, Olaf."

"No madder . . . Charlie, he no faultless pain'er. You know dat."

Poor Olaf. His English was never very good and it didn't improve. He may never have been to a roundup, but then neither had most of those others. Even those that had actually worked cattle, most of them had come from wealthy eastern families and could always trot on home when things got too tough.

As I said, Joe DeYong had taken a terrible dislike to Olaf. Called him a "blow hard," which I guess he was. Olaf liked to talk and talk about his precision-like machinist's hands and how he had started art school in Denmark when he was only twelve. Seltzer was pushing Joe out as Charlie's understudy, and Joe sure resented it. Nancy wasn't too fond of Olaf either because she was sure he always brought his own special flask and didn't mind sharing it with Charlie. She and Joe got to calling him a "keg-carrying, artistic St. Bernard." I remember exactly what he looked like, and he was kind of bulky and hairy, I guess.

Charlie often seemed more of an entertainer than an artist. One day I was outside the studio bringing in a new supply of Bull Durham for the box over the mantle when I heard them all roaring with laughter. I knocked loudly, but no one answered. I guess they couldn't hear me over the guffaws, so I went on in. When they saw me, the boisterous sounds stopped abruptly.

Charlie was standing by the big fireplace holding up a wax figure he'd just molded. It was one of his tricks. He always carried wax and would use it quickly, without even looking, to mold figures of deer, antelope, horses, bears or whatever came to his mind. This time though he'd molded a good sized figure of an Indian chief. The Indian had an enormous stiff pecker and draped over it was a tall crowned cowboy hat.

Charlie quickly hid the figure behind his back. I'd never seen them all so silent. To stifle my laughter, I put my hand up over my mouth. I stepped forward through the silence, put the Bull Durham in the box over the mantle, and walked back out. Then I heard the cackle of laughter begin again.

I didn't think much more about it until that evening when Teddy Blue arrived to play cards earlier than usual. I was still cleaning up the supper things. He took over the dish towel from Young Boy, and motioning toward the door with his head, he seemed to want Young Boy to leave.

"Ah . . . whyn't you go get us some wood fer the stove, Young Boy," he said and turned back to me as soon as Young Boy was out the back door.

"I hope you warn't offended, Miss Ovidia, by what you saw over there in the shack this mornin.' Right now I'd like to say I'm sorry. I sure am. It's jus' that when us old galoots get horsin' around . . . well, we sometimes forget there might be ladies present."

Teddy Blue was flustered. He looked down and twisted the big Montana, blue sapphire, stick pin that he always wore in his tie. I tried to put Teddy at ease. Since right after the building of the cabin, Teddy'd been joining us regularly for our evening card games.

"Don't fret over it, Teddy Blue. Just be ready to put your money into circulation tonight, or better yet, that big blue Montana sapphire you always wear."

"I cain't do that, Miss Ovidia. This here is what brings me all the luck and makes me stud-duck in this 'Lectric City' pond," Teddy grinned.

"The sapphire must be why they call you Teddy 'Blue?' Blue isn't your last name, is it? Is 'Blue' for the sapphire?"

"Nah, it's got nothin' to do with this here. Has to do with a funny incident, happened years ago, down in Miles City. You wanna hear about it?" But Teddy didn't wait for me to answer, he just launched right into his backtrailing, no way to avoid it.

"Well see, there was this here theater, Turner's Theater it was called, in Miles City, and I went there one night. You know in them days, in that kinda theater anyways, they used to have curtained boxes running all around the inside . . . . You sure you want to hear this Miss Ovidia?"

"Just go ahead and tell me."

"You won't be offended?"

"Get on with it, Teddy."

"Well, there were these girls, box-rustlers they called 'em cause they, ah . . . ah, they worked in the boxes."

"What sort of work, Teddy." Hell, I knew, but I wanted to pressure him some.

"So . . . ah, this little gal come up to me and she had on a little short skirt, like a circus girl, and some black lace tights that looked like she had been jus' melted inta them. She invited me upstairs to buy wine. Yeah, that's what she did, she sold wine."

"And then what?"

"Well shit, fer Christ's sake, it was five dollars a bottle. Oops, sorry Miss Ovidia."

"Just go ahead, Teddy."

"Anyway, so I told her, 'nothin' doin.' An' then she told me she had a room back there, and she invited me to go with her."

"You sure you want to tell me about this? Sounds more like a story for the bunch."

"Course I do, well, she'd invited me and I have to admit, it sounded better to me than five dollars for some wine, and I was goin' to go. But on the way there was this long, dark hall that ran around behind the stage. As we started along it, I remembered I had seven hundred dollars on me, tucked away in my six-shooter belt.

"Shit, oops, sorry Miss Ovidia. But you see, I was drawing top-hand's wages back then, and it occurred to me there might be some kinda deadfall back there in the dark."

"What's a deadfall?" I asked.

"It's a trap for big animals, and I'd heared stories about stuff like that. I was sure a wise guy then. Wearing Mexican spur rowels as big's a soup plate, so when I turned around quick-like thinking I'd avoid any deadfall; I caught my spur on the damned carpet and fell through a thin kinda partition right onto the stage of the theater."

"What happened to the girl who was selling wine?" I teased.

"I dunno, but I turned around and found I was right up on-stage before a big audience. Well, I thought, the audience spects me to do somethin.' I grabbed a chair from one of the musicians, and I straddled it like it were a buckin' bronc. Hell, I bucked that damned chair all around the stage. I kept yelling all the while, 'Whoa, Blue! Whoa, Blue!' which at the time was a well known cowpuncher expression."

"Did the audience laugh?"

"Hell no, but before they even got me off the stage it had already started. They was all yellin' at me, 'Hey, Blue, come on outta there.' They was all callin' me 'Blue.' And so it's been that way ever since, from the time I come outta that theater. Teddy Blue I been for more 'an twenty years now. The bunch'll always keep remindin' me. You see, I was pretty wild in them days—and young too—I'd left home when I was only twelve. Wanted to head 'em north, up from Texas. You'll not believe this, Miss Ovidia, but hell, I'm as English as old Albert Trigg. Born right there, in England."

"I believe you, Teddy," I told him.

"So I just wanted to apologize, and I hope you didn't take offense this afternoon. I don't do much carousing these days. I'm getting me a ranch and hoping to settle down soon."

It didn't take much for me to understand that Teddy Blue was trying to impress me. Like I said before, since the building of the studio, he'd been coming to the card parties more often. Mattie said he was wooing me, but I just laughed.

Young Boy had come back in. He never talked, but he had become quite a card-sharp, that's what we used to call them. It wasn't long before Joe arrived. Then Olaf Selzer came dragging in, and we started our evening card game. It was lucky Teddy Blue never bet his Montana blue sapphire because he was the big loser that evening.

Backtrailing

To get on with the story leading to the forgery, we were all getting ready to leave for St. Louis. I think I told you this before, but in late summer, right before the studio was built, Nancy had finally received word that Charlie's oil, *Pirates of the Plains*, had been accepted and would hang in the Palace of Fine Arts during the one hundred year celebration of the Louisiana Purchase. As a bonus, three other painting were to be hung in the Montana pavilion. Charlie's daddy in St. Louis may have had something to do with that, but anyway, I was to travel with the Russells to take care of Nancy's wardrobe and the packing.

We were to visit with Charlie's family at Oak Hill and Nancy was making quite a show of it. She ordered a blue wool dress with a tight bodice and long sweeping skirt. She said it showed off her small waist. There was a blue velvet collar with cream colored lace edging and a fitted coat of blue wool to match. She tried on all her clothes over and over again. We spent days in the trunk room deciding what could be taken.

I even had to go to the dressmaker. Margaret Trigg took me to Johanna Heikkila's in the dry goods store to be outfitted with uniforms suitable for an Eastern "lady's maid." I soon found out the uniforms would be mostly black with little white fringy collars and tiny white aprons, not at all like my own plain skirts and blouses what I wore in Great Falls. At the first fitting I could see that I was going to look a lot like a shiny black crow, but the material was soft, and I was even then planning how I could remake the uniforms and use them as dresses later on. I didn't think then that Nancy wouldn't let me keep them, but I was wrong about that.

Before going to Johanna Heikkila's for the second fitting when I knew I'd have to try on the uniforms, I was careful to pin my St. Olav metal to my undergarments. That Finnish woman had to be a witch, and I still couldn't understand why people in America had all but forgotten about how enchantresses like Joanna could caste evil spells on the unsuspecting.

The Heikkila Dry Goods store had little dressing rooms with curtains on semi-circular rods that attached to the wall. Margaret had to push me into one of those dressing rooms. Against the wall was a large full length mirror. She told me I had to take off my skirt and blouse this time so that Johanna could fit the garments. It had been bad enough to let her measure me. This was going to be a dreadful experience. I begged Margaret to stay with me, but she said the fitting room was too small and she left as soon as the crone, Johanna, came in. She had her measuring tape hanging from her mouth and her supply of pins stuck into a red ball strapped to her left wrist. It seemed freezing cold in the dressing room, and I started to shiver. She gave me a slow look up and down. When her glance paused on my bosoms, I wanted to run from the dressing room but I had no clothes. Oh, so embarrassing. I tried to keep my mind on our farm in Norway. I even thought of all those crazy cows.

Joanna put the uniform top over my shoulders as I held the skirt up in place around my waist. She began lifting the pins from the ball on her wrist and attaching the two pieces of the maids uniform together at the waist line. Everything went well until she reached the left side. As I lifted my arm, I felt a sharp prick just below my waist. I wanted to cry out, but I bit my lip and thought of Uncle Nils and Aunt Borgheld and St. Olav and managed to endure the stinging that persisted. For the next week I was worried that she might have scratched me with some *forgifte* and that I'd fall into her spell, but nothing happened. St. Olav must have been watching over me.

At last the fitting was over and Joanna slipped out at the side of the curtain. I dressed and hurried out to Margaret. She was waiting and called me over to the glass counter in the front of the store to look at some little lace caps. While we were selecting one, a raggedy looking Cree Indian slouched into the store. He looked over the goods on the counters and wandered casually back toward the tall hats displayed in the rear. Joanna kept her evil eye on him, but Margaret was the buyer and she quickly returned her attention to the possible sale.

"I've been told this is the latest style of headgear for ladies' maids in London. The edging has imitation Brussels' lace. Totally washable of course," she murmured to Margaret.

"Could we see the one below—there on the left? It looks very serviceable."

"Of course."

Joanna bent over to open the showcase. I was more interested in watching the Cree. He had gone to a dressing room carrying a tall crowned hat. He stepped inside and pulled the heavy circular curtain shut.

"I think you should really have two caps, Ovidia. One for general use and one for more formal occasions when you might be called upon to serve at table. What do you think, Joanna?"

Joanna raised her head. "That would seem to be a very practical idea, Mrs. . . . ah, ah . . . Mrs. Trigg . . . ." She grew stone still as she looked back toward the dressing rooms in the rear. A stream of yellow water was flowing under the dressing room curtain over the waxed floor boards and down between the aisles and toward the door. Joanna stared in shock as the Cree threw back the dressing room curtain, tossed the hat on the counter, and started toward the door.

"Well for shit's sake." Joanna looked up at the Indian. "Why you! Why you god-damned good-for-nothing son-of-a-bitch," she screamed. She bolted out from behind the counter and grabbed a heavy broom standing nearby. "You son-of-a-bitch!"

The Indian moved quickly toward the door while the Finnish witch chased after him yelling and swatting at him with the broom. "Get back here now, I say. Get back here and clean up this mess. How dare you. God damned Indians. Ought to be shot. Why can't you piss in the street like everybody else?"

But the Indian was out the door and down the street. All Joanna could do was apologize to Margaret. When we left the shop I saw the Finlander carrying a rag mop toward the yellow stream. Was it St. Olav's pay back for the nasty poke with the pin she gave me? I thought it was.

Well, sure it was true Billy. It really happened. You think I'm the one doing the backtrailing now, don't you? But you're wrong. Things in the West were real strange. But then, they were sometimes funny too. So okay, I'll get on with it. How about another coffee? Hot this time.

A week later, when I went to pick up the uniforms, I met Mattie for sodas at Lulu Disher's. She was breathless. Yes, she and Con Price were engaged. They were planning to elope and go up to Canada. Just like in Norway. When it was to be secret, we'd go over to Sweden. I wasn't to tell anyone.

The day before we were to leave for St. Louis Carl arrived on the back doorstep soon after dinner. He had been elected to the Montana State legislature along with Frank Linderman and would now be spending most of his time in Helena. He looked tired, red-eyed and rumpled. He'd been on the train all night, but he had managed to bring along a small bouquet of violets.

"Had to get up here before you left, Little Valkyrie."

"Why Carl, you know I'll be back before long."

"Brought you these here violets. For the train. So you'll keep thinking of me."

"I'm not going on to New York with Nancy and Charlie. Just to St. Louis and then back here. Joe DeYong's going with us to help Charlie at the Exposition, and then . . ."

"I hear Teddy Blue's been keeping you company."

"I think you heard wrong. Teddy only comes over to join us for a card game now and then."

"Heard he says he's been looking a long time for a gal like you—one that ain't ankle high to a June bug. Course, that's cause he's so damned sawed-off himself he can't see over a sway-backed burro."

"Why Carl, I've never heard you talk like this before. If I didn't know better, I'd say you were green-eyed, and I can see that's not the case."

"Had to see you. I think I'm gonna miss you, little Miss Brunhilde."

"I'll miss you too, Carl. But I'm happy for the Russells. It's what they've been working for . . . especially Nancy. Now her faith in her 'Cha'lie' is beginning to pay-off. He'll have his real paintings on display at the Exposition and that will prove to everyone he's an 'artist,' not just an 'illustrator.' He does paint the true West you know. Exactly like I dreamed it."

"Well, there's something going on down at the State legislature that if it works out should interest both of them. But, you've got to promise to keep it hush-hush. Nobody's supposed to know about it just yet."

"Maybe you shouldn't tell me then."

"You'd better keep the secret, or I'll chase you clean to St. Louis. The legislature has voted to commission a large painted mural to be mounted in the House of Representatives. The painting's going to be colossal, twelve by twenty-five feet. They're thinking, a big painting for the big new West. Seems Montana wants to shed its ranching past and become citified. Art and music and all that fine Eastern stuff."

"Charlie could paint the mural. He could do it, Carl."

"He might have a chance at it now that he's accepted at the Louisiana Purchase Exposition, but there's some saying we ought to get a more well known artist—someone from the East—maybe even John Alexander—or there's even been talk of Remington."

"Oh *Got* no, not fat Remington. Nancy would be moved to do something terrible—or even violent. You've got to talk to them, Carl. You've got to convince everyone there in Helena that Charlie's right for the mural. After all, he's practically a native of Montana. Who could be better?"

"One of those well known Easterners. In Helena they're saying it would make us look more progressive, more citified, if we had an artist from the East. You know. A place where there's an 'Electric City' should have a celebrated artist. Paris Gibson even agrees. He was on the train coming up, and he's all for the idea, but wants a top-notch Eastern artist."

"Well, Frank Linderman's in the legislature, he should help Charlie. He'll see that Charlie gets the commission, after all, they've been close for . . ."

"He'll help only if Charlie gets him those sketches for his book. He's counting on the publication money from Schribners. Rumor is he's got some asset problems."

"Oh, Charlie'll do the illustration all right. We heard him promise."

"Maybe not."

"But Linderman is Charlie's best friend."

"But not Nancy's. Nancy thinks Frank's stuff is just more illustrations and . . ."

"But she'll finally approve."

Don't bet on it. And . . . just keep damned quiet about the whole thing. Nothing is certain yet."

That was the first I'd heard of the mural commission, but everyone else seemed to know something about it right away. And, how could that have been if Carl said it was so hush-hush. Even Joe and Young Boy were talking about it on the way to the train station the next day. I overheard Joe say that the "keg-carrying St. Bernard," Olaf Seltzer, was trying to figure out how he could get his name put on the selection list. There must have been plenty of talk and speculation going on at the Mint Saloon.

The two were signing, but I finally heard Young Boy speak, "Gonna take heap big lotta paint," he said, and I had to smother my giggles. I'd never heard him talk English, and he sounded just like something out of one of the western dime novels.

Everyone was completely silent about the big Montana State mural project around Charlie and Nancy. Maybe the "cowboy artist" really hadn't heard of it yet.

Carl was there at the railway station the next morning to see us off.

Teddy Blue was at the station too, carrying a bunch of deep purple violets.

Confidences and Love Stories

The train going east was as sooty as the one coming west had been, but this time I was riding with the fancy tourists in the so called "palace cars." At night there were real beds made up called Pullmans with lovely fresh white sheets and a little bell to call the porter. I helped Nancy settle in her hat boxes and hand luggage, but she wasn't ready to settle down. She was restless.

"I wonder if any tourists in the parlor car would be interested in art work by an authentic cowboy artist." she said while she rummaged around in the portfolio of Charlie's paintings that she always carried around with her. She pulled out three water colors, grabbed my arm, and we headed out in pursuit of sales.

The parlor car was crowded and full of cigar smoke. It had a real playing organ, but the only pilgrim that tried to give a performance didn't know much—sounded like a bunch of alley cats at midnight. What caught my attention were the card tables. I couldn't stop looking at them. They were covered in dark green, soft looking cloth. Some seemed to be set up for Faro and Mattie had been teaching me how to deal. When three of the tourists began to sit down, I tried to edge my way over. I would have enjoyed a good Black Jack session or Poker. I could feel my hands sliding cards across those soft-covered card tables, but Nancy didn't give me a chance. She grabbed my elbow and hauled me off down toward a group wearing their lace up boots like they were still up in the Glacier, but before Nancy could pull out the watercolors and start her sales pitch, they began to sing. They'd had a few, and with that help from John Barleycorn, they launched into wailing *O Bury Me Not on the Lone Prairie* over and over. A couple of the older sightseers had tears rolling down their cheeks. Nancy finally shook her head and gave up on wooing possible sales. Unfortunately, my hopes for a card game where gone. She refused the parlor car luxuries for the rest of the trip,

Nancy insisted that I must be with her and not in second class because she might need my help if she had a fainting spell or her neurasthenia acted up, but she put little Joe DeYong in the second class car to save on expenses. She was certain her baggage would be stolen and wanted Joe to watch it, or so she said. I had the task of watching the luggage in our carriage. Since I couldn't join one of the card games in the parlor car, I settled into reading *My Sixty years on the Plains*. Nancy had sold a few illustrations to the author, W. T. Hamilton. When a copy of the book arrived in the mail she wasn't interested in reading it. She just checked to make sure Charlie's name was clearly visible on the illustrations and handed it over to me.

Nancy had stretched out awkwardly on the seat two rows in front of me. I was enjoying the clickity-clack of the wheels turning on the rails when Charlie came back in from the parlor car. I figured he'd had a pretty good snoot-full and must have been missing spinning yarns with the bunch when he took the seat beside me and started talking.

"This damned train reminds me of back in ninety-three, only then I weren't riding in luxury," Charlie confided. "That trip to Chicago in ninety-three—hell, it changed my whole damn life. I'd been drinking, and whoring, and pleading for credit every winter since eighty-eight, and after the beef roundup was over, I climbed aboard a stock train headed for the Chicago slaughterhouses. Yeah, Little Package, I got me a job walking along the top of the cattle cars with a long 'punch pole' and prodded 'em. See, the problem was that ya hadda keep 'em from lying down or trampling one another before ya got 'em to the Union Stockyards.

"That unfortunate trip was the last time. Last time I ever did any kinda cowpunching. Ain't never sung to them cows since. I never went back to wrangling for a dollar a day after that. Didn't have the spunk." Charlie pushed aside the long strand of straw-colored hair that always fell over his left eye and cleared his throat.

"But I thought you fancied those roundups so," I said, but he didn't hear me. He was staring out the window at the bare open prairie.

"Don't know why," he said, "but I wanted to go see that danged Columbian Exposition. Didn't think then I'd ever be doin' this here, goin' to showing my own paintin's at a big exposition. Didn't know then that I even wanted to.

"But it happened to me, right there in Chicago in ninety-three. Listenin' to that fella talk. All dolled out in his stiff collar, boiled shirt and lace-up shoes, he was. Big gold watch chain roping him round his waistcoat. Changed my whole life it did, his damned jawing about the frontier.

"I was gonna be thirty that next spring. Shit, I was afraid of growing old and afraid of growing up, both. Couldn't be 'Kid Russell' anymore and couldn't be—what? Hell, I didn't know. Would of liked to stay Kid Russell though, I guess. Anyways, that old fancy dressed-up geezer guy at the Exposition said that the fuckin' frontier was gone. Can you believe that, Owidi? Goddamnit, gone. He had this big map painted out on canvas, showed were everybody lived, little red dots all over that sucker. Scattered everywhere. Said there was no frontier line anymore. Well hell, I'd never heard of any frontier line in the first damned place. He kept saying it, only shitty little isolated settlements, but 'no frontier line.' Can you beat that? Woulda made the hair of a buffalo robe stand up," Charlie paused and shook his head.

"So what'd that mean for the cattle? I'll tell you, Little Package. They'd be as uncomfortable as a camel in the Klondike, and so'd I. Nesters everywhere. That's all you could see on that damned map of his, red dots. Them red dots meaning nesters. And that fancy dandy, he seemed to think it was the end of the West."

"But, Mr. Russell, you could have gone back to St. Louis after the Columbia Exposition," I said. "You could have gone to work for your Daddy making bricks and tiles for blast furnaces. Why didn't you?"

"Cause you know what was even bigger and better than the God damned Columbia Exposition? . . . I'll tell

ya what—Buffalo Bill's Wild West show. Right down the
street from where that smart as a bunkhouse rat was saying
there's no frontier. My God, old Bill, he looked jus' like
Custer, long hair streamin,' and his white pony throwing
dirt in the eyes of a jackrabbit. Ridin' around, doing what
he called 'epochs' of the West. Indians meeting pilgrims,
buffalo hunts, attacks on settlers, and then even the Little
Big Horn."

"Was he wearing buckskins?" I couldn't help but ask.
I still had it in my mind that everyone in the West should
wear buckskins.

"Shore was. Pure white buckskins. The sonnabitchin'
fringes musta been a foot long. Looked like a dime novel
on a spree. Fit him like a glove. That Billy Cody, hell, he
don't need no advice any more'n a steer needs a saddle
blanket. Shit, he knows how to please 'em."

You don't need to shake your head like that, Billy. I
was used to Charlie's language. In fact, you may think it
strange, but his profanity and Nancy's too, went right over
my head. I know you disapprove, but hell, that was the way
they talked.

Charlie shifted around on the train seat and looked
over toward me. "After Bill's show, I knew where the West
would stay. We didn't need cattle or roundups or even a
frontier. We needed show business. Bill Hart's doin' it.
Them Easterners hang on it."

"Did you want to be an actor?"

"Shit no, Owidi. I'm not a damned actor like Cody or
Hart, but at the Exposition in ninety-three, I could see that
paintin's part of show business too. It can have a dazzle. So,

I give up wrangling' and devoted my full-time to scratchin' out an existence with my brushes. Sleepin' in lofts and back rooms. Bunkin' in bar rooms. Trading a paintin' for a bowl a beans. Selling to saloon keepers and saddle makers. Trigg helped sometimes as my agent. . . . An' then, and then, my mother died. I'll never forget it. Was in June of ninety-five."

Charlie leaned back and his yellow eyes fixed on the empty air. He was totally quiet. Even his busy ringed fingers wilted at his sides. I thought at first he was dreaming and then I guessed he'd gone into the thing Joe DeYong had called "the Great Silence." I'd never seen it before. We both sat, perfectly still. I looked out the train window and watched the fields of corn and wheat move by like passing over a quilt pattern in shades of yellow and green on the plains. I'm not sure how long we sat there, and then he directed his gaze toward Nancy.

"Four months later, I met my Mame." He straightened up and looked over at her.

"She was workin' for Ben Roberts. They'd taken her in. Her son-of-a-bitchin' step-father had abandoned all of them. Her and her half-sister, and their whoring mother, Texas Annie. They was taking in sewing struggling to survive. An' their Ma, old Texas Annie, died an' Mame was shifting for herself trying to care for the little sister too. Ben and Lela Roberts finally gave her a safe haven and the only schooling she ever got."

Charlie smiled and looked down at his ring-covered fingers. "Mame was quite a little flirt, but Lela Roberts was makin' sure she behaved. An' I, well, I guess I'd always been in awe of a good woman. I think she set her mind to get me—and she did," he said grinning widely.

"She was appealin' all right. All of sixteen-year-old. She mebbe had a short rope, but she shore threw a wide loop. The two of us was walkin' down by the Missouri River one sparkling blue evening, and all of a sudden Mame suggested we get hitched. I was too damned polite to say 'no.' Hosses an' wimmen will shore make a man go whistlin' . . . provided he's still young enough to pucker.

"The weddin' was in the Roberts' parlor. Jus' the Roberts and two others. Can't remember who now. None of our families. Shit, I onny had fifteen bucks, an' I give the preacher ten. Mame made the cake, and I cranked the ice cream." The corners of Charlie's mouth turned up in a facial expression of amusement.

"Without Mame, I'd always sold my stuff for any five or ten offered. Jus' never tried to reach any further than to make a few pitchers for my friends and to pay my bar tab. She pushed. Yeah, she did. Made us move outta Cascade an' up there to the 'Lectric City.' But don't get me wrong. That first year we was purrin' like kittens in a creamery."

Billy, he did talk like that. Besides he was so drunk his breath was strong enough to crack a mirror. Maybe it sounds funny and artificial to you now, but back then that talk was part of the cowboy character. Maybe a little like some of that slang I hear people using while they're hanging on the slots here in Vegas, like: "ya know." And they keep repeating it, "ya know." I think that talk made all those ex-cowboys feel they were close to one another. Kind of a matter of trust cause they spoke the same language, ya know.

Of course, Nancy had her own version of the courtship and marriage. Not quite like Charlie's though. The last day of the train journey she told me about it as we were nearing St. Louis. I think she began losing some of her usual composure with anxiety over the Russell family reunion that would soon be taking place. Charlie was in the parlor car boosting his assurance with his customary yarns spun with the help of gut-warmer while Nancy boosted her confidence with her stock of tall tales. She launched right into her version of the romance and courtship when she could see the first tall building in the distance.

"My God Ovidia, it was so romantic," she said. We were all alone in Helena, my mother, my half-sister, Ella, and me. My step-daddy was away in the gold fields getting rich. We was sure he'd make the big strike, and I think he woulda but, while he was gone Mama got sick with the consumption so we had very little. Ella and me, we took in washing and sewing, but Mama got sicker and sicker . . . and then, and then . . . . Oh dear God, one morning Mama, she just started coughing and coughing, and then there was blood all over . . . and then she stopped breathing, . . . and then she was dead." Nancy's eyes glistened, and her voice got croaky as a frog.

"Thank God, Ovidia, everyone was so kind to Ella and me. The neighbors took us in and helped us. We bought Mama the most beautiful rosewood coffin. Used all our money and then some, but the funeral was so lovely. A granite tombstone engraved and all, and the very next day after we buried her, my step-daddy, Thomas Allen, he come back and took Ella away with him. I think he wanted me to go too, but the neighbor said I was to stay with her.

"*Ja*, that was a fortunate choice. It's never much of a good idea to stay with daddy," I told her thinking of my own experience.

"Mrs. Biggs, that was the neighbor's name, she was a scrawny little woman, looked like a brown banty hen she did. She thought I did such marvelous sewing. And then, Mrs. Biggs found this fantastic situation for me in Cascade.

"That's where I saw him first, my Cha'lie. In Cascade, at the Roberts' house. First time I saw him, well, it was love at first sight," Nancy smiled suggestively. "He had this little makeshift studio back behind the house, and when he come in that evening for supper, I was very attentive I'll tell you. He was so sightly in his high polished boots and red sash.

"It wasn't long before he was spending more time in Cascade than in Great Falls. That was when his old-timer cowpoke friends decided they didn't like me. Shit, I was stealin' him away from them. Made 'em all mad as hell. He was a natural flirt and he'd pretend I was his damsel in distress and that he was my knight in shining armor. I'd tease and call him Sir Lancelot. Yes, I'd read some of those books about knights and maidens and the courtly love they did in England. You should read some of those, Ovidia. They're so romantic . . . ."

"*Ja*, I wonder if they'd be so romantic in Norse. I've read the Norse sagas though. Oh *ja*, the sagas had many tales of Norwegian knights. But, *nei*, those Norwegians didn't waste their time wooing maidens. They sharpened their swords and battle axes and killed Danes and Swedes." Was Erik the Red courtly I wondered? Probably not, I decided.

"In the evenings, Cha'lie and me, we would stroll down among the cottonwoods growing on the banks of the Missouri River," Nancy's eyes crinkled at the corners with pleasure. She twirled the gold ring on her finger and grinned.

"Lela Roberts began inviting Cha'lie to supper more and more often, and then he'd linger until after the Roberts went to bed," she giggled like a school girl. "I remember the lumpy old red-plush chair that both of us would squeeze into in front of the big fireplace.

"Course he was still boozin'. Tried to keep it hid from me saying he was hoarse from sleepin' near a draft. Said he had to take a nip for his throat. But I knew better. And once he said, 'Don't ya wanna throw in with me, Mame?' He said it when he was full of booze and had forgotten the courtliness. Well, I wasn't having any of that goddammit. So, a few weeks later one evening he knelt down by the lumpy red-plush chair. Just like Sir Lancelot. And he said, 'Mame darlin', will you marry me?' You probably guessed, Ovidia. My answer right away was 'yes.'"

"You didn't make him wait for an answer?"

"Hell no! How was I to know but what he'd change his mind.

"Our wedding ceremony that September was so beautiful, Ovidia. At the biggest church there in Cascade with practically the whole town attendin' and some even coming down from Great Falls. I had a little blue wedding dress. Blue was the style for weddings then, but now they seem to dress in any old thing. There was cake and ice cream. The newspaper called me, 'one of the most popular and most estimable young ladies of Cascade.' I still remember those words so well." Nancy paused, smiled and looked out the train window.

She turned from the train window and looked back at me and said, "But hell, there was no market for Cha'lie's art in Cascade and I knew it, so I made the big push to move to Great Falls, and look where we are now. It's a dream comin' true. Riding here in this palace car. Cha'lie's work being honored at the St. Louis Exposition."

As we entered St. Louis and large buildings appeared close by, Nancy took a deep breath, pulled herself up to her full five-foot six-inch height and clenched her hands together in her lap. She had a determined look on her face and she concentrated again on the approaching city outside.

One thing was becoming clear to me. In the West, everyone had his own tall story. You could never be certain about anything. One story always contradicted another, so what in the hell were you supposed to believe? Probably the same today though. What in the hell can you believe?

The Louisiana Purchase Exposition

It was a chilly October day when we arrived in St. Louis. Bent Russell, Charlie's brother, picked us up in his fancy open touring car at the refurbished train station. It was the car not the weather that we were to notice. Joe DeYong waited for the wagon that was being sent to haul the baggage, but I was to stay close to Nancy since I was carrying her laudanum in a small silver flask. As we passed through the streets, it was easy to see that St. Louis had been spruced-up for the Exposition. New paint, new trash barrels, and street sweepers in bulky coveralls everywhere.

Brother Bent Russell was totally unlike Charlie. He was what in those days they called "urbane." Starched and stiff, taller and thinner, with his slick darker hair sharply parted at the midline where his pale white scalp showed through. Charlie on the other hand was always rumpled and lumpy looking with his dry straw-colored hair falling every-which-way over his eyes. But stranger yet, the family didn't call him Charlie or even Charles. They called him "Chas," and they all used precise English with a touch of a "British" accent.

Bent had the latest citified contraptions. One of the servants later told me that the fancy open automobile he drove was a 1904 Oldsmobile T-Light Tonneau. The two carriage drivers, who were part of the household, were worrying they'd be out of a job soon. But, that seemed what the Louisiana Purchase Exposition was all about: new gizmos and gimmicks, chicken cooked in twelve minutes, hot dogs in two, and electricity powering everything.

Oak Hill, the Russell family home, was indeed a mansion, a mansion that looked like a mausoleum. Three stories, solid buff-colored brick facing Lindell Boulevard with an impressive double-door entry under a large white portico. I can see it even now. A low stone column fence ran across the front, and at the street entry two white granite lions stood at guard. The covered carriage approach to the right of the mansion was an extension of the long covered entrance. Across the street was an extensive woodland. The whole thing looked like a burial ground. A bronze plaque in front of the woodland read "Tower Grove Park and Botanical Garden." What everyone told me was true. The Cowboy Artist had certainly grown up with all the advantages of wealth.

Bent deposited us on the scrubbed stoop where a footman all dressed up in polished knee-high black boots, red jacket with a black velvet collar and a white stiff shirt with ruffles down the front helped us from the touring car. Sue Russell Portis, Charlie's sister, stood waiting at the top of the entry stairs. She greeted her brother and sister-in-law with a formal light peck on the cheek and led us in through the heavy double doors. As we entered, I saw Joe and the horse drawn baggage wagon pulling up in the drive and circling to the back of the residence.

Inside were high ceilings and stained glass windows. I followed hesitantly behind the Russells keeping my mouth shut and my eyes open. When Sue Portis led Charlie and Nancy toward the parlor for tea, I was herded up the stair-case by a gruff gray-haired housekeeper wearing the same sort of black dress and white apron I had been supplied with.

Charlie was being very well-mannered, but as Sue neared the parlor doors, I saw him reach around behind Nancy, pat her buttocks, and tell her in his scampish stage whisper, "Shit, Mame, we're gonna hafta look at Wimar's damned deformed buffalo and those merry-go-round horses they got hangin' all over the parlor walls." Sue scowled, but ignored the comment.

When we reached the first landing, I whispered to the old housekeeper, "Who's Wimar?"

"He's a famous Eastern artist. He did a series of murals for the St. Louis Courthouse in what the Missouri gentry call the romance inspired Germanically balanced Dussel-dorf style," she snapped.

What a mouth full that was, and Charlie sure belittled that sort of thing. I couldn't let her put one over on me. I had to stick up for Montana, so I snapped right back. "My employer, Mr. Charlie Russell, paints in cowboy inspired Americly evenhanded Montana style."..The house keeper didn't reply. She only raised her nose in the air and lifted her eyebrows.

Once everything was unloaded and I'd unpacked Nancy's trunks and hat boxes, I was installed in a tiny back room on the second floor near Nancy. Most of the servants were housed up on the third floor rear. Joe was to stay out in the carriage house with the drivers. The auto ride had unnerved Nancy, and she insisted I have a room close by her. I'd seen her snuffling as Bent's Oldsmobile rounded each corner, and she'd been clinging onto Charlie for dear life.

When she finally came upstairs, she needed her brown syrupy medicine. I mixed it with a glass of cool water, and it turned amazingly white and milky while a pungent smell filled the room. I pulled the heavy brocade draperies and helped Nancy stretch out on the high poster bed propping her head up on the fine linen pillow cases.

"It's that snippy sister of Cha'lie's," she moaned closing her eyes and putting her wrist on her forehead. "Oh God, she's so damned hateful. What nerve. And Cha'lie—down there with Bent and old Charles Silas swapping yarns and boozing their panther piss outta crystal glasses."

"Have a sip of your medicine," I suggested.

"And we'll be here for too damned long. And Cha'lie won't paint."

"There's a lovely bathtub in the room down the hall. I'm filling it with warm water. You can soak and then take a rest until dinner," I urged. I placed a cool, damp cloth over her eyes. "The train ride was tiring."

"Who in the hell does she think she is?"

"Mr. Russell's sister," I said.

"Those stuffed shirts, the St. Louis Russells, all of them. You know what they did? They sent Cha'lie's daddy to Great Falls to check up on me after we were married.

They thought Cha'lie had married a squaw, or half-breed, or worse." she said. "But, wasn't his daddy surprised and pleased when he saw me." Nancy grinned and stretched out reaching her arms over her head. "I charmed him. Yes, I did. He said I was a diamond in the rough. When I have to I can sure hitch up a horse with a coyote, Ovidia." She laughed.

"But later, when we came here to visit, that shitty sister, hell. I overheard her tell her priggish, ill-natured, lawyer husband, Tom Portis, they didn't need to worry. She had the nerve say, 'A girl that age is like water; pour her into a pitcher, no matter how convoluted, and she takes the pitcher's shape with effortless ease.' She dared to say that about me. I may have been young, but I wasn't stupid. Charles Silas, he knew I'd be good for Cha'lie. And goddammit, I am."

After her bath Nancy calmed down. She told me that after the wedding she and Charlie moved into the hovel behind the Roberts' house, and that Charlie had an agent in Butte who was selling his paintings locally. "Well, that wasn't working, so I got him something better. I was the one wrote to the editor of *Western Field and Stream*. He thought Charlie should have a wider . . . a wider . . . awedence. I think that's the word he used. He meant more buyers and higher prices, I understood that at least. Anyway, when it comes to business, Charlie can't hit a bull's ass with a banjo.

"Mind you now, our first year in that hovel we was purrin' like kittens in a creamery, but before the year was out we moved. I saw to that. Great Falls is up-to-date and people know that. There's no boot hill and no hangin' tree."

I was not a guest at the formal dinner the next evening. Yes, in St. Louis they called it dinner, at night. In Montana, it was supper, and we all sat down together, the Russells, Joe, Young Boy and whoever else happened to be around. In the West, dinner was at noon, and I cooked it. In St. Louis, I didn't have to cook, thank *Got*, but Joe and I ate with the servants in the kitchen.

Nancy went downstairs to dinner dressed as cocky as the queen of spades. She wore a dark ivory silk brocade costume with a small stand-up mink collar that framed her face and ash blond hair beautifully. And Charlie, he groaned and complained but was forced into a get-up he called his "black clothes." Even while wearing his black clothes he still insisted on his red Métis sash and cowboy boots as signs of protest.

I learned more playing cards in the servants kitchen than I would have if I'd been seated at the fancy dinner and it was sure more profitable. The servants were card players, and it turned out that the Oak Hill gardener, the head housekeeper, and the two carriage drivers fancied themselves as risk takers. One old southern carriage driver wanted a go at Monte and the rest went along. My lessons from Mattie were going to pay off.

Billy, you'd be surprised at what an entertaining dealer I could be in those days. Any card game. I prized it. There in St. Louis, things went well—and quickly, for me. I'll tell you about it.

While we played cards and enjoyed some exception-ally good food, the young servant waiter girls, who were closely supervised by an old butler dressed all in black, came back and forth with news of happenings in the dining room and their opinions on the social interaction. They correctly guessed that Nancy was wooing potential buyers. I remember Howard Eaton was there, a fat pot-bellied guy who founded the first dude ranch in Montana, and Andrew Mellon, the millionaire art patron. It was a wealthy gathering, but the only one Charlie wanted to acknowledge was Malcolm Mackey, a New York investment banker who owned a large ranch in Montana. I got to peek in quickly and was told that the stout, balding man sitting next to Nancy was David Francis chairman of the St. Louis World's Fair. No surprise then that Charlie's painting had been selected for the Palace of Fine Arts.

The long table was lighted by tall candles in silver candle sticks, and the flames flickered off the hundreds of crystals that hung from the chandelier overhead. On the table in front of each chair there was a little white card with a name written on it.

The waiter girls reported that Charlie was in an obvious state of discomfort and boredom. He was completely silent and only answered with grunts and uh huhs when he was directly spoken to. By the time the last course was served, Charlie had emptied several wine glasses and he had suddenly come alive. The serving maids began moving more rapidly in and out of the dining room. They were trying to hear everything he said. They followed the conversation and repeated it in detail to the servants in the kitchen. I folded the cards and hovered close behind the door to listen. Charlie was playing the rascal. The wine served with each course had helped. He spoke loudly across the table to Mackey, the Montana ranch owner.

"Say, have ya heard anything about Pink-Eye Smith lately?"

"Yeah, I hear they got him hauled into the Roscoe jail for murder," replied Mackey.

While the wealthy potential buyers and other guests tried to continue their conversations, Charlie and Mackey began discussing the guilt or innocence of Pink-Eye.

"They say he took down some stall-fed tenderfoot, but . . . I don't know," Mackey continued. His face seemed flushed, but the butler refilled his wine glass when he motioned him over.

"Hell, that Pink-Eye he's always sore as a bitch wolf in heat," said Charlie.

At this, other conversation at the table stopped, and in the silence Mrs. Mellon coughed and pulled her lace edged handkerchief from her sleeve placing it under her nose.

"Yeah, an' more crust than an armadillo," replied Mackey.

"Always threw too much dust," added Charlie.

"But aloof as a mountain goat," said Mackey.

Charlie was stringing Mackey along, pulling him into the kinship of the cowboy wrangler.

"I think Pink-Eye done it." said Charlie. "Crossin' that killer Pink Eye'd be 'bout as dangerous as walkin' in quicksand over hell."

The men at the table leaned forward, but the serving girls reported the ladies were growing pale. Peeking through the crack in the dining room door jamb I saw Nancy was sending Charlie chilling glances, but he failed to react.

"Pink-Eye was mean all right, but we always thought he was as straight as a wagon tongue," said Mackey.

"Hot words can lead to cold slabs."

Sue Portis was glaring at her brother, Charlie, and I saw Mrs. Francis slump down in her chair. She was a short, heavy woman with a strong determined looking jaw line.

"That young pilgrim, he was all swolled up with mad, like a poisoned pup. Ought to have knowed better," Mackey continued. "And Pink-Eye, well, the liquor was makin' him feel like a muley-cow growin' horns."

"What I hear seems like Pink-Eye pulled his iron quicker'n he needed. I hear he jus' come down the road and without a word up an' paunched him."

"Not the best way-da-go. Doc had him there in Roscoe for three days belchin' like a beef before he died in fits. But . . . sh . . . oh sorry, Miss Portis, Mrs. Francis," stuttered Mackey.

But, Charlie wasn't quite ready to quit. "Lessen he's lucky, Pink-Eye's gonna climb the golden stair on a rope, I'd say." Charlie shook his head, loosened his tie, leaned back, and pushed away from the table.

Sue Portis saw her chance. She stopped scowling, and lost no time breaking into the conversation. "Ladies, we'll allow the gentlemen their port and cigars. We'll take our dessert in the parlor." Old Charles Silas huffed as the women rose, and Sue led them from the room.

At this point the servant girls rushed into the kitchen. "What's paunched him mean?" The youngest girl asked Joe.

"Means he was shot right clean through the stomach," Joe told them. They gasped.

"Well, what did he mean when he said Pink-Eye's gonna 'climb the golden stair on a rope?'"

"They're going to hang him," I said in an expressionless, flat voice as I turned back toward the card table grinning. The girls gasped again, then they giggled, then they rolled their eyes and quickly left the kitchen with the dessert, coffee, and wine. I can't tell you how pleasing it was for me to at last know something that others didn't. It made me feel like a real American.

You know, Billy, it always seemed strange how ready they were to hang killers in the West. Why, I wondered? In Norway we had a better way. Usually they were allowed to escape the local jail where they were held, and then they ran off to Sweden. That way things weren't so unpleasant between the people who remained. Too bad America doesn't have a Sweden, although I guess we do have something like it. We have Canada and Mexico, but it's not quite the same as having Sweden. I guess that's getting off onto another subject, isn't it?

That night I won more from the Russell's servants than I had on the Northern Pacific train going West. I was hoping to repeat the performance each night during our stay in St. Louis, but as the days went by the Oak Hill servants lost their nerve. They seemed to prefer the slower five card stud to the quicker Black Jack, and they abandoned Monte entirely. Nevertheless, before we returned to Montana, I was able to send Uncle Nils more than half of the money I still owed for my passage from Norway.

It became a ritual to go everyday to the Exposition while we were in St. Louis. Nancy and Charlie sometimes rode in Bent Russell's touring car, but Joe and I rode the street car to the entry of the Fair at Lindell Boulevard and DeBaliveve and walked up the wide Plaza of St. Louis. Although it was fall it was warm and the women carried parasols or wore straw hats for shade.

Charlie and Joe eyed the sculptures of Sioux and Cherokee warriors decorating the pavilions and groused about the Indian dress being all wrong. As for the major sculpture on the Ten-Million-Dollar Pike, Charlie dismissed it as stiff. It was Remington's. Four yahooing horsemen with six-guns in the air. It seemed to jar Charlie. The sculpture had a very special place at the entrance to the Pike, but his only comment was, "Grand, but don't interest me none." After the Exposition though, he plunged right into modeling, but all that is well ahead of my story.

The Exposition was a triumph for Nancy. She sold an oil painting of three cowboys roping a wolf to John A. Sleicher, the editor of *Leslie's*. He hoped to print it on the cover of his Christmas edition. I wondered what in the hell roping a wolf had to do with the holiday season and the birth of Jesus. I was still learning a lot about America. She got three illustrated book contracts, and Malcolm Mackey the Montana ranch owner wanted a large oil. I wondered if he bought it by way of apology after the Pink-Eye story. Anyway, Nancy was now sending out her invoices with a printed heading "In Account with Chas. M. Russell The Cowboy Artist."

On my days off I'd go with some of the household servants to see Frederick Cummins's Wild West Indian Congress and Rough Riders of the World. Not quite Buffalo Bill, but three hundred cowboys in fancy buckskin and the Apache Chief Geronimo just out of prison in Indian Territory.

One day we met, Tom Mix, the star of the wild west show out on the Pike. Are you old enough to remember him, Billy? Probably not. Tom Mix, the cowboy Joe DeYong knew and always talked about. Tom was doing rope tricks right there among the crowd on the Ten-Million-Dollar Pike. Publicity for the show I guess. He was certainly dressed for it. A bright white Stetson, a satiny red shirt with pearl buttons, pale gray California pants tucked into boots like none I'd ever seen before. They had colored tops, red and blue, with a star and half-moon on them. No one in Montana wore anything like that, but people here in St. Louis were eating it up.

Tom roped a couple of little kids that were walking along in front of their Mom and Dad all dressed up and eating sausages wrapped in bread. Everyone clapped and laughed except the kids who started to scream. Charlie and Joe couldn't hold still. Pretty soon the three of them stood there on the Pike in the midst of the crowd taking turns twirling the ropes and hitching onto the smoking guns of the Remington statue. Charlie wasn't bad at spinning and twirling, but Tom had him beat when it came to hitching, though it didn't seem to bother Charlie none. He grinned that crooked grin of his, shook his head, brushed the hair back from his forehead and told the crowd, "I jus' don't travel like a colt no more." The crowd loved it.

It was Joe who was the real star that day though, keeping two ropes in motion and never missing a hitch. Even Tom was impressed. I think he wanted Joe to join up with the Wild West Congress.

Nancy cornered Tom and whispered to him pointing toward the Palace of Fine Arts building. She saw everything in terms of its commercial potential and never missed a chance when the opportunity for celebrity publicity came knocking. Tom turned and called out to the crowd, "You all best go see this here Cowboy Artist's paintin's over yonder in that fancy building of Fine Arts." Then he threw his rope and pulled poor Charlie in. They worked this into a routine and did it as often as the crowd changed.

Later Tom Mix became a regular in and out of the Great Falls studio whenever he passed through Montana. He and Joe got to be real close while we were in St. Louis. Joe started calling him "Mixie," and the two always had their heads together about something. Joe swore that Mixie told him all his secrets, and then Joe would pass them on to me. It seems Tom had to keep up a lot of bunkum for the Wild West Congress and the movie studios. One story had it that he'd been born in Texas to a Cherokee Indian mother and a cavalryman father. Joe said it was all a studio cock-and-bull story. Part of the movie publicity. Tom Mix, the fancy dressing cowboy, known around the world, was actually a farm boy from Pennsylvania. Simply a poor white farm boy who idolized Buffalo Bill. He'd joined up with Teddy Roosevelt's army, but had soon gotten scared and became a deserter.

You know, Billy, I was beginning to doubt that anything I'd heard or even seen in the West was real. It was all like, what do you call it now-a-days? A head game? Like a magic show and you didn't know where in the hell all the white rabbits were coming from.

 SIXTEEN

Sister Ella Comes to Stay

During the three months we spent in St. Louis, I kept Nancy's neurasthenia at bay with cold packs, hot baths, and her milky looking medicine. More than the medicine, I thought her good health was probably caused by her commercial success. She managed to get Charlie's paintings into a respectable St. Louis gallery and got several commissions for his illustration work. I heard nothing more about the Montana State Legislature mural although I thought sure the Russells must have heard rumors or received letters about it. Finally, in December, Joe DeYong and I were sent back to Montana, by second class coach, to care for the house and studio while Charlie and Nancy went on to New York.

Charlie was reluctant. He'd enjoyed hanging around the St. Louis Exposition and didn't seem to care about sales. He hated New York. He said it smelled like something that had been dead for a week, and he believed the tall buildings were sure to cause it to sink into the sea at any moment.

"Cha'lie, it's where the money is," Nancy kept insisting. "It's where I can arrange to sell more paintings. "After your success in St. Louis, I'm shooting for a glorious show at the Folsom Gallery. You know David Francis here in St. Louis has some close friends in New York. He's gonna help you."

By the time Joe and I got back, I expected Mattie might have already eloped with Con Price, but it turned out Con Price had eloped with someone else, the niece of a former Montana governor. Seems he saw it as a shrewd investment. Mattie gave me the news when she called on the telephone. Like Charlie, I never got used to the telephone, but we arranged to meet at Lulu Disher's.

When I found her sitting there at Lulu's soda fountain, I expected a sorrowful expression and red eyes. Instead, she was wearing a new dark gold satin dress that made her blonde curls into sunbeams. She wasn't sighing over the pink cupids on the wallpaper anymore, and she didn't look like someone who'd been jilted.

"Oh what the hell, Ovidia, everything has its element of politics, even marriage," she said flashing her eyes at a tall, skinny engineer with a thin waxed moustache. I knew he was an engineer because he had his long slide-rule propped-up against the wall by his table. "You have to be practical about these things and understand that Miss Claudia Toole, Con's new bride, has inherited a large ranch in the Sweet Grass Hills. Con's finally got all those thousands of acres he always wanted. When I got to thinkin' about it, Ovidia, I don't want to be no damned rancher's wife. Stuck out there on the prairie. Nobody to talk to 'cept the wind and a couple of out to pasture cayuses. That's not what I want. I'm going to California."

"Mattie! You've found someone else. "A business man?"
I sputtered dripping the red soda right out on the marble
top table.

"Nah, nah, nothing like that. I'm just tired of being an
entertainer in dance halls and bar rooms like The Mint.
Dealing Faro and Monte gets humdrum. I know I could
become a star of the moving pictures," she proclaimed.

"Do you think so? But . . .*gut Got*, Mattie, those moving
pictures are mostly Westerns. All the stars are men. They're
about cowboys, with fistfights, and jumping on trains, and
robberies, and saloons. They're all about men. Not much
place for women in those films."

"Well, there will be soon, and I wanna be there when it
happens. Just think about "Annie Oakley and the Buffalo
Bill Wild West show. Hell, "Annie's a bigger draw than Bill
himself."

"I guess it's possible . . . maybe. Tom Mix was talking
about it in St. Louis. He's going to California soon, but
Mattie, it's Joe DeYong he wants to take with him. He sure
didn't invite me." I laughed. "A woman's place is tied to the
railroad tracks. That's what I heard him tell Joe, Mattie."

"Well, he's full of bull pucky. Just wait an' see."

"So you're not disappointed to lose Con Price?"

"Oh hell no, I've got some better ideas."

"But what about the cupids, and love, and kisses?" I
looked around at the decorations in Lulu's soda fountain
and at the tall handsome, though prissy, engineer.

"Had enough of 'em. Speaking of enough, Sid had a
letter from Charlie. Guess Charlie's had more than a snoot
full of New York. We all got a hoot outta the illustration he
painted on the letter though. Shows Charlie all dressed up
in his city black finery standing at a bar with some guy he

calls Jacky Rockyfeller. Charlie's lifting one, as usual, but this fancy chum of his wants him to have some milk and crackers with his New York crowd. That's what he thinks of that New York crowd, a milk and crackers bunch. Charlie told Sid he'd been trying to get outta there for more 'an seven weeks."

"I can tell you, they won't be back until Nancy gets the Folsom Gallery to show Charlie's work."

Okay, okay, Billy, don't interrupt me when I'm thinking. Just keep your shirt on. You can't rush me or it'll spoil my story. I might even forget something. I'll get back to what happened with the forged mural just as soon as you get me one of those baked potatoes over there on the buffet line. And put plenty of butter and salt on it.

When the Russells came home that spring, Nancy had a beautiful fur coat, and Charlie was wearing a fine Prince Albert overcoat which he immediately discarded. Young Boy was quick in bringing Neenah around to the house, and Charlie took off for The Mint Saloon at a swift pace.

"It's fine." Nancy signed to Young Boy. "Let him go, dammit. He's been prody as a locoed steer for the last six weeks. He can't wait to get down and jaw with the bunch," she said.

That evening Albert Trigg and Margaret came over after supper, oops no, things had changed, now we called it "dinner." Nancy had arranged to talk to them about the Montana State House mural commission. She'd learned about it, and she was sure the legislature would come to Charlie, hat in hand, begging him to do the painting. So far though she'd heard nothing from them. It was Albert who finally gave her the bad news that there was to be a selection committee. She didn't take it very well.

When I took the tea things into the living room, now called the parlor, Charlie was on his favorite buffalo horn chair leaning back, boots pushed out straight in front. Albert and Margaret sat stiffly on the velvet love seat. Nancy looking urbane in her new black lace, her hair combed into curls to frame her face, fanned herself with a white ostrich plume she had bought in New York. She leaned close toward Albert from her seat on the other evil looking buffalo chair.

"I was expecting a letter about the mural commission while we were still in New York, Albert," she said.

"It's to be a competition, Nancy."

"I can't understand that. After all, it's only Cha'lie who's the real Montana artist, the Cowboy Artist. Everyone knows that. He's the only one with proof of having been there. They all know it, from here to St. Louis, to New York, and by next year even to England. That's what I'm planning."

Charlie straightened up and chimed in. "Well, hell! Remember Mame, I've never painted a mural before. I never even tried to do anything near that size. 'Member the trouble I had finishing up that little four by six for that guy, what was his name, the wealthy New Yorker—anyways I kept changin' it and he kept wantin' more changes. An what's this thing 'sposed to be, twenty-five by twelve?"

"I'm going to send all the New York reviews to the local papers here and in Helena, Albert," said Nancy ignoring Charlie's comments. "I'm gonna tell them about Cha'lie's bronze being selected for that big International Exposition in Rome next year, an' . . ."

"Well, shit, Mame darlin'. I ain't goin' to Rome! Not even if I could see Jesus Christ hisself," Charlie interrupted.

Margaret huffed a bit at that one, but she was used to Charlie and used to hearing worse on the street corners and down at the Army's store front meeting room.

"They're not gonna push us off so easily, Albert. Committee or no committee, Cha'lie's doin' that mural."

"I'm sorry to have to tell you this, Nancy, but from what I hear down at the Brunswick, they're talking about John Alexander. He's had the experience. Besides, he's a National Academy artist who painted a mural for the Library of Congress."

"Dammit, Albert. If they want cupids and angels and Greek goddesses . . . shit. Here's what I'll do. I'll get Paris Gibson, and Frank, and Carl, and even Jesus Christ himself to talk to the governor for Cha'lie. That's what I'll do. They're all gonna help me. We'll not let this one go. Never forget it, Albert."

"I don't know, Mame. I've never painted a mural before," Charlie said quietly.

"Cha'lie, it's just a big, big painting. You're the only one that can do it right."

Life on Fourth Avenue North began to change after the triumph of St. Louis and the show at the Folsom Gallery that Nancy had been able to arrange. There was constant talk of the mural, and Charlie started doing more sculpture after seeing Remington's stuff at the Exposition. It seemed to me that he had a sort of personal competition going on with Remington, or maybe it was Nancy's contest. She had gotten Charlie's bronzes accepted for sale at Tiffany's in New York, and she set the price higher than what Remington was asking. That Charlie didn't sell even one, while Remington sold more than a hundred, didn't seem to concern her. It was the price that was important.

"It doesn't matter," she told me when she got the bad news in a letter from Tiffany's. "It's the quality of Cha'lie's sculpture that's important—that's why we charge more, goddammit."

Then she heard that one of Charlie's bronzes, *Smoking Up*, had been given to President Theodore Roosevelt as a gift, and she promptly saw to it that all the newspapers had the story. The President of the United States, an ex-ranchman and Rough Rider, admired and owned a Charles Russell bronze. That was her sell. She was sure good at using those big name celebrities. And, she knew the publicity would help Charlie get the mural commission.

Charlie's illustration work was brisk. There was artwork for the first two installments of Steward Edward White's novel, *Arizona Nights*, and then a bitter battle developed between Nancy and Bertha Bower from Big Sandy, Montana over the price of three watercolors to illustrate Bertha's first novel, *Chip of the Flying U*. Nancy insisted on one hundred dollars apiece for the illustrations, and Bertha, who used the pen name B. M. Bower, pleaded that her publisher could pay no more than twenty-five. In the end, Bertha picked up the difference, but she never forgave Nancy, and everyone said she was using her influence to stop Charlie from getting the mural commission.

You might say that as time went by we had what in upper-class circles they called a "salon." Nancy felt she now had a fashionable household with regular gatherings of writers and artists. Mattie said "saloon" might have been closer to the truth, especially when the bunch was hanging around. But as I said before, "dinner" was now in the evening in the dining room. I cooked it and served it wearing my black maid's dress with the little white apron. Nancy insisted that Charlie, with Josephine's help, make little white place cards for the table like those she'd seen in St. Louis. The invitation list always included someone who might buy a picture or someone with influence in the Helena legislature. Even with all this, Nancy's name still wasn't included on the guest list for The Maids and Matrons teas. Charlie's work pace was stepped up. Nancy liked to deny it, but Charlie's illustration work for books, magazines, and calendars still brought in the bread and butter.

About this time, it was spring or early summer if I remember right, Nancy received a telegram from her half-sister, Ella. Her long lost sister that she hadn't seen since her mother's death. She was delighted.

"Ella was little more than a baby, about six, when her daddy came and took her away. I wonder if she'll remember me. I wonder if she'll still think I'm pretty. I was only sixteen the last time she saw me. Ella always had the brightest, bluest eyes. I can't wait to see her, Ovidia," she said with small tears streaking through the white powder she now used on her cheeks. Nancy was sentimental about family. I guess because she never really had one, and she and Charlie wanted children so badly.

Anyway, I went with them when they met Ella at the train station. Nancy welcomed her with open arms even though Ella's ragged clothes were stretched so tight that one of her buttons had popped just above her waistline.

I may as well say this. To me Ella looked like a distorted version of Nancy. Like when someone stepped in front of the Fun House mirrors at the St. Louis Exposition. She was bulged out and at the same time squashed down.

I took Ella's worn carpetbag with pieces of clothing spilling out the sides up to the guest room when we got back to the house. When I hung her shirts in the closet, I noticed they all had shabby cuffs and dark oily rings around the collars. I'd need to show her the claw-foot bathtub in a hurry, and find Joe to have him put up an extra clothes line to dry all the wash.

The first thing Ella wanted when she got to the house was food. She spied the locked-up chocolate cake Nancy was saving for dinner and managed to down three large slices with two glasses of milk. The milk dribbled down her plump little chin as she mopped up the cake crumbs with her index finger and sucked them into her mouth.

"My pa's dead you know," she told Nancy between gulps. He's the one tol' me to come here. He never did find any gold in Idaho. Ended up on a stinking chicken ranch, and then he heard California was the place to be, so we went there. 'This's the land of milk and honey,' he kept saying to me even after we got there and he had no job and he took sickly."

"My poor step-daddy always was one to chase his dreams," Nancy said with sympathy as she locked what was left of the cake back into the china cabinet.

"He told me to come to you, Mame. He'd been keeping all these newspaper articles about you and your famous cowboy artist husband. He said he was sure you'd take care of me because he had tooken you in when you didn't have a home. Said you'd be sure to give me a good education since you have so much now-a-days. And after all, I'm your only sister."

Ella's voice had a pitiful whine that I'll never forget. It sounded like one of those toy dolls for little girls that squeal heartbreakingly when they're turned over.

"He was right, Ella. We'll see you're taken care of."

"I'm gonna be a famous writer you know. I want to go to the university and take a course in writing so I can become rich and famous." Ella continued sucking the smears of chocolate icing from her short fat fingers. "I'll have my name in the paper too. Just like you and Charlie."

"We'll have to see about the university, Ella. I think we could send you to secretarial school right here in Great Falls. There are always plenty of jobs for good secretaries."

That evening the Triggs and Josephine came for dinner to meet Ella. She appeared late in a dress as shabby as the one she arrived in and not clean either. All through dinner she seemed to be pouting. I was serving the remains of the cake for desert when Nancy mentioned sending Ella to secretarial school. Margaret Trigg was nodding her approval and suddenly Ella got all red in the face and jumped up knocking over her chair.

"How can you treat me like that!" she screamed. "Your only sister. What would Ma say? Phooey on any damned secretarial school. I want to go to the university. I'm to be a famous writer."

The Triggs looked flustered. I thought Josephine would faint she had turned so pale. Margaret opened her mouth. I think she was hoping to change the subject, but Nancy barged in.

"Ella, you can either go to secretarial school or not. It's your choice, but there will be no university. There's a lot more demand for secretaries than for writers. You've got to have a trade and learn to support yourself."

"Nancy, you're just as bossy as ever," Ella yelled as she turned, ran up the stairs, and slammed her bedroom door.

The next morning I was carrying Ella's breakfast tray upstairs when I ran into Nancy in the hall. She was up and about earlier than usual.

"What's this all about?" she demanded looking harshly at the tray.

"It's, well . . . it's Miss Ella's breakfast tray," I stammered. "She said she wanted to have breakfast in bed every morning, and that, and that . . . I was to bring it to her." From the hard look on Nancy's face, I knew I was doing something wrong, but I wasn't sure exactly what.

"We'll see about this. I'll take that. Come along," she said as she grabbed the tray from me. Instead of knocking on Ella's door she kicked it a couple of times but she didn't wait for an answer. She barged right ahead and entered the room.

Ella was stretched out propped-up on several pillows. "Oh, I thought it was Ovidia bringing me my breakfast." She sat up straighter and looked at Nancy with her bright blue eyes shining and innocent.

Nancy settled the breakfast tray neatly and carefully on Ella's lap. "Enjoy this breakfast, Ella, because it's the last one you'll have in bed as long as you're here."

"Well, but Nancy, what good is it to have servants if they don't wait on you?" Ella whined.

"Get this straight, Little Sister. You're welcome to stay here. I'll pay your tuition to secretarial school, I'll feed you, clothe you, but no one will wait on you. We all pull our own weight around here. From now on, you'll help in the kitchen, and you'll help with the cleaning and housekeeping like we all do. Is that clear?" Ella was speechless. Nancy turned on her heel, gripped my arm harshly, and pulled me from the room.

As we went downstairs, she said nothing. My arm was going to be bruised where she had grabbed and hauled me downstairs. I said nothing, but went outside to the kitchen porch and stamped my foot in the dust.

Young Boy watched me. He was on his way to the shack dressed in his best buckskins, blanket robe and cloth leg wrappings. Approaching me, he raised his arm palm up, fingers spread and wiggled his wrist to sign a question, then looking down at my foot, he put his closed right hand to his forehead and made a small twisting motion.

"What do?" he asked. "Look you like mind-twisted." He continued the crazy screwing motion on his forehead.

"Oh *helvete*." I stamped my shoe in the dirt again.

"Anger . . . you see spirit Miss Ella in ground under boot. Anger now rise with dust. Now be gone."

"For sure, Young Boy, you betcha."

"Anger go. You okay now." He kept signing "good" swinging his flat right hand across his chest as he walked away toward the studio.

There was another crisis later that week. This time a more serious mistake on Ella's part, and when Nancy was upset, the whole household walked on egg shells. It was going to take some adjusting and some time before Ella fit into the family.

Nancy's interaction with prospective buyers was the most sacred ritual of the house. Everything had to be just so. No interruptions allowed. But I guess Ella thought she could control Nancy to her own advantage if she did it in front of an Eastern buyer. Nancy was learning to carefully control her behavior with buyers these days. Late one morning when she was in the parlor showing Charlie's watercolors, Ella came tripping down the stairs and rushed right in.

"Hello, I'm Miss Ella Allen," she drawled in her Kentucky-tobacco-farm voice interrupting Nancy's sales conversation. "You know, I'm Mrs. Russell's only sister, and can you believe it, she's not gonna send me to the university."

Nancy coughed and almost choked. She motioned for Ella to leave the parlor, but Ella continued rambling on about the injustices.

"She's making me go to secretarial school! And besides that, we have servants and I can't even have breakfast in bed. What's the use of servants if they don't bring you breakfast in bed and don't wait on you. Why she even said, I'd have to do housework. And I'm her only sister . . . ."

The buyer's face had turned red with embarrassment, and he flipped his gloves nervously across his open palm as he looked down and stammered, "Ah, well, Mrs. Russell, I'll be going now. I can see this is not a good time. Maybe another time, ah . . . ." He turned and moved quickly through the entry hall and out the front door.

Nancy was furious. I thought at first she was going to slap Ella, but Ella must have sensed her rage and she stepped back.

"Don't you ever do that again," Nancy shouted. "If you do, you'll be on the next train back to California. Home or no home. There are two rules that you can never forget. First, you are never to interrupt Charlie when he is painting, and second, you are never to interrupt me when

I'm selling one of Charlie's paintings. Now, get in the kitchen and see if you can help Ovidia. Now!"

I never thought much of Ella. She wasn't much help in the kitchen or with the housekeeping, but she did learn to stay away from prospective buyers. She did go to secretarial school, and she finally got a job on the local newspaper. The timing was all wrong for Nancy and Ella to become loving sisters.

Nancy was continually concerned about the mural contract. She was determined that Charlie would do the mural. We all were. Only Charlie was hesitant.

"If you want something, Cha'lie, you have to go after it."

"I know, I know," Charlie would whisper.

"It's nothin' but a big, big painting," Nancy would repeat as she sat on the floor in the evening and pressed her face against his knee and stroked his thigh. "He's your good friend, Frank Bird Linderman, he's Deputy Secretary of State. Head of the selection committee. He has the legislature in his pocket. You've told me, I don't know how many times, how you both came out here as young boys. He's your steadfast friend. You go campin' together, and hunting. Talk to him, Cha'lie."

But it was going to take something more than that to get Linderman's support. I was sure about that since Carl insisted Nancy and Frank Linderman didn't get along very well although he never talked about the reason. I began to think it might have something to do with Frank's book illustrations. As far as I could see, Charlie hadn't started them yet.

SEVENTEEN

Seven Card Stud

The opportunity to improve Charlie's chance at winning the Montana State mural contract finally came one evening during our kitchen card game. Usually Joe, Young Boy, and anyone else who dropped in after supper . . . I mean dinner, joined us. Sometimes Carl came by, sometimes Teddy Blue or that big hulking Johnny Matheson, occasionally even Mattie. Ella tried to join us a few times, but just couldn't get it. She thought a winning hand was a four card straight.

Nancy and Charlie never played cards, and this particular week Nancy had taken the train over to the Mayo Clinic in Rochester, Minnesota. Her osteopath, Doc Edwin, suggested they might be able to treat her neurasthenia and possibly even her infertility. I believe Nancy enjoyed the prestige of telling everyone she was "going through the Mayo." What did that mean I wondered? How it was different from just than going to the doctor?

With Nancy gone, Charlie was spending his days at the Mint and his evenings at the Triggs' studying the Lewis and Clark journals. This pleased both Albert and Josephine. Josephine looked so rosy and was busy baking. Mostly things chocolate. Charlie's favorite. He said chocolate was what he missed most when he was up on the Judith singing to the cows.

You know why they sing to 'em, Billy? Well, I'll tell you. Teddy Blue was the one who told me. Teddy loved to sing. Knew all kinds of songs, and he was always singing to me too, but he said you had to sing to those cows. It was in case you got a storm and you had to run with a stampede. See, the other cowpunchers had to know where you were. Otherwise, they might head them into a mill right over top of you. You can guess the result of that. Both you and your horse mashed right into the ground, flat as a pancake.

What's wrong Billy? You look a little under the weather. Guess I'm off the track again.

Carl was in town with Frank Linderman. They had arrived late from Helena but had come over to Fourth Avenue to see Charlie. He was over at Trigg's place, but Frank and Carl seemed ready to test their luck. These evening card games were small stakes, sometimes even Penny Ante, but they were proving to be quite profitable for me. I never pushed my luck and avoided scaring everyone off though I sure loved to play.

I threw a thick gray felt blanket that Young Boy had come in with over top of the bare wood kitchen table, and the five of us sat down. We were just about ready to deal the first hand when Teddy Blue arrived carrying a bunch of those damned violets and signing to Young Boy. Carl scowled, but Joe and Frank clapped him on the back and invited him into the game. He accepted, of course, and sat down next to Frank. Teddy was dressed to the nines with a new set of Montana sapphire cuff studs in bright gold settings.

"Where the hell you been Teddy?" Frank asked. "Look like you was the one been over in the 'Big Teepee.'"

"Managing, of course, just managing. Like a steer, I'm still trying. Been transporting bullion from the Spotted Horse Mine for old Granville Stuart. Planning on gettin' my own ranch up there soon."

"Well, that kinda money's only going to bring you grief. You better stop and breathe your pony. Sit right down here so as we can relieve you of all them worries," said Carl.

I tried to sit where I wouldn't be "under the gun" and have to make the first bet. Young Boy was the lucky one. He almost always drew high card to win the first deal, so I wanted to have someone sitting between us. The stakes were not high that evening, but sometimes pots got to be as big as two or three dollars. I knew all the players pretty well. Joe was a bluffer. Carl played it tight-aggressive, often sandbagging, waiting for someone else to open even though he had a strong hand. I knew less about Frank than the other players, but as I said, I was alert and focused since the stakes could get high. We were friends, but this was a money game.

Like I anticipated, Young Boy won the first deal. I placed the sugar bowl we used as a dealer button in front of him. We were playing five card draw. During the first two hours or so, play went routinely. We had a one dollar limit, but few hands came to that. I won a couple of small pots. Young Boy kept drawing pairs and doing well with it. Joe had no exceptional hands, but raised the ante a few times by bluffing. It surprised me that no one noticed him fidgeting with his bow tie every time he used his bluffing strategy. Carl kept his best poker face, and Frank finally won a nice pot on three of a kind. I'd folded early on that hand and was making coffee.

Frank was pulling in his winnings when the front door slammed and Charlie shuffled into the kitchen. Looking around at the group gathered around the table he nodded to me and said: "I see these slick cowpokes tryin' to part you from your daily bread again, Little Package."

"Well come on in here," both Teddy and Joe chorused to him.

"We all been waiting for you. I gotta tell you this new one," said Teddy.

Charlie pulled a chair up and sat across the seat leaning forward on the back of the chair. "Suppose I gotta hear you airin' your lungs, I reckon."

"Couple a lines, couple of lines. Happened just the other day. I was over to Miles City. They got a new school teacher, young and kinda sprightly. She comes up to me and says: 'Oh, Mr. Abbott, tell me about you boys all riding your ponies. Didn't you all have fun on the trail?'" The whole table snorted except for Young Boy and me.

"Hell, Charlie, I couldn't believe it. So's I turned to her and said: 'Madame, there weren't no boys and there weren't no ponies. They was all pure men and horses.'"

The table broke up with amusement and Charlie mumbled "True, true."

"Sit in for a hand or two. Do you good," said Frank.

"I'll pass on that one. Tried a few times and never could find 'nough spots on my cards. 'Sides my pockets always seemed to spring a leak."

"Sure, couple a hands'll do you good," said Carl.

"Promised Mame, 'fore she left. No late nights."

"Ah, sit on down. Nancy ain't ever going to know," Frank continued. But Charlie was already pushing his chair back from the table.

"Right now I'm runnin' down faster'n a two-dollar watch." Charlie lifted his Stetson and with a grand King Arthur bow toward us he turned and started toward the stairs.

The room was silent until we all heard the upstairs toilet flush and the sound of the bedroom door closing. Joe spoke up then signing and questioning Frank. "So who's got the edge on the mural commission this week?"

"Rather not talk about that, Joe."

"Ya otta give it to 'The Chief,' ya know, or . . . maybe even to me. One of us real cowpokes."

Frank looked at Joe and sighed. "What in the hell are you saying, Joe? You ain't never, even every, sold one single damned painting. How could we put you up there?" said Frank.

Carl interrupted leaning back in his chair. "We might as well have Olaf Selzer."

"Oh no, you don't." yelled Joe. "That St. Bernard gets it, and shit, I'm leaving Montana. I know a helluva lot more about cowboyin' than any of 'em."

"Ya probably do, Joe, but we're lookin' for a painter not a damned wrangler," said Frank.

"How 'bout that boy over in Belt, the one that does all the horses?" Carl smirked sarcastically.

"Charlie, the Cowboy Artist, has my vote," said Teddy Blue.

Frank was getting pissed. I noticed a sweat breaking out on his forehead, and he'd taken off his glasses and stared straight up at the ceiling as he rubbed them off with his handkerchief. I could see the muscles in his jar clenching.

"Damn it! This here ain't the State Legislature, and none of you got no say in this." Frank's face was red. "Jesus-H-Kee-ryst, everyone wants their favorite. It's been driving me nuts for months. Feel like I been studying to be a half-wit."

"Who's deal? Yours Young Boy?" I said trying to ease the tension. "I'm feeling lucky."

Frank paused, looked at me, and shook his head. "I'd even bet that Ovidia there'd probably want some guy to come over here from Norway and paint a bunch a reindeer and God damned Viking ships all over the Montana legislature walls."

I had to suppress a giggle. It did seem like a farfetched idea, but I couldn't say I didn't like it. Why not? More Norwegian speakers in America than in Norway—especially in Montana.

"You guys are all so God damned rustic. Parochial, I think that's what you'd call it. Hell, we've got two locals already. Edgar Paxson and Ralph DeCamp both of 'em got commissions for other parts of the building. The big one for the House of Representatives needs a serious artist. Ever think that this is the chance for the State to have someone like Whistler." We were all silent.

"Maybe even John Alexander." No one said a word.

"Someone with formal training in Europe." Teddy Blue and Joe groaned.

"Charlie once told me he couldn't see how a Dutchman or a Frenchman could teach him how to paint things in his own country," I said.

"You simply don't understand, Ovidia, and neither does Charlie. Well, I recognize that. You're all great friends of Charlie's and the West. I agree someone from the West should probably do the mural, but the one I'm thinking of has formal training. Name's Sharp, Joseph Henry Sharp. Lived over on the Crow Agency for years. Had his stuff purchased for the Smithsonian in Washington even. He'd get my vote."

"You just won't support Charlie 'til you get your book illustrations." said Teddy Blue, and Frank looked at him with an ugly scowl.

"Then there's Remington," interrupted Carl. "Right now the odds seem to be in his favor down in Helena." We all groaned.

"Kee-ryst, I'm fed up with this whole thing," Frank mumbled.

"There's this guy down in Texas, name's Reaugh I think. They call him the dean of Texas painters," said Teddy. "He 's good. Sure knows cattle."

"Well, I heard of a guy, Charles Adams up in Colorado," said Joe. "He's 'posed to be good."

"Nah, not that one," said Teddy. "All he paints are those damned rivers."

"There's always Jim Ballinger down in Arizona."

"I heard of a guy named Forsyth."

"Another's Ben Brown."

Frank slammed his fist against the table making the cards and coins jump. "What in the hell are you guys doing? You should hear yourselves. You think you're a bunch of art critics? Since when? I'm fed up. In the end it's my decision, and I'm gonna make it. Everybody carping and jockeying. Never ends. I'm up-to-here." Frank gestured, shook his head, and thumped both his open fists down on the table again.

"Enough! Shit, I'm getting' outta it. Outta it, dammit! We're going to deal these cards. Whoever wins is going to choose. Once and for all . . . and then it's over. And, I guarantee I'll lobby to see that everyone on the God damned committee sticks to that choice. But, seven card stud this time."

I almost dropped the coffee cups before I could sit down. I couldn't believe he was serious. My hands were shaking. The table was tense and silent. Everyone shifted in their seats. Frank had a nasty determined look on his face, but we cut the cards for the deal, and Young Boy won again. I could hardly believe it. It looked like Frank was going to go through with it.

What if we could really choose? Surely Teddy, Young Boy, and I would choose Charlie, but maybe Teddy really did like his Texas painter, and Joe? As much as Joe idolized Charlie, I had a sneaky suspicion that Joe might try to pick himself . . . a new unknown cowboy painter? I was less than certain about Carl. He actually did like and admire the kid from Belt. It was his hometown. And Frank had already said he wanted Joseph Sharp. This could be my best, or only, opportunity.

The table got stiller than the grave as Young Boy shuffled. We all anted-up our silver nickels. Young Boy started dealing for seven card stud, two down and one up to each of us. While five card stud is mostly a game of high cards and pairs, seven card stud can be wide open. The betting round began with the high card dealt since we never played with a bring-in back then. It was Young Boy's King of Diamonds and he checked. Carl was to Young Boy's left with a Four of Diamonds showing. Without a word, he turned his up card face down and folded. I think he just wanted out.

I was to Carl's left. I had pulled pocket Ten's. Not bad, but tricky, and I had a Jack showing. The pair of ten's was a better hand to play against a small number of people. The more players, the more likely someone would have a face card or Ace that would pair up with the next up card. I was looking to scare some of them off. I bet fifty cents.

Joe was to my left. With only a Nine of Clubs showing, he called, but given his bluffing pattern, I didn't figure him for much. Teddy with a Four of Spades showing hesitated and then folded, and we all looked to Frank. His Queen up card could mean a high pair, but he only called, and there were four of us left for the second round: Young Boy, me , Joe, and Frank.

I got my third Ten, Joe a King, Frank pulled an Ace of Spades, and Young Boy found himself with the Ace of Clubs. His King, Ace gave him the best poker hand showing, and he bet fifty cents. My *Got*, I was nervous. I was silently thanking Mattie for her lessons on how to keep your hands from trembling. I looked straight across the table and imagined the heat flowing into my fingers.

Was Young Boy bluffing? It wasn't his style. I called the fifty and raised a dollar. Joe with his King, Nine called. I was expecting more from Frank, but he seemed to want to see the next round before committing, and he called as well.

Young Boy dealt the third up card. I almost gave myself away when I saw my second Ten fall. I choked down a grin. My hand was unbeatable, four Tens. Frank, who had gotten another Queen, looked like he might have three of a kind. Joe had gotten another King which now gave him the high pair, and he opened the third round by betting our limit, a dollar. Frank called and Young Boy with only a King, Ace, Eight showing, finally folded.

I raised, figuring my opponents would be thinking I had a full house, Jacks and Tens. It seemed the best Joe could have was two pair. Both Joe and Frank called, and we were ready for the fourth up card. Nothing was changed by the deal, and Joe again had the first bet with his King pair. He checked, Frank bet a dollar, I called and Joe check raised a dollar.

This was probably the biggest pot the kitchen table had ever seen. It looked like the three of us were in until the end, and Young Boy dealt the final down card. It was still Joe's turn to bet because the down card did not change either hand. Joe checked, Frank bet a dollar, and I called. With the close of the betting round, the three of us remained so the showdown would decide the fate of the mural commission . . . if Frank was to keep his promise. I remember every card that was played that night, Billy.

And, I was right about Joe. He had two pair, Kings and Nines, only Frank had fooled me. His was a full house, Aces full of Queens. He had taken me in with the pair of Aces in the pocket, but my four of a kind were unbeatable. As I raked in the coins, Teddy and Joe let out a whoop.

"Guess I don't need to ask who you want doing the mural then," said Frank quietly.

"You've got it Frank. It's got to be Charlie," I said.

"So, you got my word. I'll lobby for him, but God dammit, this'll make two he owes me now." Frank mumbled as he and Carl pushed back their chairs and stood to leave.

"An' keep your traps shut about this." Frank raised his hand in a threatening gesture and pointed at each of us. "I hear any rumors, even the slightest gossip or hint, and the deal's off. You can count on that."

"Not a word, Mr. Linderman, it's our secret even after the letter from the commission arrives. Sworn to on St. Olav." I touched my medal as I spoke.

"Well, I hope to hell you can keep him sober and on track. I sure as hell can't." Frank shook his head and adjusted his glasses. "The State legislature doesn't have much patience."

"We'll be looking for the commission letter from the Selection Committee," I said just before the back screen door slammed.

EIGHTEEN

Show Business at Bull Head Lodge

We kept a stony silence about the poker game waiting for the letter commissioning the mural to arrive. I warned Teddy Blue that if he said a word to Charlie or any of the bunch, he'd better be looking for a change of pasture— quick. We worried, I think, that Frank might have second thoughts about the high stakes game once he cooled down. In truth, I was sure he would change his mind. He hadn't shown much conviction that Charlie could do the job, and Joe knew he was still waiting for the illustrations of his book and that Frank was pissed off about it.

Nancy came back a week later. Home from the Mayo Clinic all smiles and gaiety. They had indeed confirmed the diagnosis of neurasthenia, and she was slightly pleased to have such a stylish malady. She brought back a trunk full of new clothes, a cosmetic case full of new medicine, and William S. Hart on her elbow. He was dressed as cocky as the

King of Spades, plaid shirt with matching scarf and a heavy wool vest covered in multicolored flower embroidery. His hair was parted straight down the left side and slicked flat making his forehead look high and his eyes coldly piercing. He was trying out a new more colorful image on his way to California for an acting contract with the movie industry. Nancy was decked out in a black dress covered with bugles and jet and wore a big hat with nodding plumes.

In spite of her chirpy mood, Josephine confided that the Mayo Clinic had been unable to do anything about her infertility. Josephine said Nancy cried and moaned but was trying to hide her disappointment because Charlie wanted a family so desperately. Nancy was convinced Charlie would work harder and stop drinking if he had the child he had so long wanted. She was blaming herself for his lethargy and drinking.

Three days later, the letter from the selection committee at the State legislature did arrive. Nancy habitually rushed to open the mail before the postman could even leave the front porch steps. But this time, instead of coming in she stopped on the porch. "Oh my God, oh my God, my dreams have come true, my prayers are answered," she screeched. "They do love my Cha'lie down in Helena."

I rushed out of the kitchen thinking she had perhaps gotten dizzy and was ready to faint, but she was jumping joyfully up and down waving the letter and I knew right away what it was.

Both sister Ella and Bill Hart came hurrying out the front door. Joe and Young Boy were rushing around from the barn, and Charlie plodded slowly out the heavy door of the shack still holding his brush and palette. Nancy kept shouting, "We did it. We did it."

The Triggs, next door, must have heard the commotion and hurried over from their place. When they saw Nancy jumping up and down, they guessed it was about the mural commission. Joe grabbed old Young Boy and started a howling dance on the front porch. Josephine ran toward Charlie, took his hand and pulled him quickly up to where Nancy stood still waving the letter.

"Hush now, hush up everyone. I'm gonna read it to ya. Every word. Just listen. Here's what it says:

> Dear Mr. Russell:
> On behalf of the entire great State of Montana, it is my deepest pleasure to inform you that you have been selected to paint the mural for the new House of Representatives wing. Upon your acceptance of the commission the selection committee will forward to you a contract in the sum of five thousand dollars to be paid upon completion of the twenty-five by twelve foot mural. Congratulations on your success. Sincerely yours.

And it's signed with heavy black pen and ink, Edwin L. Norris, Governor of Montana."

Nancy caught her breath and squealed, "Five thousand dollars, Cha'lie. Five thousand dollars. They're finally taking you seriously, Cha'lie. You're a great artist. The only true Cowboy Artist."

"I don't know 'bout that, Mame," Charlie scowled. "But, they sure as hell ain't gonna get cupids and angels."

"What you gonna give 'em, Chief?" asked Joe.

"Well damn, I dunno."

"A buffalo herd maybe," I suggested.

"A round-up?" said Joe. "Or, maybe a cowboy camp?"

"Maybe the jerkline wagons up out of Belt?" Albert said. "I doubt if they'd want a saloon scene."

"Five thousand dollars," Nancy whispered.

Margaret Trigg broke up the speculation shooing us all inside. "I think it might be wise to send some ideas to Governor Norris for his approval before you get too far ahead of yourself. Meanwhile, let's get off this porch, and give Charlie some breathing room."

"I dunno," mumbled Charlie. "Twenty-five by twelve feet . . . I may need some help from the bunch."

"The bunch needs to be left out of this one, Cha'lie," said Nancy.

From that moment on, everything had to do with the mural because Charlie didn't know what to paint. I was concerned about his hesitation, and in spite of what Nancy wanted, more of the bunch seemed to be hanging around the shack and Olaf Selzer was there almost every day. Charlie's trips to Sid Willis' saloon became more frequent. He said he was getting ideas there.

It was finally Young Boy who realized that the mural could never be painted in the log cabin studio because the ceiling wouldn't take a canvas twelve feet tall. No work could begin until the studio roof was raised several feet. Nancy insisted we should all go to Bull Head Lodge while the work was being done. I remember thinking Charlie might have been better off getting right down to painting, but I think Nancy wanted to take Bill Hart up to the Glacier.

The Russells had built a cabin at Lake McDonald about a quarter of a mile from the tiny Apgar settlement.

They had named the cabin Bull Head Lodge and mounted the usual a dead buffalo skull on a large tree near the boat landing. There were no roads, but a small steam-powered launch plied the lake and delivered passengers, all of them wealthy tourists, to the newly completed Glacier Hotel.

"Cha'lie can do his sketches up there where it's quiet. The place is slower than a snail on crutches. Besides, it's far away from the bunch and The Mint. It'll be enjoyable for Bill Hart to see what a pretty place it is and have a nice rest before he goes to California," she told me.

So, as soon as Charlie had signed the State contract, we all packed up for Bull Head. Bill Hart agreed to come along. The spring and summer were to be spent "rusticating."

I didn't like Lake McDonald or Bull Head Lodge at all, and during the time I worked for the Russells I tried to avoid going there if I could find any excuse. When the sun was high, the lake water was a clear, deep, beautiful turquoise, but in cloudy weather it turned black, a pure *soten* black. At the head of the lake was a thousand-foot massive stone structure, steep and scalloped that the Indians believed was a rugged path to the sun that reached up to the other side of the world . . . a frightening thought.

The Russell's Lodge was a real log cabin this time. Cold, small, and cramped. Always uncomfortable. The place was constantly full of guests, but the two-hole outhouse was at least forty feet from the back door, and the surrounding dark hemlock and cedar forests were full of evil trolls and wood sprites.

Billy, I'm going to go ahead and tell you why I didn't like Bull Head Lodge. It's something you should know. You take terrible risks when you make images of trolls, wood sprites, and gnomes, and then leave them around in the forest where their empty eyes can taunt the real creatures who always live in that sort of area. But, Charlie, didn't seem to know or care about this.

All Charlie did at Bull Head was to go around continually modeling clay figures of those creatures. To make matters worse, he'd dress them in moss, and bark, and tree leaves and lose them under logs, tuck them in rock crevices, hang them from hemlock branches, or even sit them on the porch railings grinning with their teeth showing and ready to bite.

One night, there was only a half-moon, I was hauling water buckets through the heavy growth of tamarack and cedar down to the narrow lake shore. The moss was glistening with moisture and the high rocky cliffs gleamed where the water came trickling down toward the lake. As I knelt down and bent over to fill the buckets with the black water, I saw in the mirror of the lake that someone was standing to my right among the birches and leaning toward me. I abruptly straightened up into a kneeling position and turned to look over my right side.

At first I saw only a large rock and the berry brambles clustered at the base, but suddenly a face was here among the leaves. A woman hiding with a pale face and flowing yellow hair. She was wearing a gleaming silver necklace and silvery brooches covered her tunic. Her nostrils flared pale-pink and her large gray eyes clouded. She raised her hand out of the brambles and held out a wreath of red holly berries and beckoned to me with her outstretched hand. Her fingers were all covered with rings like those Charlie wore, and she kept motioning me toward her. I screamed as loud as I could and dropped the buckets into the black water, then I ran still screaming toward the flickering light of the oil lamp burning in the lodge.

When I heard rapid footsteps on the gravel path behind me, I ran faster. I was nearly to the lodge when Charlie and Bill Hart appeared coming down from the Indian tent where the two were camped.

"Fer god's sake, Owidi, what in hell's goin' on?" said Charlie.

"Calm down, calm down. What happened?" Bill asked. He put his arm over my shoulder. I was shaking and my whole body had broken out in a cold sweat. It felt like my heart was hammering a hole through my chest it was beating so rapidly. I heard Nancy's footsteps coming toward us through the pine grove. Margaret, Josephine, and Ella were with her.

"I . . . was . . . getting . . . water," I stuttered.

"What's all the racket?" asked Nancy. She was in her heavy night clothes and robe with her hair wrapped in the frayed curling rags she used at night.

"The buckets . . . I dropped them. Someone waved to me down by the lake . . . she wanted me to come."

"Who was is?" asked Nancy. "Who waved? Charlie had gotten a blanket from the tent and wrapped it around me.

"A woman. She beckoned me to come with her."

"Where?"

"Into the water. I think . . . she wanted to give the holly wreath to me. So dangerous." I was sobbing. "One of the Christmas trolls." I could barely whisper the name.

"Well hell," Nancy said as she turned to address Charlie. "I told you to stop showing her those trolls and stuff, Cha'lie."

Bill Hart understood and wanted to help. He pulled out a tiny doe skin bundle on a bead chain and hung it around my neck against my bare skin. Immediately I stopped shaking. "This'll keep you safe. It's what the Cree use. Full of good medicine," he said. "But just maybe we'd better guard our tongues. The Cree and Black-feet Indians say you never know who's under the stones listening."

"It was a Christmas troll. I know it. They live here, *got-dammit*. Right in this forest." Charlie and Nancy exchanged glances. I know they didn't believe me, but Bill seemed to understand.

I turned and faced him. "The Indians know it, don't they? They know the trolls guard the path to the sun," I said.

Josephine took my hand and started to lead me back to the lodge. "Don't be afraid, Ovidia, maybe they're good trolls. Aren't there some that won't harm you?"

"*Nei*, Josie, that troll wanted me to follow . . . right down into the lake. She wanted to take me up that awful trail to the other side of the world. They don't want us here. They don't want us here." I kept repeating even after we'd gotten back up the dark path to the lodge.

Margaret Trigg hadn't said a word, but now she spoke up in a firm voice. "We'll take care of this right now, she said. "Ovidia, look at me. I want you to pick up seven of those nice, round, white rocks. Over there, near the steps to the porch."

I hesitated, but tucked the blanket more closely around me and did as she said. "Now, take the rocks and lay them out in the shape of the holy crucifix there on the path to the lake." I bent over and did as she asked.

"Now," said Margaret, "we'll all join hands in a circle around this holy sign we'll say a prayer of protection to the Lord Jesus Christ."

Charlie and Bill, looked at each other and blinked, but they joined the circle and listened to Margaret's prayer. While she spoke, she made the sign of the cross over each of us and we all whispered, "Amen."

When we looked up, Margaret brushed her hands together and in a nonchalant voice said. "Well, that's that for the trolls. Now, let's get on with it."

"But I'm not getting water from the lake at night. *Nei*, not ever again," I said. And, I never did. And, I was careful and wore the doe skin bundle plus my St. Olav medal every time I had to go to Lake McDonald. Looking back, I wonder if the Christmas Troll was giving warning about all the trouble that was to come.

Charlie's did some strange things at the lake. It sounds funny, but he liked to pretend he was a horse. At least it wasn't dangerous like the trolls. Morning and evening he'd hunker down by the lake. First he'd douse his whole face in the frigid water, then he'd bend back down and closing off one nostril with his thumb, he'd nosily suck up water with the other nostril. Then, he'd raise his head and forcefully blow the icy water out the other nostril in a slimy spray. He'd repeat this procedure several times. Disgusting display. I couldn't watch it. I had to look away, but he insisted it was the only way to avoid head colds. "You never seen a horse with a head cold, did ya?" That was his response when I asked about this unsightly practice. Life was going well for Charlie, but he wasn't making any progress on the State House mural.

In spite of the commission for the Capitol mural, the largest amount ever paid by the state for art, Nancy didn't forget that there were potential sales to tourists staying at the Hotel. For this reason we frequently went by the steamer, Klondyke, up the lake to the grand new Glacier Hotel. The Klondyke had two decks, and when it was warm enough you could watch the lake scenery over the railing up top.

The Glacier Hotel looked like a Norwegian castle to me, but I heard it was supposed to look like a European chalet. One hundred rooms with timber porches for viewing the lake and the high snow capped mountains beyond. The three story lobby was filled with stuffed animal heads, bear skin rugs, and heavy hickory furniture. The rusticating well-heeled tourists could lounge in front of the immense hearth on chilly evenings.

John Lewis, the builder and promoter of this palace, made the Russells welcome and even gave them complimentary meals. Nancy had convinced him to hang Charlie's art prominently in the lobby where she could explain the narrative stories of the paintings to the wealthy potential buyers. Both Nancy and Lewis were money minded, and the Russells became the local color that Lewis knew tourists doted on.

Charlie fell naturally into his roll of entertainer. He'd tell stories to any listener, and the Russells devised an Indian Sign language ritual that they performed in front of the crowd gathered around the hearth each evening. Charlie loved it as long as it was on his own terms.

Nancy and Lewis gathered the hotel guests near the hearth and had them sit crouched on floor cushions in a split semicircle. Lewis and a couple of Cree Indians then distributed blankets and draped them around the tourists' shoulders. Nancy, dressed in full Indian costume and black wig, would distribute feathers for the tourists to wear. She'd giggle and tease them into pretending to be Indians. If an important client was visiting, there might even be a real feather "war bonnet." Sometimes Lewis could get one of the Crees to sit to the side of the circle and beat a drum softly.

When all the tourists were settled and in the right mood, Charlie would enter regally dressed as a Chief in beaded buckskins, fringed leggings, and feather bonnet. He'd have an ugly scowl on his face and his arms folded across his chest. Behind him came a Scout carrying a long feathered coup stick, his bare chest and face decorated with paint and his long black hair braided and tied with beads and hide. This entrance, in the flickering fire light, generally brought a gasp or two from the ladies.

Sometimes Joe DeYong played the scout, sometimes Frank Linderman, and when Bill Hart was around he loved to do it. Actually, Tom Mix even played the Scout a few times at house parties in Great Falls. It was a role they all loved.

Anyway, the two "Indians" moved majestically to a center spot in front of the fire. Charlie settled on the floor and took a long pipe and a leather pouch from his buckskins. He slowly filled the pipe and waited while the Scout pulled a burning stick from the hearth fire. The chief took a long pull on the pipe but did not speak. Everything was done in Indian sign language. Nancy stood elegantly to one side. She was the sign language translator for the tourist audience. She'd begin by waving her palm back and forth at her shoulder telling the tourists it was the sign for a question.

When Charlie finished his first signing, she'd start the translation somberly and slowly. Everything was scripted, and Nancy translated the signs that went something like this.

CHIEF TO SCOUT:	Where you home?
SCOUT:	Across prairie beside good river.
CHIEF:	How you come here?
SCOUT:	I ride over prairie. Go good river valley. See many Indian. Want fight. Many Sioux. Many Cheyenne. Come Sioux Cheyenne camp. Two chief ride. Two chief meet. Talk long time.'"
CHIEF:	What Indians do now?
SCOUT:	Indians go forth. Make fight with soldier.
CHIEF:	Yes. Indians fight little while. All understand fight bad medicine.
SCOUT:	You wise chief. Talk true. Tongue no crooked like snake.

At this point there was usually a long pause while the Chief took some heavy puffs on the pipe and passed it to the Scout. The Scout then returned the pipe to the Chief. There was another pause.

CHIEF:	Why you come here, my camp.
SCOUT:	You many good horse.
CHIEF:	Where you horse?
SCOUT:	Horse swim river. Climb mountain. Go across prairie. Horse foot go down. Prairie dog hole. Break foot. Shoot horse. My heart on the ground.
CHIEF:	You want trade horse?

SCOUT: Yes. You good horse. White-man trader he
                bad egg. He bad horse.
CHIEF: White-man bold as brass.

Here there was another pause for puffs on the pipe and
Charlie's fierce hostile glances at the audience.

SCOUT: You many woman.
CHIEF: You want wife.

At this point, the Scout broadly signed female by comb-
ing his fingers down through his hair.

......SCOUT: Yes. Want wife.
......CHIEF: Trade woman.

Then Charlie repeated the sign for woman and for
trade by vigorously striking his hands with index fingers extending past each other. He repeated this several
times.

......SCOUT: Good.
......CHIEF: Yes. Good.

Charlie then slammed his two index fingers with their
many rings together, pointed them aggressively toward the
audience and pushed them rapidly forward.

Nancy would gasp dramatically. She'd look startled,
open her eyes wide, shake her head signaling "no," and
then she'd turn slowly away from looking at the audience
and look severely at Charlie the Chief.

"Why Cha'lie" she'd exclaim, coming out of her Indian
role. "You know I can't say anything like that."

She'd say it with a whimper in her best sweet Southern accent shaking her head and casting her eyes down. The audience would break into the loud guffaws and the tittering giggles that ended the show and began the sales.

One evening, after the show, I heard John Lewis telling Nancy that the thing to do was to sell the West. To sell it not only to those who hadn't lived it, but even to those who had. "Sell it all." he said. "Hats, boots, spurs, buffalo, elk, cowboys, gunslingers, lawmen, gamblers, whores, and—especially Indians."

Lewis and Clark on
Montana Soil

We lingered around Bull Head Lodge and the Glacier Hotel for most of the summer. I had no more trouble with Christmas trolls, but I was like Charlie in New York—wanting to leave every minute. Bill Hart finally left for California. His departure sent Nancy into a bad spell. Joe had come up from Great Falls and was playing the Scout at the hotel performances. Charlie did a couple of pencil sketches for the mural, but that was about all. Gloom settled in heavily at Bull Head.

"What they both need is a child," I confided to Margaret Trigg one morning as we were washing up the dishes after breakfast.

"Well, there certainly isn't going to be one."

"Why not, Margaret? They're old—but not too old yet. In Norway, my father is still having children, and he must be at least fifty."

"It's not Charlie."

"If my mother hadn't died, she'd still be giving him a baby every year or so."

"The problem is Nancy."

"The neurasthenia?"

"The clap," Margaret whispered and put her finger over her lips. "They found out at the Mayo Clinic. Pelvic adhesions they said. Poor thing, let God love her." She shook her head.

"What's pelvic ad—ad—heeon . .?" I asked her.

"Better you don't know. It comes from gonorrhea, a serious disease. Comes from running with the wrong crowds like they were. Either one of them may have had it. She might have even gotten it from him. Promiscuity, sin, and now . . . God makes them pay the penalty. Bless their souls."

"Well, can't we do anything?" I asked Margaret. "Maybe God could find a baby for them?"

"I don't know. . . ."

"In Norway what we say is 'Got helps those who help themselves.'" Margaret gave me a strange look, put down her dishtowel, and walked outside heading down toward the lake.

"After Margaret and Albert had returned to Great Falls, Tom Mix arrived to visit. He was on his way to California, but he took over the role of the Scout in the sign language drama at the Glacier a couple of times. Mixie promised Joe a job out there and for awhile I thought Joe would leave with him. The cowboys all seemed to be getting Hollywood fever.

When we finally moved back into Fourth Avenue North, I confess I kissed that monstrous white bath tub and those creepy buffalo horn chairs. Great Falls was wonderful, totally free of trolls and wood sprites even though there might be a few Finnish witches. Besides, the house was much more comfortable and had real bathrooms.

Young Boy had been put in charge of the task of enlarging the log studio before we left for Lake McDonald and Bull Head since the mural was to be so large. Four more logs had been added to handle the twelve foot height of the canvas. That meant that the roof had to come off and everything inside was moved. Nancy didn't like the price, but somehow Young Boy and his Cree friends had managed to get real logs this time.

They'd done a good job of raising the roof, but Charlie was disappointed. He rolled a cigarette and stood staring up at the building. The low sloping roof was now broken into two sections. "Ain't like Jake's old place no more," was all he said. Then he turned to Young Boy. "Don't blame you none, Young Boy. It's them down in the Capitol. I'd like to knot 'em and hang 'em on a bob-wire fence. Always wanting stuff bigger an' bigger. Gonna mess up things worser'n a hen in a pile of cow dung." Charlie put down his anger by clearing his throat and walked on into the house.

It was true. The studio was different. The place looked immense, barn-like, as if it had been cleared for a major battle. The old atmosphere was lost, and nobody felt it more than Charlie.

He at last submitted three ideas for the mural to the governor. His favorite notion was a painting of Lewis and Clark trading with a band of Indians. The other proposal was a wagon train under attack by Indians, and the third was a cowboy camp during roundup. Although there was some talk of a railroad scene and much lobbying in favor of it down in Helena, the governor finally approved the Lewis and Clark idea on one condition. The scene had to depict the explorers on Montana soil.

Nancy and Josephine were delighted. They knew how much Charlie loved history and how much time he spent pondering over the Lewis and Clark journals.

"This is just up Charlie's alley," Josephine said. "He knows everything about Lewis and Clark."

"Why Cha'lie darlin' it's a wonderful idea," Nancy said. "Why your daddy once told me you knew ever so much about the explorers. Said it was cause your great grand-daddy, Silus, he helped 'em get good prices for their supplies from them cheating fur trader Frenchies."

"Not about trading, Mame. S' bout Montana," Charlie grunted.

I knew nothing at all, but Josephine told me that in 1805 Lewis and Clark were on soil that was to become Montana. They had encountered a group of thirty-three lodges of friendly Eoote-lash-Shute, members of the Flathead Tribe, at Ross' Hole.

With the help of Joe and Young Boy, I began setting things up for the painting of the mural. While we worked in the studio, they gave me their version of the Lewis and Clark meeting.

"Those Indians were called the Salish people," said Joe.

"Is that the same as the Flathead? The Eoote-lee-e-sh . . . . Oh hell, I can't pronounce it."

"Yeah, yeah, sure, the same," Joe said. "Used a bunch of different names depending on who was talking. By late summer, August it was, the men with Lewis and Clark had already explored a few miles of the Salmon River, but the Shoshone Indians told them that the canyon was impassable."

"So they must have turned around," I said.

"Hell no, Ovidia, they was stubborn and had to find out for their own selfs. So they purchased a bunch of under-nourished, sore-backed, ill-trained horses to carry their baggage across the Bitterroot Mountains to the Columbia."

"Why didn't they just go where the Indians told them to go?" I asked. "The Indians were the ones who knew the country."

Young Boy grunted and looked away.

"Ovidia, you hafta to understand. They wanted to take the shortest route. The Indian trail wound back over the Continental Divide to the east. It woulda been a lot longer and slower. Least that's what they thought. So instead, they sweated like a bunch a hog butchers up the North Fork of the Salmon River."

"White man always big hurry," said Young Boy signing.

Young Boy had climbed the old wooden ladder, and Joe was propping-up the heavy canvas that had to go almost to the ceiling.

"Wild game was so damned scarce that time of year that they had nothin' but their emergency food," Joe continued. "It was God damned tough all right. The slopes of the Bitterroot Mountains were thick with timber, and the underbrush so heavy they had to hack their way through it. And then too, the mountainside there was rocky and steep. The horses kept sliding and falling down."

"Did they turn back and try the Indian route?" I asked.

"Shit sake no. And to make things worse there was an early-season snowstorm, then rain, then sleet. They musta been shiverin' like a bunch a lizards lookin' for a hot rock."

"Salmon River country . . . cold," Young Boy signed.

I was handing nails up to him to anchor the canvas to the wall frame.

"Finally, with their fingers aching from cold and their moccasins frozen total, they made their way down the steep North Slope of the Bitterroot Divide through ankle deep snow and came out on a flat, grassy valley ringed by mountains. It was what the trappers later on would always call a 'hole.' And there they was—the Salish Indian lodges."

"Then did they shoot the Indians?"

"Shit no. For God's sake, Ovidia, don't you understand nothin'? They needed 'em. And besides, they noticed that they had some damned good looking horses. They sure as hell wanted them horses.

"Young Boy, you go ahead, talk damn it. Tell her what your people say 'bout it. Tell her what the Salish thought when they saw the explorers."

"Try think that time," said Young Boy, hesitating, and he paused and tilted his head back. "Mebbe think crazy. Come out mountain that time year." He seemed to be joking, but he didn't laugh. Joe was holding the ladder steady and lifting the canvas at the same time, while Young Boy was teetering dangerously up near the roof.

"Tribe have stories of meet white man. Few story. See people as they be in that time."

He was more serious now. Young Boy didn't have a deep voice. I hardly ever heard him speak. I don't know why I always thought he must have a deep voice. Instead, his voice was quiet, with a sort of melodic tonal quality, almost like singing.

"Old Charlo . . . he son of Old Victor . . . he son of Old Chief who meet Lewis 'n Clark. . . . One time Old Charlo say . . . Salish look at Lewis 'n Clark as be light from the East. That good . . . cause sacred place in east . . . with sun. Salish tribe old . . . very old sun worship."

"Did they think they were *Gots*, Young Boy?" I asked.

"No, no, think they be light . . . some good thing. No understand what Lewis 'n Clark all 'bout. Salish understand explore. Salish accept. Explore, Salish accept." Young Boy signed "accept" several times as he spoke. He had turned and was now sitting comfortably on the unsteady top rung of the ladder.

"Explore good, mean pass through . . . not stay. Not take land. Take food . . . go.

"Another side story," Young Boy continued slowly. "Old Chief that time see couple thing. One . . . think mebbe they be warrior 'cause man call 'York,' he all black. Warrior go to battle, paint self black. Black sign death. Black sign move to side. Red sign life. So, Salish Chief confuse."

"Understand, Ovidia," Joe interrupted. "That chief was just using common sense. The explorers' actions warn't hostile, they even had a squaw with 'em. Sacagawea, and she had a baby by then. 'Nother thing, they were out in the open on the flat, not concealed, so the chief he must've thought, let's just wait and see," said Joe.

"Two thing . . . mebbe Indian see white man before. Long time past. Not first white man Indian see. Salish have story, tell of warrior 'Shining Shirt.' He Indian. But he wear breastplate made hard silver. He prophet. Come out from Southwest."

"So they were friendly right from the beginning?" I asked.

Young Boy signed "yes" and continued, "Set bad habit. Later must keep up. Always treat like visitor. Always give food. Give horse. People say 'Oh, you visit us?' White man say, 'Well, we gonna be here for short while.' Then see fence. See shotgun appear."

"Yeah, that first contact with the Salish seems like it was real good," said Joe. "Lewis and Clark was wise. They did things that mark a good man. They were generous, and they was interested in the Salish horses 'cause that was their key to moving on. But the trade goods and all that stuff, that was like a nibble."

"I'd like to see that place, the place where they first met. Is it beautiful?" I asked Joe.

"Hell, they's not a tree there big 'nough for a short dog bothering to lift his leg on. But you're gonna see it," Joe laughed. The governor's pissed 'cause Charlie ain't started the mural, so Frank Linderman's pushed Charlie into a trip to The Hole so he kin do sketches an' get going. Gonna be a regular chuck wagon camp. I'm to go pick up the Baines Wagon in Butte tomorrow.

"Linderman's boiling mad. Says he stuck his neck out for Charlie, and Charlie ain't even done his book illustrations yet, but Charlie'll rustle 'em up. He'll do the sketches. The Chief ain't gonna let him down."

No one said anything about the Seven Card Stud game. It was never, ever mentioned, but Joe DeYong and I exchanged knowing glances. We knew Frank had good reason for his annoyance.

When we had the canvas hung, I could see that Charlie was going to have to work from a platform high up on sawhorses to paint. He'd never done that. In fact, it seemed he mostly liked to paint sitting down, but anyway, the next day we began packing up for the trip to Ross' Hole.

TWENTY

The Salish Medicine Tree

Joe headed to Butte to meet Linderman and Carl. The whole household was going to Ross' Hole. Young Boy was needed to tend the wagon and horses. Nancy wanted to keep an eye on Charlie, but thank *Got,* Ella was now working at the newspaper and had a new beau, so she was staying in Great Falls. A relief for me, since she never was much help anyhow. At the last minute Teddy Blue came along saying it'd be a chance to see the old trails he came up while herding the Long Horns from Texas.

Charlie was like a kid. He couldn't wait to leave. He kept telling me he was going to do all the cooking: beans, bannock, and bread pudding to go with the beef cooked on the open fire. Teddy was taking over the breakfast chores with his cream gravy and Brazo biscuits. It was fast turning into another party and Charlie was loving it. On the way to what everyone was called "The Hole," our borrowed wagon felt like each wheel must have been different size.

It barely lurched along. Like Lewis and Clark, I guess, I felt I was never going to get there. Nancy had refused the offer of a saddle horse and rode in the wagon with me. Joe handled the team. It was a butt splintering trip. And sometimes cold too, I'll tell you.

Teddy and Charlie swore they found the old wagon trail all right, but I couldn't see it. At least, the weather was holding pretty well. Finally toward evening, a couple of days out of Helena, we started dropping down into a small, flat grassy valley ringed by mountains. As Joe had said, there were no trees, but once into the valley you could look in all directions and see nothing but mountains, some already heavily capped with snow. The sky was a clear, pale blue with pink tinted clouds that turned lavender with the setting sun.

Charlie rode close beside the wagon and he kept talking about his first trip to Montana all the way down onto the flat prairie of The Hole. Of course, Teddy encouraged him and my *Got*, his slow drawling voice droned on and on.

"Back in the mid-eighties it was, Teddy. We got to Ogden and then boarded the narrow gauge Utah and Northern rail that was brand new then. Took us onny far as Red Rock. Then Pike Miller and me hadda hop a stagecoach on up to Helena. Goddammit, I was so dumb then I couldn't a tracked a fat squaw through a snowdrift."

"Don't talk like that Cha'lie," Nancy interrupted.

"Jus' 'cause I'd had that little pony back in St. Louis, I thought I knew a lot about horses, and 'cause I was a cheeky little greenhorn I asked the driver to ride up top of the stage. He give me a hand up. After we gits going he says to me, 'Whar you from, Bud?' an' I says, 'Missouri.'

"That driver, he looks at me dumb struck-like, eyes popping wide open. Then he quick put all the reins in one hand and clamped the other hand right smack over my mouth and whispered, 'My God boy, not so damned loud, someuns gonna hear ya.'

"He looks around suspicious-like, and then took his hand away. He spit tobacca juice over the side, and croaked, 'Missoory.'

"Dammit, son. Don't for the like of ya tell nobody in Helena ya be from Missoory. Why those cow pokes in Helena be meaner'n a bitch wolf in heat. They got a tree there down in a gulch what they use onny for hanging people from Missoory on. Hangs 'em right along, jus' as fast as they come inta town.'"

"That wasn't true, was it?" I insisted. Charlie liked to tease me. The stories were meant to impress the greenhorns and pilgrims, but I'd been with the Russells for too long by then.

"Well, how's I to know if that stage driver was telling the truth or not. I just decided I'd best stick close to old Pike Miller on account of when we got there the damned place didn't look exactly like my dreams of the splendid new frontier."

Between Charlie and Teddy there was plenty of story-telling. While we were coming down onto the flat part of the Bitterroot Valley, we came upon a small tree. I think it was some sort of pine. Up about ten feet embedded in the trunk something poked clear through the tree. I couldn't recognize it, but it was a strange sight.

"What's that, over there in the tree?" I called to Frank and Carl who were riding up in front of the wagon. I pointed toward the tree and Joe brought the horses to a halt. Jumping down from the seat, I walked over to get a better look. Young Boy had dismounted by now. He knelt beside the tree and began chanting in his native Cree language. When he finished, he and Frank spoke quietly for some time.

"Good time for a break," Frank said. "Whyn't you build a small fire Joe, and we'll let Ovidia boil us some coffee."

"I'm ready for that," I said. Any excuse to get off the wagon for a while. Joe and I went to work, and soon we were warming our hands and sipping hot coffee out of the tin camp mugs.

I watched Young Boy. He had taken feathers, some beads from his medicine pouch, a few leather strips, and grasses he gathered from nearby and had fashioned a stiff sort of rope that he wrapped around the tree just over the object.

"What's he doing?" I asked Frank Linderman. "What is it?"

"That's the Sacred Salish Medicine Tree. Legend says all travelers leave gifts and prayers. Young Boy's praying . . . to keep us safe."

"What did he say? Do you know?"

"Well, I can translate it, but. . ."

"Will it keep the evil sprites away? I hope to *Got*.

"Yeah, Ovidia, it should do that. The prayer's about the wind and our ancestors. Says something like:

> In the skin at the tips of our fingers
>   we see the trail of the wind;
> It shows us where the wind blew
>   when our ancestors were created.
> It was the wind that gave them life.

It is the wind that comes out of our mouths now
  that gives us life.
When this ceases to blow, we die."

I looked down at my fingers and saw that it was true.
The lines did look like the trail of the wind and a kind of
shiver raised the small hairs on my arms.

"Probably be a good one to use against the trolls,"
Frank laughed.

"*Nei*, too powerful," I replied.

"Well then, ask the tree to give Charlie some help on
the mural," Nancy shouted. She was up from her nap in the
wagon, poking her head out from the cover.

"Wish the tree'd give him some help on my book illustrations," Frank murmured before he turned away, but
Nancy called after him.

"Hey Frank, what's that damned thing sticking through
the tree?"

"A ram's horn."

"Well how'n the hell did it get into a tree like that?"

"Young Boy says that it had to be done . . . to make the
land safe for the human beings who weren't on the earth
yet. Salish myth says that long ago before humans came the
land was full of them killing monsters."

"Just like evil wood sprites," I mumbled.

". . . And Coyote, who had strong medicine, was traveling all over killing 'em fast as he could. Story says Coyote
heard about a real wicked monster who took the form of a
bighorn sheep named Ram near the south end of this here
Bitterroot Valley. That monster was destroying everything
in the Valley, so Coyote knew he had to kill it."

"So what did he do, grab it and throw it, or poke it into
a tree?" Nancy asked.

"Nah, he couldn't do that. Ram was too powerful. Heavy, and much bigger than Coyote. So one day when Coyote saw Ram, he told Ram how wonderfully powerful he looked. Ram agreed, of course, saying sure, he was the strongest creature in all of the Valley. Coyote said he'd like to see how powerful, and he pointed to a tree and said, 'Can you knock over that little tree there?' Ram laughed. He couldn't wait to show off his strength. He snorted a couple of times, kicked the dirt back with his hind hooves, and thundered toward the little tree. Smashed right into it with his great head, and as he did, one horn penetrated all the way through the tree and out the other side."

"He was stuck there, wasn't he? Pinned down by his own horn," I said.

"Sure as hell was. But Young Boy tells me that's not the end of the story."

"What happened?"

"Coyote didn't waste any time. He took out his flint knife and cut off Ram's head with three swift strokes. And from then on, the Bitterroot Valley has been safe for human beings. That's why they bring gifts here to thank Coyote for making the land free of danger."

Nancy and I got down from the wagon. We each placed an offering at the base of the Medicine Tree. I tried to repeat Young Boy's prayer, in *Norge*. Nancy had some hair ribbons and whispered that she wanted a baby. I laid down a button I had pulled off my shirt and wished that Charlie could get going on the mural. I heard Frank mumble something about his book illustrations when he put a silver coin down. Joe kept saying, "Hollywood, Hollywood, Hollywood," and set down an arrowhead tied-up in grass.

We camped later that day at what we imagined must have been the Lewis and Clark meeting place. Charlie got out his sketch pads and paints almost as soon as we arrived. Every day he did several sketches, mostly of the prairie and the surrounding mountains. He loved camping out and the chuck wagon cooking. I don't think I'd ever seen him happier. I watched him pull out his Bull Durham and slowly roll a cigarette while watching the clouds with a fixed gaze.

It was on our third day there in The Hole that an unexpected thing happened. Charlie had done his morning sketching, and we'd finished up a meal of Dutch oven stew, when we saw dust rising from the trail leading down into the valley. We watched the approach of a horseman leading a pack mule, and it wasn't too long before we recognized who was coming toward us.

I'll bet you can't guess who it was, Billy. No, I'm not starting off on some new story. What I'm telling you is important. We're getting there. No, I'm not going to promise no more stories. I can't help it. The stories start flowing out of me. Keep your damned shirt on.

It was the *Gotdamned* Dane. Trotting across the prairie as big as you please. I'll bet you guessed. Yeah, the keg carrying St. Bernard, Olaf Selzer. Even from a distance we could see he was all grins and happy as a flea in a dog house.

Joe DeYong spotted him and bellered, "That sonnofabitch. Sticks onta ya like cockleburs on a coyote. Totting his barrel of grog, same as always, I'll bet. Want me to tromp his britches, Chief?"

"Nah. He's harmless as a pet rabbit, Joe," said Charlie.

"Closest he's been to a cow is a T-bone steak," Teddy laughed and turned to spit tobacco into the fire.

Charlie nodded, pointing his nose in my direction, "I think he's jus' come out here to do hisself some heavy courtin.' He's got an eye for the Little Package there."

"Well, ya ain't never gonna hitch up a horse with a coyote," said Teddy.

I was wounded. My face was blazing hot. I stamped my foot, gave them both a cold stare, and turned to carry the supper plates to the chuck wagon. Carl followed me.

"Is he still wooing you, Little Valkyrie?" asked Carl.

"*Got* no, Carl. It's only . . . well, all this talk about me and Selzer is annoying. People seemed to think Denmark and Norway are one and the same, and they sure as hell aren't."

"If he gets to discommoding you, you let me know."

"It's all right, Carl. I can take care of myself."

"Same goes for Teddy Blue there," Carl added.

"I said before, Carl. I can take care of myself."

But I did wonder what in the hell Selzer was doing out on the prairie. It didn't take long to find out. Selzer always had his flask of whiskey handy and didn't mind sharing it. He acted like Charlie'd invited him along. At first I didn't think so, but the next day they were together happy as clams at high tide sitting side by side on packing boxes doing sketches and passing the bottle.

"Yeah, like you say, I think that'd do it." I heard Selzer tell Charlie. "Right there. Just off center canvas. Lewis and Clark, big and bold, smack up front and maybe some painted Injin lodges way over in the distant left."

Olaf told me Charlie was showing him some methods he could use to get more action in his painting. I told him, "Olaf, you're a *Gotdamned* liar."

TWENTY-ONE

The Calgary Stampede

The inspiration for the mural painting finally took place there at Ross' Hole. Joe swore that Charlie had just needed time to cogitate before he got going. I was more worried that Nancy was finding too many other things for him to work on. The smaller paintings were bringing in more immediate cash while the immensity of the mural seemed to create a block for both of them.

Can you believe it, Billy? Charlie was to be paid five thousand dollars. Five thousand dollars. In those days it was a fortune. Like you say, something that big was pretty unusual.

Ever since the log cabin studio was built, it had always been pretty much open to anyone dropping by. People could stop in and shoot the breeze with Charlie as he worked, but shortly after we got back from The Hole all that changed. Nancy insisted Charlie wanted no interruptions.

The studio was closed, day and night, so he'd have no interruptions. I couldn't even go in to clean up or prepare brushes and paints for Charlie. They even hung sacks over the windows on the east side. No one could even peek in. And another strange thing happened, Charlie had always hated to use the telephone, but suddenly he wanted one installed in the studio.

At Lulu Disher's soda fountain one afternoon, I told Mattie how puzzled I was about the lock up of the studio and new phone.

"Easy to figure that one out, Ovidia. I know what he's doing. He's calling up other artists."

"How can you be sure," I asked. "Why would he want to do that? He's got the wonderful sketches from Ross' Hole now."

"He's asking for advice. He don't know how to begin. That's what Sid Willis tells me. Sid says he even called John Alexander."

"Oh *nei*, what's John Alexander going to tell him. Nancy admires Alexander, but she says he's only a society painter."

"But remember, he's done a couple of murals, so he knows how."

"Well, what advice did Mr. Alexander give Charlie then? Did Sid say?"

"I'm not sure, but Sid didn't seem to think he helped much. Sid says Alexander paints women." Mattie paused and grinned at me. "And, everyone knows all Charlie's women look just alike. . . . I gotta say though, his cows all look different enough." We both snickered and stirred the cherry red bubbles in the soda glasses, but I was worried.

"But Mattie, he's keeping the true West alive. You know he is, and besides, there weren't many women with Lewis and Clark at Ross' anyhow."

"Just the one Indian woman. Sid did say that Alexander told Charlie to go right on and start painting just like it was an ordinary size canvas."

"*Got*, I sure hope maybe he can do that," I said, but I had some misgivings. I couldn't forget Carl always saying how stubborn Charlie could be.

A few days later Josephine was lettering place cards in the dining room, and she motioned to me to come sit down. She looked all broody and anxious.

"What's going on, Josie, what's wrong?"

"I just heard him," she whispered.

"Heard who?"

"Charlie," she hissed. "He was on the telephone, here in the house. Just before he went out."

"Guess he couldn't get Nancy to make the call for him," I ragged her.

"No, no. He was calling New Mexico. Joseph Sharp, that fellow that paints Indians down in Taos. He wanted help. He doesn't know what to do with the mural."

"Oh *Got*. And he's been calling John Alexander too." We both took a deep breath. "And he was chasing after Selzer out there on the prairie too," I said. "I can't believe Olaf Selzer know a thing about murals though."

"How about Ed Borein? Has he called him?"

"Not that I know of—so far."

"Does Nancy know?"

"She must have some idea," I mumbled. "And he's sure tippling more than two down at The Mint these days."

"Poor dear. Daddy tells me it's more like swigging than tippling when he comes into the Brunswick. The poor dear, he must be totally blocked." Josephine shook her head and made a quick sign to hush.

Nancy was coming in the front door with the usual stack of mail and headed to her desk in the living room. I went back to scrubbing greasy pots in the kitchen. When the phone rang, Nancy scraped her chair back and answered in her sweet-talker voice.

"The Charles M. Russell residence and studio of The Cowboy Artist." She never said just "hello" anymore. She had taken to answering the telephone with what she said was a more fitting response for a famous artist.

Nancy was using her society voice. What now, I wondered. I thought maybe it was the uppity Mrs. Paris Gibson on the line. Maybe the Maids and Matrons were at last inviting Nancy to join them now that Charlie had the mural contract. Or, maybe another deal to paint calendar illustrations. As I dried the big skillet and hung it back on its hook over the sink, I tried to guess what was going on. The telephone conversation went on for some time. Someone must have died . . . or another long lost relative was coming to stay . . . maybe that old no-good daddy of hers.

Finally, I confess, I moved toward the living room and stood lurking in the hallway, eavesdropping. It was a habit I'd picked up from the serving girls at the Russell mansion in St. Louis. They'd warned me it was best to always know what was going on before it happened.

". . . Stage coach races? Well, I know, Mr. Wea . . . Weadoo is it? Oh, Weadick, Mr. Weadick. But . . . well, trick riders . . . contest winners . . . silver buckles, but . . . well . . . Charlie don't do . . . roping, ah well, a rodeo . . . he isn't . . . .

"Right now? But you must have heard, Mr. Weadick. Yes, a large commission . . . with the State of Montana. . . . Oh, you'll have a real exhibition gallery . . . twenty paintings . . . well, I don't know."

It sounded like someone wanted The Cowboy Artist for a large exhibition. I wondered if the Russells would be heading to New York again. Or maybe Colorado. There'd been some talk of an exhibition in Denver.

"You see, Mr. Weadick, he's doing a large mural to hang in the Montana State Legislature building, and . . . ."

There was a long silence. I could hear Nancy tapping her pencil rapidly against the top of the desk. She was impatient.

"But well . . . rh, rh, royalty you say?" she stammered. The tapping stopped.

"The Duke of Connaught, you say. He's going to be there? . . . Prince Arthur, Duke of Connaught, Queen Victoria's son," her voice squeaked. "Queen Victoria's son . . . and the Duchess too?

"Well, of course, Mr. Weadick. Naturally . . . I hadn't realized. But of course in that case . . . The Duke and Duchess of Connaught. Well, we, we can't disappoint the governor general of Canada or the Princess Patricia . . . or the Duchess. . . . The Calgary Stampede can count on Charlie and I. The fifth of September then. Twenty paintings.

I heard her click the phone back on the hook and turned to slide back to the kitchen.

"Ovidia." She hollered from the living room. "Ovidia, oh my God, quick, bring some water quick. I think I'm going to faint."

Josephine had hurried into the living room when she heard Nancy's voice calling me.

"Oh Josephine, go. Go real quick. To the shack. Get Charlie. This is so exciting. Get on out there. No, don't shake your head. Yes, I know he won't let you in, but pound on the door. Tell him anything, but get him in here."

Before I had time to fill the water glass Josephine rushed through the kitchen and headed out the screen door toward studio. When I got to the living room with the water, Nancy was clutching a large ivory sheet of paper to her heart and then using it to fan her face which was flushed a bright scarlet. The hysteria again, I decided. But no, she was smiling and started waltzing around the room waving the sheet of paper.

I handed her the glass of water and asked hesitantly, "You've got good news?"

"Glorious." she sang. "We're going to Canada, Ovidia, Calgary. The Prince Arthur, Duke of Connaught, can you imagine. Royalty . . . real English royalty . . . we'll meet Queen Victoria's son."

"Canada has royalty?"

"Of course, Ovidia. The Queen's picture's on every coin and bill." Nancy was humming and glancing at the paper.

The screen door slammed again and Charlie hurried in. He had a paint brush in hand, but I noticed it was clean and dry.

"Mame, darlin' are you . . ."

"You're not gonna believe it Cha'lie." She was breathless.

"You're gonna have a baby after all."

Nancy's expression became melancholy, but she inhaled deeply. "Oh Cha'lie, you're only teasing me again. It's something even better."

"Can't think of anything better'n that."

"Cha'lie, we're going to meet the Prince Arthur," she blurted out.

"Who the hell is Prince Arthur? Shit, I thought old King Arthur had to have died long ago."

"We're going to Canada, Cha'lie."

"Why for God's sake?"

"It's the Stampede, The Calgary Stampede. This real nice man, his name's Guy Weadick called. He's master-minded a week long rodeo. Says in Canada they call it a stampede. He's hired a hundred Indians to parade around in war paint, and he's invited every cowboy he has ever known to come on up to Calgary and compete. He's giving away thousand dollar prizes, silver buckles, new saddles, and twenty-five dollar Stetson hats to the winners."

"Sure as hell I ain't competin'. Only ones that'll come'll be the sonnabitch glory riders."

"Oh Cha'lie, don't be that way. Did you know Mr. Weadick was a trick roper for the Miller Brothers Wild West Show?"

"Did Mr. Weadick ever work for Buffalo Bill, Mrs. Russell?" I interrupted.

"I don't think so, but he told me he'd married a trick roper, named Flores LaDue, and I think she was with Buffalo Bill."

All of this was grabbing my attention. The Stampede sounded like it might be the real West. Like Buffalo Bill's show with buckskin shirts and tents and . . . . Charlie was scowling and cleared his throat.

"Them folks that pay to go take in ridin' contests don't ride a damned thing but sofa cushions."

"But they're wealthy Cha'lie, remember that. Prominent people from Alberta. Even English gentry. And I know they'll want your paintings. And the royalty'll be there."

"Shit. Them rodeos, if the damned hoss unloads you, they say you can't ride. An' if you scratch the hell out of anything that wears hair, they say the hoss didn't buck."

"Well, Mr. Weadick's invited Ed Borein."

"Hell Mame, Borein couldn't even ride in a covered wagon while tied to the seat."

"Well, hell, of course not Cha'lie, 'cause Borein's not going to be riding. He's going to be exhibitin' paintings. Weadick said he'd pay all our expenses in a downtown hotel."

I looked straight at Nancy then and asked boldly, "Am I going to get to go too?" A real Wild West Show at last. Maybe not Buffalo Bill, but almost as good. This was a trip I couldn't miss.

"Course you're coming, Ovidia. You and Joe too. How could Mr. Weadick expect us to be there with twenty paintings and no one to help us with the exhibit?"

"Jesus-H-Kee-ryst, Mame. Twenty? I ain't even done those illustrations for Linderman yet."

"So then, it's all settled. We're going to Calgary. We're going to meet royalty and the Prince. We're gonna sell paintin's."

And we did too. Thirteen out of the twenty. At top prices, mind you. Weadick later claimed Charlie had sold a hundred thousand dollars worth of art. A big exaggeration, of course, like everything Guy Weadick did. But that's ahead of the story.

We got up to Calgary by the second of September, the date Mr. Weadick had arranged with Nancy. Weadick and his wife Flores LeDue met us at the train station. She was a tiny little thing, but decked out like a tall Christmas tree. All shiny gold satin and sparkling colored beads with a big floppy hat over her dark auburn curls. The feathers were so big they must have come from a very old ostrich bird. On her ample bosom two gold world championship medals hung from purple ribbons and at her teensy waist was a heavy silver belt with a huge buckle depicting a trick roper doing a fancy "Texas Skip." What's a Texas Skip? Hell, it's nothing but a jump through a vertical loop. Bet you could do it, Billy. You don't see much of that fancy stuff anymore though.

And Mr. Weadick, well, he was dolled up like the quintessential cowboy. He had the biggest, highest ten gallon Stetson, I'd ever seen. A well, mannered one too. The brim rolled just so on each side and dropping to a soft point slightly to the right of his long straight nose. Gave the impression he was nodding to you with romancing attentions. But what I couldn't stop looking at though were his eyebrows. Real heavy they were, with long uncurled black hairs. His eyebrows stretched perfectly straight across his forehead, a bit under the brim of the Stetson. Embroidery eagles decorated the pockets and back of his fancy shirt and a large red silk scarf hung loosely around his thick neck.

Not only the Weadicks, but another celebrity was waiting there on the platform for us. Tom Mix was standing there next to Guy Weadick, more colorful than ever, slapping Charlie on the back and hugging little Joe like he was his long lost brother. Mixie'd been hired to put in a guest appearance on opening night. During that Stampede rodeo, I saw enough buckskin, silver, gold, leather, and Stetsons to last me a lifetime.

Nancy and Charlie waited the whole week for their royal audience in the exhibition gallery. On the final day of the Stampede, the gallery was cleared of everyone except members of the vice-regal party and a few of Charlie's bunch so the royalty could view the pictures privately. Nancy was beside herself. She'd been practicing her bow all week. She even made me learn to do it. She'd had a new gown made all covered with lace and big red satin roses. Flores LeDue must have told her where to find that big old ostrich bird because when the Prince Arthur, Duke of Connaught, and his Duchess entered with the Princess Patricia, Nancy's deep bow caused her feathers to sweep the floor clean and stirred up a small cloud of dust. I was a little afraid she might fall right over from bowing so low.

I stood way back to one side talking to Ballie Buck and Johnny Matheson, both of them part of the bunch. They'd come up for the stampede and managed to slip in to view the royals. When the Duke's outfit entered, instead of making a big ado, Charlie, kind of sidled away and over toward us.

I wasn't paying much attention to them. I could only watch the royalty. The Prince had such a regal face. White hair topped by a black velvet helmet with soft white drooping feathers. A cleft chin and thin lips under a white moustache waxed so perfectly that the ends curled slightly up pointing toward his sparkling blue eyes. He was old, I guess, but it didn't matter. I had fallen in love at first sight.

"Oh my *Got*, Ballie. Just look at the Duke," I whispered. "He must be the most beautiful man I've ever seen. I think I'm in love with him."

"Teddy Blue, ain't gonna like to hear you say that," Ballie whispered.

"Neither will Carl," Charlie added. "Well where the hell's Teddy anyway? Why ain't he here?"

"Went back on up to Granville Stuart's place, I heared," said Ballie.

The Duke's costume was majestic. Not even Flores LeDue could outshine him. The entire left side of his chest was covered with gold medals, and the right side held ribbons and chains looping from his gold encrusted shoulder boards. The braid on his scarlet tunic reached clear up to his elbows, and at his side was a silver sword. His leather boots even sported pointy golden spurs at the heel.

Nancy was leading the party around the exhibition hall speaking in an unusually quiet voice describing the paintings to the royal couple and telling stories about the action. About half way down the first wall, the Princess Patricia had broken away and walked slowly over to where Charlie stood with his cowboy cronies. She went directly to Charlie and asked in English I'd never heard before, "My dea-ah Mistah Russell. Please tell me. Do you, yourself, do all the things these riders and ropers are doing in your paintings."

"Oh, no, I was just a common dub cowpuncher. Most times I'm jus' as likely gettin' caught in my own loop," he said and cleared his throat.

Charlie's self-deprecation always played well. The Princess knew exactly what he meant and got a big laugh out of it. Calgary loved Charlie, and going to the Stampede did pay-off, not only in sales. The ripples from the big splash in Canada traveled. The next year Charlie and Nancy were invited to England. The Doré Gallery in London wanted an exhibit. But, that's getting ahead of our story again.

Damn, I know, I'm off on another track, Billy, and you'd like to get right to the time when I found out about the forgery. I'm coming to it. I have to take things as they happened so you'll understand all about why Charlie couldn't do the painting. I not sure he ever wanted to do it, Billy. He seemed to take issue with the pompous nature of the thing.

You remember I mentioned that Joe DeYong came to Canada with us. He'd set up the art exhibit there at the Stampede, but when it was time to leave, he'd already gone. Can you believe that? Maybe all the western falderal at the Stampede had roped him in. He left—with Tom Mix. Joe had confided to Ballie Buck and Matheson that he was following Mixie on the trail to the California movie studios. Mixie had gotten him a job as a paid consultant. He was to be a technical advisor to the studios on Indian costumes.

TWENTY-TWO

The Lifeline

The Calgary Stampede had been heady stuff for all of us. I even found myself dreaming about the handsome Duke even though he was pretty old. Nancy was so taken by the British royalty that she dropped the "Cha'lie" and began using "Chas." Good sales and high prices, but back home at Fourth Avenue North everything fell into dismal desperation after our return. Joe was gone. Charlie tippled his scamper juice heavily. Ella was putting on airs. She was keeping company with an Englishman, a Mr. Frank Ironsides. Charlie said she was going to sink old Ironsides, and he took to calling her Mrs. Stonehenge.

The worst part though was the angry letter from the governor. Over a year had passed since the mural contract, and Governor Norris was not amused when he learned from Frank Linderman that Charlie hadn't even started the Capitol painting. The two other Montana artists had already completed commissions for other parts of the building, and Governor Norris wanted the mural done by the end of September. A matter of less than a month.

Linderman too remained pissed-off. He felt he'd helped Charlie get the big Montana Legislature contract with the notion that Charlie would first complete the illustrations for his book. Frank had a fall deadline with his publisher, and now it looked like Charlie wasn't going to complete the mural or the illustrations. I was outside hanging laundry when Frank came to the studio the day after we returned from Calgary. Even from the clotheslines outback I could hear them arguing on the front porch of the studio. I carried my basket of laundry up closer to the side of the studio so I could hear better.

"You screwed me, Russ. You knew they been pounding me for those illustrations. Now they're maybe not going to publish this season at all, God dammit, and I needed the money. What in the hell am I going to do? I've earned next to nothing the last two years. Nothing. You know the State don't pay me a pittance and nobody's buying the insurance I'm selling. I'm begging you Charlie, make up any old thing damn it, in any old way, just so's I can get by on this one."

There was a mumbled response from Charlie, but I couldn't make it out. I didn't have the empty glass to put against the wall as a listening tube. That's what the housemaids in St. Louis used when they had to know what was going on. Probably wouldn't have worked with the thick log walls anyway.

"Why the hell'd you go up there to Canada anyway?"

More mumbling, but I still couldn't get it.

"Mame? Mame crap." yelled Linderman. The argument continued for some time.

Frank finally walked off the studio porch smacking his Stetson against his leg. "I always thought I could count on you, Russ," he yelled back as the studio door swung shut behind Charlie. He stood there looking sullen as a sore-headed dog, and then stomped off growling to himself.

That evening at dinner I heard Nancy say to Charlie, "For god's sake, Chas, I bet his damned publisher never wanted the book anyway, they only wanted it 'cause of your illustrations." Charlie just cleared his throat and said nothing. "The truth is—everyone wants you to do their books. Teddy Blue was just asking about it last week, but you aren't going to do anymore books, never. You're an art-ist, not an illustrator."

We all worried about the mural though. I think Nancy finally realized she'd hovered over Charlie and had pushed his work a little too far. One afternoon when I brought her tea into her desk where she was working, she looked up at me with a sad expression. "I guess we shouldn't have gone to the Stampede, Ovidia," she confided. "I understand that now, it was a mistake. It's just that I so, so wanted to see the Duke and Duchess. And we did, we did, but now . . . I don't see how Chas can do that mural in such a short time," she said.

"He's got all the sketches from Ross' Hole though."

"Here's what we're going to do. Joe's gone, Ella's no help, so it's up to you and Young Boy. You've got to see he stays in the shack and works on the painting. All day, every day. Nights too if necessary. No more trips to The Mint Saloon. And no more Rot Gut. Don't allow any visitors. And, forgod's sake, keep that St. Bernard, Olaf Selzer, outta there."

I suppose Nancy had good intentions, but she didn't know how to stop pushing Charlie, and there was no way I could manage Charlie's friends or his drinking.

"You gotta stop drinking, Chas," she told him time and time again.

"Why, Mame darling, I'm as sober as a muley cow," he'd always answer. Charlie and Young Boy went to the studio early every morning and spent the day there. One morning Nancy caught Olaf Selzer sneaking around the back and chased him off with the yard broom.

Margaret Trigg came by almost every day to hear more about the Canadian visit, but I think she was there more to try and keep Nancy calmed down.

"Tell me again, what exactly did the Prince look like?"

"Like he was puttin' on more dog than a Mexican general, Margaret. But Mother, Chas keeps lapping up likker like a damned fired cowhand."

"If I remember right, the royalty always went in for a lot of fancy rigging."

"He's not paintin'. And he's got less than a month now."

"And the Princess . . . was she beautiful?"

"The Princess? Oh, why of course, she looked like a mail-order catalogue on foot. . . . But the studio, it's all set-up with the canvas hung and everything. Paints waitin'. I think that damned Selzer is slipping the stuff in somehow."

"And, the Duchess of Connaught? I've seen pictures of her. Elegant, simply elegant."

"Oh, Mother Trigg, please, I just can't remember," Nancy cried. "I can't think. What'll I do?" Nancy threw herself onto the buffalo horn chair and put her head down between her hands. "I'm near hysterical with worry. The governor's pounding us. Chas has got to stop drinkin' and start paintin'."

"Well why didn't you say so before," Margaret said quietly. She bent over and lifted her up from the chair, got out a lace edged handkerchief and wiped Nancy's eyes. Holding her closely, she looked sympathetically at her swollen face. She smiled and clasped her hands together.

"Nancy dear, didn't you know? I'm the one that got Buffalo Bill Cody to stop drinking, and he, well, his was a difficult case . . . . A long time, heavy drinker. Loved the stuff. Didn't I ever tell you about his rescue. My, my, what a prize trophy of grace he was. And Charlie will be too."

"You cured Buffalo Bill? You mean he was a sot?"

"Sure thing. Bill's rescue saved the whole Wild West Show and Congress of Rough Riders of the World. So, I'll be leaving you for a bit, but I'll be back. Ovidia, you get her medicine. Make her rest now. I'll be back before dark with exactly what they need, and I'll be bringing the lifeline with me. We're going to rescue the perishing." Margaret raised her chin in a gesture of determination before heading out the front door murmuring, "Hallelujah, praise to Glory."

I had all the house lights ablaze by four-thirty that evening when the Salvationists arrived. Adjutant Hallelujah Pickles was at the head of the troop, Smiling Alice followed with a stack of blankets and diapers, and Happy Jenny as rear guard with a squalling baby boy in her arms. Nancy couldn't believe it when Margaret said, "He's yours, all yours, yours and Charlie's. You're both responsible now to me, to this little boy, and to God. No more drinking or you'll answer to me immediately and to God almighty when the time comes."

"Oh Margaret, give him to me," Nancy pleaded with tears rolling down her cheeks as she took the baby from Margaret's arms.

Margaret turned and looked directly at Charlie, "You hear that Charlie Russell? To God almighty."

"You got it, Margaret. You got my solemn promise. I'm done with all that. This day forward." Charlie was overjoyed. He took the baby from Nancy and rocked him with tears in his eyes, repeating over and over, "He's a peach, he's a peach, he's sure a real little peach."

"I'll love him forever and ever. Finally Charlie we have a real family. How I've longed for a family."

"You've got it now, Mame, darlin'."

Nancy oh'd and ah'd over the baby's little toes saying they were the most cunning thing she'd ever seen. She and Charlie took turns handing him back and forth while the lifeline carried in baby supplies and stood around grinning and praising *Got*.

Happy Jenny said the baby was supposed to be three months old, but he looked younger to me. I doubt if he weighed even ten pounds. Young Boy signed to me in the kitchen, "Boy look thin . . . weak. Him hungry," and he rushed out in search of a milking cow.

Charlie wanted to name the baby Childe or Mason, names from his family, I guess, but Nancy won the day. The baby would be called Jack Cooper after Nancy's no-account disappearing father.

Josephine told me confidentially that Margaret had been keeping an eye out at the Salvation Army Post for a long time looking for a child they might adopt. She whispered the secret to me as we were refilling the tea pot. A young girl had come in from Fort Benton and had taken refuge in the barracks. It seems the baby's father ran off when he heard the news that she was in the family way. The girl had agreed to the adoption without difficulty, and she'd already left Great Falls headed to the gold fields of Alaska to find her true, heart's-desire, love. She wasn't planning on looking for the baby's daddy.

That evening, before the Salvationists left, Charlie and Nancy knelt, baby in arms, and received salvation. It looked like the baby would be the lifeline they needed after all. Margaret kept saying that you just had to find out what the real need was if you wanted to stop the drinking. That's how she'd saved Buffalo Bill. She knew the Russells' need had been for a baby. I wondered what Buffalo Bill Cody's need had been, but Margaret never told us.

From that night on, our lives centered around the baby although Charlie was still confined to the studio lock-up during the day. He substituted range ballads for the lullabies he didn't know. In the morning he always sang "I'm Only a Cowboy and I Know I've Done Wrong" to the little boy before he went out to the shack. Charlie's bunch all appeared one evening and presented the Russells and Baby Jack with a buggy decorated with two silver buffalo skulls.

Nancy spent more time going downtown and always came back with something new for little Jack. I'll remember the white rabbit fur outfit she bought for him. It did make him look like a small bunny with big dark eyes shining out from under the silky haired cap. She kept busy with plenty of cooing and gurgling and had less time to keep pushing Charlie. It seemed a good thing to me. Maybe now he would concentrate on the mural.

No, Billy, well sure, the baby kept things from falling apart altogether, and Charlie stopped drinking, but he still couldn't get started painting. I guess you could say he was "blocked." It was the big canvas, but I was confident he could do it.

Of course, I was a lot busier now, what with the baby and all. When Nancy went on her baby shopping sprees, I cared for Baby Jack. He was a spoiled baby, wanting attention every minute, so Young Boy had taken over supplying the studio. Mattie stopped by to see the baby one afternoon while Nancy was out shopping. When I told her the good news about Charlie's really painting on the mural and not drinking anymore, she looked surprised.

"Maybe I shouldn't tell you this, but Ovidia, Charlie's down at the Mint almost every day. Sometimes even in the morning."

"I don't believe it. He made a solemn promise . . . he loves Baby Jack so and . . . "

"Well, he's not drinking; he is sober, but he's sure buying and jawing with the bunch. Scoots out the backdoor though if he sees Frank Linderman come in."

"Oh Mattie, I don't know how that could be. Nancy has him in a regular lock-down out there in the studio."

"He's gettin' out somehow. He's clever. Why hell, Ovidia, he can just leak out of the landscape. He's sly as a fox. If it's a lock-down, he's sure as hell found the key."

"Then how's he going to finish the mural in less than a month?"

"He's not."

I thought my heart would stop. I had been so convinced Charlie was painting. Mattie knew I was upset. She took my hand in hers and we just looked at each other, puzzled. I had to find out what was going on with the mural. I didn't dare ask Teddy Blue or Carl. Teddy'd certainly tell tall tales for Charlie, I was sure of that, and Carl never had much confidence in Charlie in the first place. Carl had gone along with the seven card stud game to get Frank Linderman to agree to award Charlie the State House contact, but I didn't want to push him any further.

TWENTY-THREE

Deception

The only way to find out what was going on inside the studio was go in there myself. Just after dark that night, I saw Young Boy coming from the side of the studio heading toward the barn. I hurried out and maneuvered him into the horse stalls. There was a bright harvest moon, and I noticed right away that his old shirt and cast-off gray pants had paint smudges and spots. Drips and drops were all over him. Why I'd never seen it before, I don't know. We'd all been so busy with Baby Jack.

"Where's all the paint coming from Young Boy?" I motioned toward his clothes.

He looked straight ahead and didn't say a word. Finally I grabbed his sleeve. "Where's it from?" I repeated. He turned away from me.

"The mural. You're doing it, aren't you?" The accusation seemed to come blurting out from nowhere. "It's not Charlie's, is it?"

Young Boy said nothing. I dropped my grip on his sleeve and he turned away toward the buckets and the cans of turpentine. He started cleaning the brushes. I could smell the acrid turpentine. It made me a bit dizzy, and I had to take a deep breath. I made another try.

"What is going on? Is Olaf Selzer sneaking in there?" Young Boy continued his cleaning, now with the bar soap and water.

"I want to see it, Young Boy. You've got to show me the mural." I had to be wrong. He didn't move. "I'll go to Nancy then," I said and started to turn back toward the house.

Young Boy still said nothing, but he put down the brushes and turned toward the studio motioning for me to follow. Before we left the stalls, he stopped and signed, "no . . . talk," then stood blocking my way. His expression was blank, but I knew what he wanted. He wanted to assure my secrecy. I hesitated and then reluctantly signed, "Agree . . . no talk." I was trembling. I followed him as he went toward the north end of the studio, away from the house, to a side wall of the shack that had been replaced when the studio was enlarged for the mural canvas.

It had grown very dark with clouds now covering the moon. Young Boy knelt near the northwest corner of the studio. He pulled away some sod then rolled two pieces of the lower logs away from the building. I couldn't believe it. With the logs gone, there was a secret crawl space into the studio. He motioned for me to enter.

I got on my hands and knees then flattened my body and started pulling myself slowly through the opening. I caught my heel in the hem of my skirt, and it tore with what seemed like a loud rip. Young Boy hissed. The entry had no real sill, only the rough edge of another log and no light at all. As I pulled myself through on my elbows and forearms, I hit my forehead painfully and gasped, but I continued hauling myself in.

Once I was inside, I could do nothing but hunker on the floor. It was pitch-black inside, but I could smell fresh paint. The windows must had been covered. I could hear Young Boy crawling in after me.

As I waited I understood that Mattie was right. Of course, Charlie had been sneaking out of the studio, how could I have doubted it, and now I understood how he did it. The crawl space was on the far side, away from the house and completely hidden. If you knew what you were doing you could slip in and out easily and quickly.

Young Boy was crouched beside me on the floor now. He must have reached out and quietly pulled the logs back into place after us because the darkness inside the studio seemed to intensify. I squatted on the floor not knowing where to move. I was afraid I could knock something over or hit my head again.

I heard a sharp scratching sound and realized Young Boy was trying to light a lantern with a match that must have been damp. I could smell the sulfur and then the burning kerosene as the lamp finally took. A faint yellow light began to spread across the dark log walls.

My *Got*. There it was. The mural, covering the whole wall. Even in the dim light I could see that it was almost completed. Only some dry grasses in the far lower corner needed filling in. It looked like Charlie's work, but yet, what was different? The colors were more vivid, almost shining. In the center foreground were two horses. A black and a white. They were both moving.

The lantern was glowing brighter now and I could see more clearly. Charlie was always good at horses. I felt some

relief. Maybe he had painted this after all. The white horse
glowed like moonlight reflecting the pale blues and lavender of the sky and the snow covered mountains in the distance. Flanking the white horse was the spectacular black
laying back on its haunches while wheeling to the left in a
quick movement. A third horse raced forward at a full reck-
less gallop to the left of the white. But . . . the riders.

I stared at the painting in the yellow light. The horses
carried riders that were unmistakably Indian. Arms raised
high, they held hooked lances topped with feathers that
seemed to be moving with the shifting position of the horse
and rider. The scene was Ross' Hole all right. Even I could
recognize it. A grassy, all but treeless, valley surrounded by
the high mountains. I stood before the painting with wide
eyes searching for Lewis and Clark. They weren't there—
only the horses and the Indians.

I looked at Young Boy. He was walking slowly back
and forth in front of the mural holding the lantern high
above his shoulder. The light reflected off his high cheek
bones and produced deep shadows on the lower part of
his long face. His two scrawny black braids reached down
well below his shoulders, and a heavy lock at his forehead
partially covered his right ear. I had no idea what he was
thinking.

"Is it Charlie's work?" I asked quietly. "Tell me truth-
fully."

"Charlie idea. Lewis 'n Clark meet Flathead. Ross
Hole."

I looked back up at the mural. Several scraggy gray and
dun colored Indian dogs ran snarling or sat howling in the
foreground. They loomed large as part of the action, and
there was plenty of action. All kinds of action. In the lower

left corner, almost buried in the prairie grass, I thought I
saw Charlie's buffalo skull trademark, the only thing that
wasn't moving, and then I realized, it wasn't a buffalo skull
at all. It was a ram's skull with one large ridged horn curling
back and then forward again. My *Got*, of course, the monster Ram who was killed by Coyote in Ross' Hole.

I thought I was beginning to understand what was
going on. It was Ross' Hole all right. What Charlie planned
to paint. Pure Montana, like the governor had ordered. I
hadn't been mistaken about that. I searched the painting.

"Lewis and Clark?" I signed and asked. I turned to look
at Young Boy and moved my open palm back and forth at
shoulder level signing a question again. "Where are they?
Where Lewis, where Clark?"

Young Boy set the lantern on a nearby table and lifted
the scaffolding. He carried it from the center of the room
to the far right and returned for the lantern. Climbing
onto the high scaffold, he raised the lantern, shining the
light more brightly onto two distant figures standing near
a blanket on the ground. An Indian woman with a cradle
board knelt in the grass in front of them. Trading was taking place.

The tiny figures, dwarfed by the Indian horsemen in the
foreground, were the American explorers, Lewis and Clark.
Even Sacagawea, the Shoshone interpreter, was placed more
central. As Young Boy held the lantern, I could see an even
smaller figure that identified the Lewis and Clark expedition. There on the right in the far back was Clark's black servant, York, holding the fagged out horses of the expedition.

"It's breathtaking, Young Boy," I said. ". . . But, Charlie
didn't paint it. And Olaf Selzer couldn't get that action.
You did. You can't deny it. Charlie may love Indians, but

he'd never have painted this. Your signature is right here."
I pointed in the flickering light to the ram's head. "The
Monster Ram's head. The location in your terms. The valley made safe for humans to live, your many lodges clustered in the distance, ready to welcome the exploring white
men who only travel through. The Indians are the ones
central and permanent. You painted this, Young Boy."

Young Boy climbed down from the scaffold. "Long
time . . . watch paint. Joe, he show . . . teach . . . try . . .
practice. Save Charlie. Do mural." He helped me to the
secret entry, snuffed out the lantern and followed me out. I
don't remember crossing the yard from the shack to return
to the house.

TWENTY-FOUR

Shared Secret

The house was dark when I returned. I went to my room off the kitchen and pulled the string for the electric light. In the mirror on the wall across from the door, I thought I saw a ghost, or one of the terrible wood sprites. Straggly hair, tumbled down over a white, white face, pale eyes, and a line of dark dried blood traveling down from near the hair line across the cheek to end in a smear on the quivering chin. My *Got.* It was me. I hardly recognized myself. My blouse was stained with dirt. I lurched forward and tripped on the ragged hemline of my torn skirt. I quickly pulled the light cord again. What if someone were to come in and see me like this. What would I say?

I needed to think. Should I tell? Who should I tell? The mural was due in a matter of days. I paced back and forth. What if Nancy saw the cut on my forehead? I hurried to the bathroom. Above the big white pedestal sink was a medicine cabinet. Charlie sometimes left the bathroom door ajar when he shaved, and I'd seen him take a waxy white stick out of there when he cut himself. I quickly found it propped up next to the shaving mug behind his bristle shaving brush. I wet a wash cloth with very hot water and held it to my forehead. The dried blood quickly loosened, but the water had opened the wound, and it began bleeding again.

I wiped away the smear running down my cheek, pulled the white styptic pencil out of its narrow container, and held it to the cut on my head. "Ouch, damn it." I whispered. It stung like hell, but I tried to keep quiet and waited. The wound seemed to be closing up, and there was no more bleeding. Maybe Nancy wouldn't notice. Maybe no one would notice. I cleaned up as quickly as I could. turned off all the lights, undressed, and hid the stained, dirty clothing I had been wearing in the bottom of my Odegard trunk. I got into bed. Then I tossed and turned, worrying what to say if someone saw the cut on my forehead.

I shouldn't have worried about it. The next morning everyone was so busy they paid little attention to me. Charlie grabbed his coffee and hightailed it out the back door. Ella sat at the kitchen table feeding on the breakfast waffles and talking about her beloved Mr. Ironsides. Nancy worked nervously at her desk in the living room. Baby Jack was sucking his thumb propped up in a high chair that was still too big for him. Josephine was the only one who said anything at all that morning at breakfast.

"Dear me, Ovidia, what did you do to your head?" she asked.

I hadn't thought of an answer. I could feel my cheeks turning red. Young Boy who was bringing in the fire wood saved me.

"Neenah," he said. "She give sugar. Neenah want more. Throw head." Young Boy motioned lifting his chin quickly, and then he dumped the logs into the big wood box by the stove with a loud crash. I wanted to look at him, but I couldn't. From the corner of my eye, I saw him sign, "no."

"Well, it doesn't look infected anyway." Josephine stacked the finished hotel menus and turned to pick up Baby Jack who had started screaming when Young Boy slammed the back door on his way out.

I cleared away the remains of breakfast like always, but my head was spinning. Should I tell? Who should I tell? Charlie surely must know. Did Nancy know? How could Young Boy paint so much like Charlie? The light had been so dim. Was the painting really as good as I thought? What if it wasn't? Would it be rejected? Would Charlie be shamed? So damned many things running through my brain. Why had I ever come here in the first place? Because of a stupid Buffalo Bill poster? . . . Or was it the buckskin coat with fringes? It all seemed so foolish. I should have gone to Minnesota and Erik Trygstad and his thirty-two fine milk cows.

I took the baby who was now in a full voiced rage from Josephine and asked. "Does Young Boy paint?"

"Oh no, I don't think so. I remember Joe was always trying to teach him. Joe once told me that showing Young Boy how to do perspective and action helped him remember more clearly what Charlie taught him. Joe always wanted to be an artist, but no, Young Boy's never want to paint."

"He used to always take leftover paints and brushes from the studio though," I said.

"Most likely he used them to paint symbols and signs and such on the Cree lodges. The lodges are big, you know. Takes a lot of paint."

Nancy came into the kitchen looking agitated. "Oh, don't bother with those now, Josephine," she said. She ruffled her pale gray wool skirt and adjusted the bow at the neck of her ivory satin blouse as she moved back and forth.

"Give me Baby Jack, Ovidia. Him just loves him's mummy so. Don't he . . . don't he? I'll just hug you forever, Baby Jack, darlin'." Nancy covered the baby with kisses. Josephine and I had secretly started calling Baby Jack 'the boy with the golden pants.'

"Oh wonderful, Ovidia, you've already got this cleaned up. We have plenty to do this morning. First, Bob Hayes is due here any minute.

"Who's Bob Hayes?" I was so jumpy. The question had just come out. I shouldn't have asked, but Nancy didn't seem to notice. Anything frightened me.

"He's going to take some pictures of Chas working on the mural." She sat fussing over Baby Jack and then got up again just as quickly. "Elite Studios," she sighed. "The finest photo studio in Great Falls. Just wait until those Maids and Matrons see these pictures of Chas in the *Great Falls Tribune*. The studio wants the pictures now before the canvas comes down. It'll be shipped to Helena next week."

Then he certainly had to know I thought. Charlie must know Young Boy has done the painting. So why's he having his picture taken with it this morning? Did Nancy know Charlie hadn't done the work? I had to talk to someone.

"And that Governor. All that silly complaining. Getting us all so distressed. I knew Chas could do the damned mural in a month. After all, he is the famous 'Cowboy Artist.' And next year—we're going to England. The Doré Galleries, London. We're callin' the show 'The West That Has Passed.' Here, Ovidia, take Little Jack. I think I hear Bob Hayes. Elite Studios . . . , finest in town," she said turning toward the front door.

I didn't see the photos being taken. Instead I called Carl while everyone was out of the house. I still disliked the phone. I felt reluctant to call, and the phone offered little privacy. It just wasn't something women did. Calling a man. Embarrassing at the very least, but I did it. All I asked was for him to take me to the library that evening . . . late. Josephine had taught me about the library. It was the best place to meet quietly, secretly, and in total privacy.

When Carl arrived after dinner was cleaned up, the two of us left the house. Carl carried my heavy book bag. I'd filled it so no one would wonder where we were going or why. Carl had remembered to bring a little bunch of violets, but it didn't cheer me at all. I was getting fed-up with violets. I didn't know how to tell him about the forged mural. As soon as we were settled at a table in the far corner secluded behind the stacks, I just blurted it out.

"Charlie didn't paint the mural."

"Well now, I've been told it's finished and ready to ship on down to the State House." Carl was never ruffled.

"Sure, Carl, it's ready, but Charlie didn't paint it."

"Then who in the hell did?"

"Young Boy."

Carl laughed. "You're dreaming, Little Valkyrie. Washing all those diapers getting to you already? Marry me and we'll go on over to Belt. I promise, no diapers, least not for a while," he teased. "I been working on the place. You'll like it, guaranteed. I've been waiting a long time."

"I'm serious, Carl."

"I am too. Marry me."

"Carl, please, please listen to me. Charlie didn't paint the State House mural."

"Well, then, I guess you are serious. You think Young Boy painted it?"

"I know he did."

"If you're serious and Young Boy painted it, tell me, what in the hell does it look like then? A Cree Lodge with a bunch of magic spirit symbols?"

"No Carl, it looks just like what Charlie would do . . . almost."

"Then maybe Charlie did it."

"It looks like Charlie, but not like Charlie, Carl." How could I explain? It didn't seem possible.

"Well, that makes things much clearer. You've been taking some of Nancy's medicines."

"Don't joke, Carl. There's a ram's skull down in the corner."

"Well shit, Ovidia, maybe Charlie's just gotten tired of buffalo skulls."

"There's lots of action, just like Charlie paints."

"Okay, then it's Charlie's work."

"But it's all about Indians. Even Indian dogs running all over the place, right up front in the painting. And the ram's skull. It's the sign of the Salish."

"It's true, Charlie doesn't much like dogs, but he sure paints plenty of Indians."

"Oh but not like these. Oh please, stop it Carl. Listen to me. I'm worried. I don't know what to do. I was in the studio last night. I cornered Young Boy and made him take me in."

"Why'd you do that?"

"Cause Mattie's been telling me Charlie's always hanging around the saloons. She said he's not drinking anymore. He's sober, but he's buying and hanging around.

How could he have finished the mural if he's in the saloons all the time?"

"I thought Nancy had him locked in. The bunch all say she jailed him and threw away the key."

"They're only covering up, Carl. He's got a secret escape route."

"Okie dokie. So tell me."

I explained how Young Boy took me into the studio. How we moved the logs. How the painting was like Ross' Hole. How the horses were so beautiful . . . how Lewis and Clark were there . . . but only just tiny figures in the middle distance. I even showed him the cut on my forehead.

"Okay, what's the mural look like?"

"Beautiful. But the Indian horsemen are the important central figures. You hardly notice Lewis and Clark. It's probably the best thing Charlie's ever done. But Charlie didn't do it."

"You're sure?"

"Young Boy admitted he did the painting. He says he had to save Charlie. Those were his very words. 'Save Charlie.' So what are we going to do?" I pleaded.

". . . Nothing."

"Nothing . . . But Carl, Charlie . . . ."

"Yeah, he's getting five thousand, a big price for it, but if Young Boy really did paint it, he's doing it because he's getting something he wants. Mebbe something he needs."

"But Carl, it's all a lie."

"Not really. Only if we say so. If Young Boy's asked, which I hope never happens, he'll deny painting it."

"It's cheating."

"Who's cheating? Charlie or Young Boy?"

"Those tiny little Lewis and Clark stick figures."

"I'd say Young Boy maybe wanted to make it clear who was here in Montana first. Sounds like he wanted unambiguous evidence of the historical past of this State hanging right up there in the Statehouse."

"Chicanery, Carl, pure and simple."

"Well, people may prefer it to the real 'Cowboy Artist' thing."

"So you're suggesting we let it ride; we shouldn't tell."

"Yep, if not, Nancy's liable to up and leave for California. Probably move in with Bill Hart. It'd look bad for the governor. I don't even want to think about what would happen with Frank Linderman. Decision by Seven Card Stud? He'd be out but fast. But, it's your decision really."

"Oh *Got*." I was on the verge of tears. Carl put his arm around me.

"Not to worry, Miss Brunhilde. Not to worry."

We talked a long time. The library finally closed and we had to leave. I agreed to keep the secret of the painting. Carl would too. Maybe he was right. What purpose would it serve to reveal the hoax? Charlie symbolized Montana and its worthy achievements. It seemed unlikely that Young Boy would be seeking recognition for his work. The work would always speak with calm certainty to him and his Cree people of their vanished past. A cowboy could paint fine art, but so could an Indian.

TWENTY-FIVE

State House Honors

Charlie was asked to appear at a special joint session of the State Legislature to be honored for his work on the mural. I have to tell you, Billy, he sure didn't want to go even though the mural had been received with enormous approval. Finally, Frank Linderman was appointed by the governor to come up to Great Falls and make sure Charlie got to Helena. Frank was still brooding about the illustrations for his book which Charlie had never completed, but he told Charlie it was absolutely necessary that he attend the ceremony. I overheard them quarrelling in the living room and peeked through the crack in the doorjamb.

"Well, it don't matter what you think Russ, you've got to go. It'd be a blot on the whole State if you don't. Shit, all you gotta do is strut around like a turkey gobbler in a hen pen. Just sit there, look pretty, and listen to a bunch a fancy speeches. Hell, the paintin's something to be proud of and the governor's keen on it. Get your God damned half-breed sash tied up. We're getting' outta here even if I have to call the bunch and hog tie you."

Charlie cleared his throat but didn't respond.

"My God, wait till you see it up there. It looks just like Ross' Hole hanging up there behind the speaker's station. Big as the building is, the paintin' covers the entire wall. It's like sitting smack in the middle of Ross' Hole. Nobody's gonna mistake it. Everybody says it's the greatest painting you've done. They fancy it, and I ain't told anyone . . ."

"What ain't you told anyone?" Charlie interrupted angrily.

"'Bout the Indians, of course."

"What about the Indians?" His eyes had taken on that angry yellow light, the exact color of a wolf's.

"Their costumes, of course."

"What's eating ya about the costumes?"

"Hell, Russ, you've read all the Lewis and Clark journals. I know you have. You must have forgotten. Clark never mentioned them having cloth garments." Frank chuckled. "You got that horseman there in the front wearing a blanket robe, even cloth leggings. Not like you to forget that."

"Musta made a mistake, Frank." Charlie cleared his throat.

That was all he ever said. He tied up his métis sash, I polished his cowboy boots to a satin shine, and he reluctantly went off to Helena with Frank. Frank had promised Charlie all he'd have to do would be to sit there, but that wasn't to be the case.

Carl told me what really happened. "Ovidia, the mural's spectacular. So powerful that lookin' at it gives you goose bumps. But after the eulogies were over, Charlie was asked to reply to the formal acceptance speech. 'Course everyone expected Charlie to stand right up and go to the speaker's stand, but he didn't. The whole room got as quiet as a sick cow in a snow bank. Finally Charlie stood up, but then . . . I guess he panicked and absolutely stampeded for the door, pale white, and frightened.

"You should have seen it, Ovidia, almost caused a riot. All those ex-cattlemen jumped to their feet. They mobbed him and literally dragged him back to the speaker's stand. They was laughing and howling, acting like it was some big joke. Terrible ordeal for Charlie though. He stood there behind the speaker's stand looking dazed. His mouth opened once or twice, but he didn't utter a damned word, or at least none that I could hear.

"He stood there still as a stone cow, and then his right arm came up toward his forehead, and his left hand raised in a quick gesture. I thought maybe he was going into some of his sign talking, but he didn't. That was all. He gives this embarrassed nod to the cheering audience and bolts from the room."

Nancy and Charlie never talked much about the mural afterward. We all settled back into a routine. I stayed on at the Russell's to care for Baby Jack while Charlie and Nancy traveled to England that next year, but London wasn't the triumph Calgary had been. In London, sales weren't as good at the Doré Galleries as Nancy had hoped, but she came back with a fine English accent.

Not long after the Russells returned, Carl and I were married. My wedding ring was a small, but beautiful, blue Montana sapphire. Can you guess what I wore for the ceremony, Billy? No white dress and veil for me, no old-fashioned dark blue dress either. I had a pure white buck-skin jacket and skirt. Hell, the fringes on that jacket must have been a foot long. I had it at last, my buckskin jacket, just like Buffalo Bill. 'Course, it got to be pretty useless over on that homestead we had in Belt, but . . . .

Because the State legislature was in session, Carl and I traveled down to Helena on our wedding trip. We had never talked about the forgery again, after that night in the library, but I wanted to see the mural in place. When I entered the House of Representatives and looked toward the speaker's station, I had to catch my breath.

"Oh my *Got,* it's dramatic all right," I said to Carl who had taken my arm. "Ross' Hole right here in this room."

"Yes, vivid. The cattle people love it."

"But, Carl, even you say there aren't any more cattle people."

"Well, there's supposed to be. A good prop for the western image, anyway."

"It's the pictures that will last, Carl. I've just been chasing an impractical vision."

"Call it an icon."

"*Ja,* an expression of the Montana native character." We moved behind the speakers station to get a closer look at the painting.

"And the Indians?" Carl asked.

"They're right up front," I said.

"Lewis and Clark, even York way back there in the corner . . . tiny, not too important. And, Ovidia, look there. Don't you think those explorers are, well, they're way too clean after all those months of travel?"

"How was Young Boy to know, Carl?"

"Yeah, his interest centered on the people who were here first. Not those passing through."

"My *Got*, those explorers, so determined. They'd been traveling for months and months, syphilitic and all, I've heard. "

"Yeah, and nothing was going to stop them."

"Remember Carl, the morning after I first arrived in Great Falls. Margaret and Josephine were giving Nancy her elocution lesson. I remember you came in and said the Cowboy Artist would never do anything he took issue with. I think he took issue with the notion of such a grandiose mural. I think he didn't want to do it because it was just too damned big.

TWENTY-SIX

Ovidia's Epilogue

That's the story, Billy. Charlie Russell, famous as he is, never did paint the mural he's always been so noted for. He's a Montana hero regardless. His statue standing there in the Washington, D.C. capitol and all. I never told anyone until now—only Carl, and he's dead and gone. I kept the faith and my agreement with Frank Linderman.

Carl always thought that Charlie was just playing a trick on the greenhorns there in the legislature, a trick only he would know about. He didn't have much conviction about them knowing anything. They kept squawking about wanting some famous artist, a celebrity, and what they finally got was unknown Indian.

A few years later, Charlie and Nancy got themselves a big fancy house in Pasadena, California and hob knobbed with all the Hollywood movie people. Make no mistake though; Charlie continued painting successfully for years and years, right up to the day he died. They say he completed more than four thousand works during his lifetime.

Seems like a lot to me though because Charlie was always a bit lazy. Carl used to say he reminded him of a hound dog in the sun.

He even put me in a painting one time. It showed me out back behind the shack hanging up washing on the clothesline. I was wearing my blue dress, and my red sunbonnet had fallen off on my shoulders. It must have been summer. There was a cowboy in full regalia to my right sitting on his horse and flirting with me. I always kind of thought it was supposed to be Teddy Blue. Charlie gave me the painting. Wish I still had it, but I think it was lost or sold around the time of the Great Depression.

Remember how Teddy Blue was courting me? Good thing I didn't take him seriously. He'd started working up north there with Granville Stuart, and it wasn't long before he got approval from old Granville to marry his half-breed daughter. They said Teddy'd been in love with her for years. But I don't know. At the time I kinda wondered if Teddy was looking more for a bundle of land than a bride.

Charlie really did stop drinking after they adopted Jack. He loved being a daddy. Took Little Jack on his pony all the time. By the time Jack was a year old, he was plump and talkative and nothing was too good for him. The boy with the golden pants, and well on his way to being a real brat. Never amounted to much though, I've heard. Last news I had he was working highway construction in the California desert.

And Mattie, yeah Billy, she did go to Hollywood. She left before Carl and I were married. She took the screen name Louise Lester. Became a big star. She portrayed Calamity Anne in a series of films. *Ja*, she was a real serial film queen. Made plenty of money I heard. She was right.

There was a place for women in the Hollywood westerns. But like Bill Hart suggested, she spent a lot of time tied to railroad tracks or under bursting dams. She died a few years back. Hate to tell you, but I heard she may have committed suicide.

Joe and Tom Mix became quite an item in Hollywood, though it was all very hush, hush in those days. Joe got to be famous as an authority on western Indian and cowboy paraphernalia. Kept busy advising the movie studios on costumes and riding. Yeah, I think he and Mixie lived happily ever after.

Margaret Trigg kept on saving souls. She finally started a rescue home for foundlings there in Great Falls. But poor Albert. He met an early and unexpected demise. In 1917 he cut his hand on a broken whiskey bottle there in the Brunswick and died a couple of weeks later of blood poisoning. A shock to everyone.

Josephine? Well, things didn't go that well for her either, poor dear. She married that guy that smelled of printer's ink, Will Ridgley. They never did get along. She finally divorced him after the death of her baby girl, and then she spent most of her time hanging around the Russells. She'd help with Little Jack, and she and Margaret kept things together during those dreadful summers at Lake McDonald.

Frank? His second book was never much of a success. Publication was delayed a year or more. He got another artist to do the illustrations and never really forgave Russ for that. I've heard that his daughters still held that grudge even after their daddy was gone.

When Charlie died in 1926, he was enthroned by his fellow artists who said his pictures were of inestimable value and truth in preserving the West. And do you know what? Olaf Selzer actually did complete some of Charlie's commissions back then. And was Nancy ever furious. I heard she said the paintings could no longer be considered as being Chas' work. Selzer was always copying Charlie. Every once in a while I still see something in the newspaper about another Russell forgery surfacing done by that old St. Bernard.

Funny story I heard about another collector of Russell art, Billy. This guy wanted to collect Russell bronzes. You know why? He thought the bronzes where more than art. He really believed he could talk to Charlie's ghost with them. He held séances and Charlie would speak to him. Don't joke about it, Billy. You've got to keep in mind that this was back in 1929 and just about everybody was a little bit irrational then.

Remember I told you about Sid Willis and all the Russell paintings he had there in the Mint Saloon. Well, I know this to be a fact, because I read it in *Time Magazine*. Back in 1952 Sid sold the whole damned collection, ninety paintings, to an ever so rich guy in Fort Worth. Gave all the Montanans a real slap in the face. They sure wanted them, but Sid, he was eager for the Texan's big bucks and to hell with Montana.

Now Josephine, she was different. She had a lot of Russell stuff and she gave it all to the City of Great Falls. Her house and land too. That's how they were finally able to build the museum there. Right on the site of the Trigg's old place where Charlie went to read the Lewis and Clark journals.

Nancy sold the log cabin studio to the City of Great Falls in 1928 for only one dollar, but then, typical Nancy, she wouldn't turn the property over until the City raised twenty thousand dollars more to buy the house and land around it. I thought maybe she was trying to get even with those Maids and Matrons who were never very nice to her.

Gossip has it that Nancy didn't have to spend her old age entirely alone. There was a twilight romance with Bill Hart. He was supposed to be living as a straitlaced old bachelor with his elder sister, but I heard he always kept a picture of Nancy right there beside his bed. Carl and I suspected something even back in the early days in Great Falls.

I totally lost track of Young Boy. One morning, not long after the mural was sent the Helena, he just stopped appearing at breakfast. I think he returned to the Cree Nation. Charlie used to see him once in a while I've heard. They used to meet there in Great Falls in a cigar store near the Mint Saloon. I picked up that he moved up to the Rocky Boy Reservation north at Box Elder, Montana near the Canadian border in 1916. But when Charlie died he wrote to Nancy. None of us thought he could write either, but his letter was quoted in the *Great Falls Tribune.* The letter to Nancy read:

> I am going to talk to you not to think so hard you wont be so lonesome you lost your husband. [G]ot made our life. [W]e cant live all the time. [H]e good man every place. I sure think of him and feel sorry for him just like my own relation. [T]hats all I could tell you to day."

Wasn't that nice. So why'd Young Boy do the mural? He sure didn't get any money or recognition. I still believe it gave him spiritual rejuvenation. He saw the dynamic Indian horsemen up front in Montana while the explorers, well, maybe sometime they'd finish trading all their goods and move on.

Nancy worked hard to keep Charlie's image alive. Did a pretty good job of it too. Maybe better than pretty good. After all, Charlie is still idolized and idealized. Of course, she was always manic. Her driving energy and ambition never stopped. She always wanted a book written about his life. It never happened during her lifetime though. She tried, with a bunch of different writers, but she never believed anyone could do her Charlie justice.

Made in the USA